A
LOVELY & COMFORTABLE
HERITAGE
LOST

A Unique History
of
Early El Dorado County, California

Enjoy!
Ellen Osborn

ELLEN OSBORN

Cover Design: Antelope Design
Cover Photo: The Crystal Range
"Snow covered Sierra Nevada as viewed across miles of open forest."
Courtesy: @Benedicks Dreamtime.com Sierra Nevada Crystal Range

PronghornPress.org

John C. Johnson
Courtesy: California History Room, California State Library, Sacramento, California

Dilapidated and deserted cabin near top of Echo Summit: *Photo by Author*

Touch me gently, friend of mine,
I'm all that's left of '49;
Many a long-forgotten face
Hath watched me in my good old place;
Many a heart once true and warm
Hath watched through me the threatened storm.
A moral on my face is cast
Which all must truly learn at last—
Man's hopes and fears are all, alas!
Like me, a fractured pane of glass.

The author is Senator William Frank Stewart. This verse was written on a pane of glass in the log cabin of B. F. Post. It was often quoted in early day histories and was said to have been written on April 19, 1865, the day of President Lincoln's funeral.
Mountain Democrat 03/18/1969 *Reminders of Bygone Days*

TABLE OF CONTENTS

ILLUSTRATIONS

PREFACE

This is a history of the earliest development of El Dorado County California, beginning with the conflicts between the Native Americans and the newly arrived miners and settlers. If your interest in history draws you to look beyond textbooks, to question popular beliefs, to look for answers in the words of the people who lived those tumultuous years, then you will enjoy this fresh look at Gold Rush history.

This is the first published account of the El Dorado Indian Wars that is based on primary source documents, including the unpublished diary of one of the soldiers, and is told from the perspective of the men and women who lived it. Also included are the in-depth accounts of three Native Americans. They are: Indian Hattie, a native Californian; Fall Leaf, a Delaware Indian army scout; and raiding Apaches on the Mexican-American border, who had very different experiences with the advancing frontier of the United States.

This is the history of what has been called the most storied and romantic road in American history. It is the tale of how a Native American trade trail became a popular Gold Rush route and grew into California's first highway, Highway 50.

Finally, it is the story of one man, John Calhoun Johnson, who lived it all. His efforts to tame his part of the West have had a lasting effect on El Dorado County and California.

John Calhoun Johnson was my great great grandfather. For over thirty years I have been interested in his story, his life, and work. At first, I was just curious, but before I knew it I became his biographer. Along the way I realized that to understand a nineteenth century man, I would also have to learn about the world in which he lived, a world very different from our own.

I approached this work as if I were reconstructing a fractured pane of glass, finding pieces here and there, fitting them together, doing my best to re-assemble the parts into a clear window on the past. This window is still not complete, but the time has come to share what I have discovered.

1

JOHN CALHOUN JOHNSON, PIONEER

In 1849, like so many young American men, John Calhoun Johnson was caught up by the exhilarating news of the discovery of gold in California. When the word reached his home in Harrison County, Ohio, all the young men were filled with excitement and met almost nightly during the winter of 1848-49 to plan their trip west in the spring.[1]

As is often the case, in the end the company of gold seekers actually departing for California numbered only fourteen. Included in this number was John's cousin, Asbury Johnson, who left us his reminiscence of the trip and his experiences in California.

In early March 1849, they started out by steamboat down the Ohio River, stopping briefly in Cincinnati where John was completing his education to become a lawyer. It would be hard to imagine that he would have passed up this chance to meet with his friends, neighbors, and relatives from Harrison County on their way to get rich in the gold fields. How he must have wanted to join them! It took real self-restraint

---

1 *The Lillie Porter Collection of Harrison County Ohio*

not to just drop everything and leave with them. Instead he stayed, but as soon as he passed the bar, according to family tradition, he headed west "alone and on horseback." Alone meant not that he was riding alone, but rather that he wasn't traveling with familiar companions.

No one on the trail to California needed to travel alone. One emigrant described the trail as a line of white-topped covered wagons as far as the eye could see in both directions. Younger men without families often chose to make the trip without the encumbrance of a wagon and household goods. Instead, they took just what they needed for the trip and packed it on mules. This made for a much quicker passage. They would travel during the day at their own speed, then look for a larger group to camp with at night for security.

Since he departed in May, John may have hoped to catch up with the Harrison County boys, but he did not. They arrived in Weberville in El Dorado County late in June of 1849. John Calhoun Johnson arrived in California a month later. None of the Harrison County boys are listed as residents at his ranch in the 1850 Census. It doesn't appear that John and those friends ever connected again in California.

J. C. Johnson came west for adventure. Instead, he found a home and a place where he could make a difference. What has been written about him is largely about what he did, rather than who he was. The majority of the records tell of his accomplishments, not of his personal life, his thoughts or ideas, except those of a political nature. However, enough can be pieced together to present a picture of who he was as a person.

Take his name, for instance. He was christened John Calhoun Johnson. There does not appear to be a Calhoun branch of the family. It is likely he was named in honor of the Southern Senator, John Caldwell Calhoun, the fiery orator. The assumption here is that his parents were impressed with the senator and wanted to give their firstborn son an impressive name. Giving a child the name of an admired public figure

Watercolor portrait of John Calhoun Johnson by an unknown artist.
In the original his hair is chestnut and his eyes blue.
Author's collection

was a fairly common naming practice in the nineteenth century, and it was probably safer to select a dead public figure, because it was impossible to predict if one would continue to agree with what that public figure stood for or did in the future.

John's parents, however, appropriated the name of a living man. At the time of Johnson's birth, March 18, 1822, the politician from South Carolina's star was definitely rising; he was serving as secretary of war and about to be elected vice president of the United States, with the expectation that he would eventually be elected to the office of president. It might have been embarrassing for Johnson when in 1850, his namesake opposed California's bid for statehood in the Senate. Apparently, it didn't deter him from following this same naming practice with his own first-born son, George. For George, he chose the name of a political figure from his home state of Ohio, George Hunt Pendleton[2].

Johnson most commonly referred to himself as J. C. Some people called him Jack, and John Studebaker fondly remembered him as Jackie.[3] The honorific title of colonel recalls his participation in the El Dorado Indian Wars. With a name as common as John Johnson, people had to have a way of knowing to which Johnson was being referred. After his death, and probably before in private conversations, he was referred to by the descriptive sobriquet of Cock-eyed Johnson, a reference to his crossed eye. This name didn't appear in print prior to his death, which suggests he didn't care for it. Persons who did not know him in life were the ones who most often used this nickname.

His cockeyed appearance was caused by the inward turning of his right eye when looking at an object. This condition, known as strabismus, was more commonly seen among adults in the past than it is now, due to improved treatment for the condition. He certainly lived a full life in spite of probable depth perception loss, double vision, and vision loss in general.

Here are some words used by his contemporaries to describe Johnson: D. R. Leeper in 1891[4] recalled him as the eccentric cockeyed lawyer. The *Mountain Democrat* editor Dan Gelwicks wrote, "Johnson is of irreproachable veracity[5]." On a later occasion the same editor described him as a "restless and indefatigable pioneer." In the announcement of John and Emily Hagerdon's marriage in 1854, the editor of the *Empire County Argus*[6] referred to him as "the gallant

---

2 It is also possible that Johnson named his son in honor of George Pen Johnston, a colorful and active participant in politics, law, and journalism in California's early days. Johnston, most closely associated with San Francisco, was also active in El Dorado County. He is often remembered for his fatal duel with William Ferguson on Angel Island.

3 *To Old Hangtown or Bust* page 44

4 *Mountain Democrat* July 26, 1978

5 *Mountain Democrat* July 10, 1858

6 *Empire County Argus* January 7, 1854

Emily Jane Hagerdon as she must have looked at the time of her marriage to J. C. Johnson. The original is a cabinet card by photographer George H. Gilbert, Placerville, California. *Author's collection*

colonel." Following Johnson's death in Arizona, Dr. O. P. Ingram remembered him as a man of fine education and untiring industry.[7]

Johnson was capable of decisive action. As his future wife, Emily recorded in her reminiscence of her early life, when John spotted her in the stream of arriving emigrants, he immediately commented to a companion, "There goes the girl I will make my wife."

He followed her family until he caught up with them and offered her stepmother a job as a housekeeper. His courtship was successful, with marriage following on January 1, 1854, just three months after he first saw Emily driving an ox team, with her hair loose down her back and barefoot. She had torn her skirt off at the knees

---

7 *The Citizen*, September 23, 1876

because of the heavy mud on the road. She must have really stood out from the crowd![8]

Johnson also could be implacable if he thought he was in the right. One of the soldiers in the El Dorado Indian Wars recorded in his journal that as the war wound down and funding dried up, the soldiers came near to having no supper when they returned from a long ride because Mr. Johnson, in his capacity of adjutant of the militia, had left orders for them to have nothing more on the government account. Mr. Phillips, Johnson's partner, must have had a softer heart because he relented and fed the men and their horses.

Sportsman's Hall on the emigrant route twelve miles east of Placerville.
Emily remembered that is where she saw John for the first time.
Courtesy of Library of Congress, Prints and Photographs Division,
Lawrence & Houseworth collection.

---

8 See *The Life of Emily Hagerdon* in Appendix F.

In the 1870s, when a conflict arose between Johnson and Alburn J. Blakeley, his neighbor, Blakeley had some very hard words to say about him. Blakeley called Johnson "dishonest, habitually intemperate," and accused Johnson of threatening violence.

In the early days Johnson established his reputation as an indefatigable party-giver. In June of 1853 this advertisement appeared in the *Placerville Herald*:

> *Fourth of July Ball at Johnson's Ranch*
>
> *The new hotel of Col. J. C. Johnson, upon the immigrant route from Carson Valley to this place* [Placerville], *will be the point of attraction on the day of our approaching national anniversary. A grand ball is to come off in the evening. The mountain boys are ever ready."*[9]

These parties at the ranch required participants to purchase a ticket. As late as the second of July, the newspaper was still advertising the availability of tickets with the promise "the elite and ton [fashionable] of the mountains will be there," which did include over one hundred ladies who attended. Since in 1853 the ratio of men to women was so great, it can be assumed as many as three hundred people were present. Here is how the editor of the *Placerville Herald* described the festivities on the Fourth:

> "Sweet music echoed through the vale, and soon the merry dance began, which participated in by a very large party of ladies and gentlemen from Placerville, White Rock, Diamond Springs, Georgetown, and all the smaller villages of

---

9 *Placerville Herald* June 11, 1853

the mountains, making one of the largest and most decidedly genteel parties that ever convened in El Dorado County, upon a like occasion. To speak of the merits of the supper discussed, the ices, the ice-creams, the champagne, would be entirely a one-sided speech, telling of their great abundance and excellent quality[10]. "

It is possible that, in addition to the ice cream, champagne, and dancing, the guests were to be witness to an "affair of honor," as promised by the *Placerville Herald:*

"It is probably well understood that an affair of honor is to come off on the afternoon of the Fourth of July at that place.[11]" An affair of honor generally meant a duel. With a crowd of unruly men drinking toasts to Independence, it would be expected that spontaneous fights might occur, but in this case, one was scheduled! Probably the affair of honor either didn't take place, or no one was seriously injured, as there was no follow-up story in the newspaper. This ball must have been a success, as Johnson advertised another just a few weeks later.

An interesting tale that may or may not have actually happened during one of Johnson's parties, one that has been repeated and attributed to other occasions elsewhere, is nonetheless too good to omit.

As the story goes, the young mothers attending the party put their babies together in one room. While the festivities were in full swing, a few wags stole into the room and switched the babies' clothing, resulting in the mothers taking the wrong baby home, and was followed by general bedlam as they sorted out the infants.

Johnson continued the party-giving tradition at his ranch on July fourth for several years thereafter, saying in 1856 that he intended to give a ball on every return of the anniversary of our National Independence, until he is too old to dance.

---

10 *Placerville Herald* July 9, 1853
11 *Placerville Herald* June 15, 1853

In December of 1856, he also gave a Christmas ball. The *Mountain Democrat* commented that Jack "has become famous for his pleasant parties, and we doubt not, this one will be well attended."[12]

Observances of Independence Day were among the largest of any annual holiday at that time. Great effort was made for lively celebrations, even among the emigrants who found themselves far from home on that important day.

From the journal of James Fyffe[13], there is this colorful account of the Fourth of July celebration of the El Dorado County militia in 1851:

> *July third—We are making preparations for a tall celebration on tomorrow. One committee writes toasts. Another tends to getting flowers. Another hunters were sent out and having returned with a deer... General Winn presented our flag to us this evening in a somewhat lengthy speech. Some emigrants have arrived and intend participating with us tomorrow.*
>
> *July fourth—This was ushered in with a salute of thirteen guns while at sunrise our flag was unfurled to the breeze of the mountains. At ten o'clock a Battalion Drill. The General reviewed the troops who then passed in review after which we listened to an interesting oration from Major Hall. After[ward] Dr. Keane[14] had read the Declaration of Independence. After the proceedings were over we sat down to a fine dinner of roasted ox. The pies created some fuss being a rarity. At the drinking of the toasts*

---

12 *Mountain Democrat* June 21, 1856, and December 20, 1856

13 From the unpublished journal of James Perry Fyffe.

14 B. F. Keene, M.D. was unanimously chosen to fill the office of state senator in 1851. His untimely death in 1856 cut short what surely would have been a great career contributing much to the development of California.

the boys got a little obstreperous. Came near having several fights but finally everything passed off. The snow pyramids that decorated our table looked nice. The one on the right was in the shape of an inverted wine glass three feet or four high. The one on the left was a square structure three feet wide and four feet high ornamented with wreaths of flowers and having beautiful variegated colors.

This party took place at a camp thereafter called Camp Independence. It was located about fifteen miles from Johnson's Ranch.

On the various issues of the day, Johnson generally had well-developed opinions that guided his actions. His relationship with the local natives is a good example. While he was an active participant in the El Dorado Indian Wars, he later took a paternalistic interest in the natives living on his ranch or nearby. He took the time to learn their language well enough to communicate, evidenced in several contemporary newspaper articles where he is described as the "interpreter": on the trip to Lake Bigler in 1853,[15] and again for the men who, in June of the same year, visited the Diggers Fandango (as it was styled by the *Placerville Herald*).[16]

In 1856, Indian agent, Tom Hensley, appointed Johnson as his agent to supply the needs and wants of the local Indians because Johnson was familiar with their habits and language.[17] Two years later, Johnson intervened to protect the local tribe when an Indian from the Cosumnes River came onto his ranch and murdered one of the leaders of the tribe living there.

On the other hand, among the older family members who'd had a chance to listen to Emily's memories, there was a story of a

15 The full account is in Appendix A *The Origin of Lake Bigler.*
16 *Placerville Herald* June, 18, 1853
17 *Mountain Democrat* October 25, 1856

native sneaking up on the Johnson house with the intent to murder the occupants. Emily, his wife, is said to have foiled the attempt by alerting the neighbors. If this story is correct, there was at least one Indian who didn't care for Johnson.

His relationship with the Chinese miners was similarly conflicted. The June 15, 1867, *Mountain Democrat* carried the following article about the proceedings of the local Democratic Convention, to which Johnson had been elected secretary. In addressing the topic of the Chinese in California, the committee passed the following resolution:

"Resolved, that the continued emigration of Mongolians to this State, to be used as the ill-paid slaves of capital are evils of startling and increasing magnitude, that to the utmost extent consistent with public faith and humanity, should be corrected by Federal and State legislation."

This resolution was unanimously approved. It was a popular sentiment expressed repeatedly throughout the diggings where the number of Chinese had grown, until by 1852, in some mining camps the ratio of Chinese to all others was three out of ten.

One response to the influx of Chinese was the passage of the Foreign Miner's License Law of 1850.[18] This law was largely enforced only on the Chinese. One correspondent of *The Mountain Democrat* went so far as to opine that the Chinese were supporting El Dorado County![19]

While serving in the Sixth State Assembly in 1855, Johnson sponsored a bill that provided for a graduated tax on those foreign miners who were ineligible for citizenship.[20] This included the Chinese. Following a long and inglorious period of restrictive local laws and acts of violence, the issue was resolved to the legislators' satisfaction in 1882, when a bill to exclude all Chinese emigrants was approved. This law was extended well into the twentieth century, and effectively prevented further emigration from China.

---

18 John W. Caughey, *California 2nd Edition* page 383—392
19 *Mountain Democrat* February 28, 1857 page 2
20 *Assembly Journals Sixth Session, 1855* page 417

ELLEN OSBORN

The Chinese issue became a personal one for Johnson when he found a little Chinese boy wandering in the streets of Placerville alone. John and Emily took Sam Wam into their home and raised him. When some years later a photographer visited the Johnson Ranch, he took pictures of all the Johnson children. Photographed with John Jr. was the young Chinese man, Sam Wam. Pictured in Western clothes, his serene face is a contrast to the rebellious expression on little John's face. Note the firm grip on the wrist of camera-shy John Jr.

Sam Wam, the Chinese boy the Johnson's took into their home with John Calhoun Johnson, Jr. Photo taken at Johnson's Ranch, circa 1870.
Author's collection

The 1870 U. S. Census confirms Sam Wam's presence at the ranch. He was also listed as an occasional laborer in the records of the Vallejo Mining Company in 1867. The family story has it that Sam Wam returned to China as an adult where he enjoyed success in the export business.

While both Emily and John were related to Protestant ministers, religion doesn't appear to have played a large role in their daily lives. According to an anonymous emigrant of 1850, the Sabbath was observed at the ranch, at least if the circuit preacher was present. The circuit preacher, Israel Deihl, had married John and Emily at the ranch. Later, when their daughter Annie married Milo Oldfield, Rev. C. C. Pierce, of the Episcopalian faith officiated at the ceremony in the Johnson family home on Cedar Ravine Street in Placerville. While living in Placerville, Emily was just a short walk from the Methodist church located on Main Street at the end of Cedar Ravine Street, but she was not listed among their members. When George notified his mother of his father's death, he sent the telegram by way of Rev. Newell, the local Presbyterian minister.

Johnson was a lawyer by profession, although he preferred farming. When he registered to vote in El Dorado County, he listed his occupation as farmer. He attended Cincinnati Law School in 1848 and 1849.[21] As previously mentioned, he only stayed long enough to complete what he had started, that is, to become a lawyer before heading west to California and the exciting life he knew lay ahead.

D. R. Leeper, author of *The Argonauts of Forty-Nine*, lists Johnson among the early day lawyers. *The History of El Dorado County* includes him in its list of early day attorneys.[22] However, his

21 Personal letter from Cincinnati School of Law
22 *The History of El Dorado County* pub. by Paolo Sioli page 220. His name is listed incorrectly as P. C. Johnson.

name rarely appears in the official record as an active attorney. While his handling of various events in his life evinces a very good grasp of the law, the practice of law, or the making of laws as a legislator, was not his first choice[23].

Another early day attorney, L. A. Norton, is to be thanked for the one story of Johnson practicing law in early El Dorado County. He included this anecdotal tale in his book *Life and Adventures of Colonel L. A. Norton*.[24] To set the scene, this took place during the trial of Billy Sutton for stealing a turkey belonging to Mary Ann Crowley, a widow. L. A. Norton was retained by "Uncle" Billy to represent him. This story must be read carefully, as the prosecuting attorney was also named Johnson.

Norton wrote: "Cock-eyed Jack Johnson, an assistant to the prosecutor was present [in the court room]." In order to win the case for his client, Norton decided to run off the chief witness.

Norton's narrative continued: "Cock-eye Johnson (or Jack Johnson) saw me return alone, when he exclaimed, 'Where is the witness? I will bet a hundred dollars that cuss has run him off.' At this he [Johnson] looked out the window, through which I was watching the progress of my friend [the witness] when he exclaimed, 'Yes, by G-d, there he goes!' Hopkins had just stepped into the room, when he and Jack Johnson took after him, but my young racer soon distanced them and they returned panting."

Norton went on to relate how he got Uncle Billy Sutton off on the charge of stealing the turkey. Mr. Sutton paid Mrs. Crowley for the turkey. Apparently she forgave him, for later they were married.

---

23 A descendant of J. C. Johnson has a lovely pendant necklace. Family tradition says Johnson received it in payment from a lady to settle a debt. This debt could have been incurred when Johnson provided a defense for her. 24 *Life and Adventures of L. A. Norton* pages 279—284. The whole story is well worth reading. This is a shortened version.

Johnson's penmanship indicates he had a very good education. He had both a formal and informal style of handwriting. During the nineteenth century it was standard for educated people to use both. The best source for examples of his handwriting are the letters in the State Archives written during the El Dorado Indian Wars, or the ledger from his time as treasurer of El Dorado County.

The *Mountain Democrat* carried letters, or "cards" as they were called then from readers who wished to express their opinions. Most often those cards were signed with a pen name, concealing the identity of the author. However, Johnson did sign some of his. These provide examples of his ability to express his ideas in words and also his high level of literacy. One example is this excerpt from the July 10, 1858 *Mountain Democrat*:

> *As to myself, there is no need of misunderstanding me. I am and have been a sincere admirer of the political course of Stephen A. Douglas; and at the sitting of the committee was in conversation with Mr. Hoover in relation to the position of that gentleman on the Kansas question; and said to him were it not for widening the breach in the Democratic ranks, that I would offer a resolution endorsing Douglas....*

Almost from the date of his arrival in California, Johnson was active in politics and public service. He was elected to serve as El Dorado County's first treasurer on April 6, 1850.[25] He served in that capacity until the election of 1851, when his partner, John Phillips followed him as treasurer. The Governor's Executive Act of 1850-51 appointed Johnson notary public on March 7, 1851. He served a two-year term. The same executive act also appointed him adjutant of the militia. He was elected to represent El Dorado County (14th Assembly District) in the sixth session of the California State Assembly on September 6, 1854.

---

25 El Dorado *County Court of Sessions Book A*

In the Assembly, he was appointed to the House Standing Committee on Agriculture and the Committee on Public Lands. These appointments must have pleased him, as they most closely followed his interests. From the earliest date, he realized that he and his fellow farmers were in danger of losing their lands and improvements if laws were not passed to protect them.

He sponsored Assembly Bill 303 that clarified the laws applicable to the rights of persons who made peaceable entry onto unoccupied land. The wording looks very much like a response to the issue of squatter's rights. This act was approved on April 11, 1855.

As a member of the El Dorado delegation to the Assembly in 1855, Johnson worked with the delegation from Amador County to finalize the southern border El Dorado County shares with Amador County by amending the previous statute.

He was not on the Roads and Highways Committee, but he continued to work to bring about his dream of a year-around road over the Sierra Nevada into El Dorado County when he was elected to the Three County Wagon Road Convention[26], and in May of 1854, he was appointed a road commissioner. He was also the road supervisor responsible for the maintenance of a large portion of the emigrant route into California, the road he had pioneered. Known as the Johnson Cutoff, it was the predecessor of modern Highway 50. Although his discovery of a better emigrant route made him somewhat famous at the time, he never appears to have been motivated by self-promotion.

J. C. Johnson's personal politics were well known and consistent. He was a life-long Democrat. He made many speeches before the public and the Democratic County Central Committee. He regularly attended Democratic state conventions and took an active part in them for over twenty years. He often served as a teller, secretary, or on the credentials committee for the El Dorado County Democratic Committee. His ranch was a voting precinct for many years.

---

26 The counties were: El Dorado, Sacramento, and Yolo counties.

In the July 10, 1858 letter quoted in the *Mountain Democrat* earlier, Johnson clearly stated he was an admirer of the political course of Stephen A. Douglas. In this matter, Johnson and the *Mountain Democrat's* editor, Dan Gelwicks, did not see eye to eye, with Gelwicks supporting, instead, John Breckinridge who was pro-slavery. However, the election results on November 10, 1860, showed overwhelming support for Douglas in El Dorado County.

Douglas tried to keep the Union together by crafting a compromise on the slavery issue. When the Civil War did come, he rallied his supporters to the Union cause. So, by inference, Johnson's position was probably the same as Douglas's on the most important issue of his time.

As early as 1850, to secure his ranch and protect the settlers and miners living there and the emigrants entering California, he found himself caught up in the escalating conflict between the Native Americans who were themselves trying to protect their way of life. As the conflict progressed from skirmishes to war, his ranch became the headquarters for the newly formed militia.

2

EL DORADO INDIAN WARS

In the history of El Dorado County, the El Dorado Indian Wars of 1850-51 has received scant serious attention. The little that has been written about the conflict contains many errors. In more recent years, the subject was treated as a joke, and a bad one at that. Some otherwise reliable historians, contend it never happened, that it was a "hoax," even called it a "burlesque." To call it so is an injustice to the dead on both sides of the conflict. Other writers who lived a little closer to that time have called it a "wretched affair" or "a war of extermination."

Although the Indians who lived in what is now called El Dorado County were not considered war-like, the rapid increase in the number of American settlers and miners pushing into every corner, even into steep remote mountain canyons, made conflict inevitable. Other parts of the brand new state of California were experiencing the same type of difficulties.

As the Indians defended their homelands and lifestyle, Americans and gold seekers from around the world were insistent about imposing the lifestyles and values they brought with them. That blood would be shed seemed unavoidable.

John Calhoun Johnson found himself in the middle of the El Dorado Indian Wars because his ranch, located on the emigrant route, was considered the last outpost of safety at the time.

The Sacramento Daily Union newspaper on May 13, 1851, wrote: "It is not safe for a small party to go five miles beyond Johnson's Ranch on the emigrant road, so great is the probability of their being attacked by the savages in that vicinity."

Indian depredations along the western slope of the Sierra Nevada caught the emigrants in a generally exhausted and weakened state. Their provisions were running dangerously low, with just enough left to complete their journey. The Indians would help themselves to food, or clothing, or anything that caught their eye. Assaults on the emigrants themselves were reported, but the most frequent target of the Indians was the worn out cattle and horses, those faithful creatures that had brought the emigrants across a continent.

Of known surviving diaries of emigrants coming into California on the Carson River Route, more than a dozen contain narratives of Indian attacks on the western slope of the Sierra Nevada during the 1850 emigration season.

A most gripping account is that of Franklin Langworthy. Mr. Langworthy wrote well and in great detail. Two days after he left Leek Springs his party encountered:

> *...a young couple of Tennesseans, a man and his wife. They had been wounded the day before, with arrows shot by two Indians, two miles east of this place. When attacked, they were traveling on foot and by themselves, and driving before them their two oxen, upon which their goods and provisions were packed. They had left their wagon on the desert.*
>
> *Unfortunately, the man had no firearms at the time, but kept the Indians in check by hurling at his assailants pebbles picked up from the road. He says*

he dodged more than twenty arrows, till at length, one struck him in the shoulder blade, disabling his left arm. At this time he had retreated, facing the enemy, until he found himself and wife at the summit of a long and very steep descent. Here they both turned and fled with winged speed down the hill, the enemy gave up the pursuit, and the fugitives arrived at this post, leaving their oxen behind.

The attack of the Indians seems to have been made through mere wantonness or malignity, and not for plunder, as the oxen were soon afterwards discovered in the woods with all the baggage safe. The woman was severely wounded through the breasts, at the commencement of the attack. Her husband did not notice it, having at the time his attention drawn another way, and she, although but eighteen years of age, was so much of a heroine, that she made no complaint, and her partner knew not of the wound, until both had gained a place of safety."[27]

This appalling attack was reported in Placerville where it served to inflame the settlers against the local Indians.

Sporadic conflicts between the Indians and the miners had been occurring throughout the mines since the gold rush began. A couple of especially bloody encounters happened along the Middle Fork of the American River.

In April of 1849, a group of five miners were attacked and killed. A search party from Coloma went out to examine the scene, and followed tracks to an Indian *rancheria*, where they pursued and killed two Indians. This was quickly followed by a similar event that may have been retaliation by the Indians. In that case two miners died. However, neither of these events triggered the mobilization of the militia.

---

27 Langworthy, Franklin *Scenery of the Plains, Mountains and Mines.* Also *Sacramento Transcript* October 25, 1850

In the same article cited earlier, *The Sacramento Daily Union* gave voice to the thoughts of many of the citizens that an army post along the emigrant trail was what was needed:

> *"It seems rather strange that the General Government is not willing, or able, to defend our citizens on the frontier. Where are the U. S. troops? Are they defending our frontiers and protecting our citizens, who are thus exposed to the merciless hands of these savages or are they lolling in idleness in Benicia?"*[28]

By May of 1850, the clouds of war began to gather on the horizon. For accounts of events during the first episode of the El Dorado Indian Wars, the Sacramento newspapers were the most reliable source. A correspondent of the *Sacramento Transcript* reported the following incident:

> *One of our citizens was out yesterday morning hunting mules, and in passing a party of Indians, who were mining, one of them shot him in the neck with an arrow; he drew his revolver and wounded the Indian, and they all immediately retreated into the bushes. Captain Bee left town in the afternoon with a party of about thirty men well armed; they came up with the Indians at their ranche [sic], about four miles from here* [Placerville] *and made a descent in two parties upon the camp; the Indians discovered their approach and took to their heels, setting up*

---

28 *Sacramento Daily Union* May 13, 1851. Benicia Barracks was established in 1849 as an army post by the Second U.S. Infantry. It was used as army headquarters for the Department of the Pacific 1851-1857. The site is now California State Historic Landmark #177.

an unearthly yelling, which was imitated by about a thousand dogs that they had with them. One Indian was captured, and one was supposed to be severely wounded. All the guns, knives, and ammunition that could be found were brought away. The Indians in this region have generally been peaceable, but they have been purchasing arms from time to time from men here, and now are pretty well armed.[29]

On October 25, 1850, the *Sacramento Transcript* ran a large article under the headline "Highly Important! Great Excitement in El Dorado County!! Threatened Indian Hostilities!!!" This was in response to a rumor, later found to be baseless, that the Indians had banded together and in three day's time planned to sack and burn all the towns within three leagues of Sutter's Fort.

This, in addition to continued depredations, fanned the communities of Placerville, Ringgold, and Weberville into a frenzy of action. Meetings were held, picket guards placed around the towns. Not waiting for the government to act, each community began to raise a volunteer force of fifty men each. Subscriptions were raised to pay the volunteer army and to defray expenses. The citizens of Coloma and Diamond Springs quickly followed suit.

In the meantime, Sheriff William Rogers received an order from the Governor of California to take responsibility to keep the Indians at bay and keep the emigrant trail open. Governor Burnett was acting under the provisions of the 1850 Act Concerning the Organization of the Militia. Under this act, the county sheriff was responsible for calling out the militia.

The militia in El Dorado County consisted of three companies, each headed by a captain, assisted by three lieutenants. Because of the small size of the force, Sheriff Rogers only received the rank of Major. Judging by subsequent newspaper articles, military rank for the officers frequently changed. Ready or not, Sheriff Rogers found himself leading an army of two hundred volunteers against an elusive

---

29 *Sacramento Transcript* June 3, 1850

Sheriff William Rogers, also known as "Uncle Billy" or Colonel.
Courtesy of the El Dorado County Historical Museum

enemy. By Rogers's own estimation the job needed twelve to fifteen hundred fighting men.

The editor of the *Sacramento Transcript* went on to express his opinion of how the Indian difficulties would proceed:

> *Although from the character of the California Indians, they cannot be considered formidable enemies in regular warfare, still they can do immense mischief. If the State should send a strong force to chastise those now committing murders along the*

immigrant trail, the probability is that they would flee beyond reach, and as soon as the State forces were withdrawn, their present system of shoot-in-the-dark warfare would be renewed.

With this statement, he accurately predicted how the Indian wars would go.

The citizens of El Dorado County seemed to believe all the natives they encountered to be of a single tribe, one they called "Diggers." They did not consider that the Indians they encountered south of the Cosumnes River would not be aligned with the ones on the northern shore, that one tribe might not even share a language with another, or that they might be in a state of hostility toward one another.

Caught in the net of the El Dorado Indian Wars were the Nisenan, Maidu, Miwok, Washoe, and even Paiute tribes. Retribution by the settlers was carried out hastily and without regard to which tribe had actually committed the act. To be fair, the Indians did not calm the situation as they continued their depredations and murders. Provocative acts on the part of individual miners continued, as well.

The militia came together fairly quickly. On November 5, 1850, the *Sacramento Transcript* published a lengthy list of volunteers from Placerville. These officers were elected: William Rogers, Colonel; L. H. McKinney, Lieutenant Colonel; J. C. Johnson, Adjutant[30]; John Brown, Commissary; J. L. Slaughter, Surgeon; and B. F. Ankeny, Quarter Master. All of the several militias throughout the state answered to Brigadier General A. M. Winn in Sacramento.

The gold rush attracted a number of men who had recently seen action in the war with Mexico. Their military experience was an asset to Sheriff Rogers as he tried to pull his force of eager, but inexperienced, volunteers together.

One such man was Leslie H. McKinney. In the Mexican War, he held the rank of major, and so brought valuable military experience

---

30 Traditionally the role of adjutant is as the commander's personal assistant. To him fell the job of communicating with headquarters the needs in the field and seeing to non-combat needs.

to this greenhorn militia. In a letter written at Sly Park, dated October 29, 1850,[31] Lieutenant Colonel McKinney provided an eyewitness account of one of the early encounters:

> *We have commenced operations against the Indians, and God only knows when it will end. The Indians are numerous, and disposed to fight it out. They are in large numbers about thirty miles from this place* [Sly Park] *and on the Cosumnes River. This morning we shall start with mounted force for that point. Yesterday we had some fighting and some fun, and the Indians have many white men among them. After fighting them a good part of the day, we returned to camp, and while in the act of cooking our evening's repast, the fire again commenced upon us from the timber which surrounds the Park. Our horses, luckily, had just been staked down, and were beyond the reach of their guns. Well, Judge* [Vinal Daniels[32]], *to make a long story short, some of us have had some fighting, and I think by tomorrow night some of us will smell hell. You have but little idea of the immense numbers of Indians that visit this trail for the purpose of murder and robbery.*

How could Lieutenant Colonel McKinney know his prediction would hold true for himself, and would come to pass less than one week later?

On November 4, 1850,[33] Colonel Rogers wrote that the body of a white man was found among the Indians killed in a skirmish the day before. Several accounts mentioned white men had been seen

---

31 *Sacramento Transcript* November 1, 1850
32 Vinal Daniels was *Alcalde* of Placerville prior to statehood in 1850. *Alcalde* was a Mexican office with a wide range of authority invested in a single man by appointment, that combined the duties of judge, justice of the peace, and mayor.
33 *Sacramento Transcript* November 8, 1850

among the Indians, assisting them. None gave a full description of or name of a particular person. It is possible these assertions were simply ethnocentric in nature; the men making those remarks might have assumed the Indians could only be effective fighters if assisted and directed by white men.

Meanwhile, a letter penned by Judge Vinal Daniels, gave this account:

> *A scouting party, ten in number, fell in with a party of fifty or sixty Indians, about twelve miles east of Placerville, located in a deep ravine, upon which a smart skirmish ensued, but were forced to retreat after fighting a short time, with the loss of Dr. Dixon of St. Louis, and a Delaware Indian[34], killed, and Captain Francisco wounded severely in the lower jaw. They report eight or ten Indians killed, and many wounded. Our party retreated as far as Johnson's Ranche [sic], six miles above Placerville, and sent into that place for reinforcements; and I learn that some two hundred volunteers will start for the scene of action tomorrow. I have just learned that the body of Dr. Dixon has been recovered, horribly mangled, being literally cut in pieces by the savages.*

Judge Vinal Daniels went on to express the high-minded opinion that: "From the known character of the officers in command, there will not be a useless slaughter of the Indians, but their only object will be the protection of the lives and property of our fellow citizens."[35]

Lieutenant Colonel McKinney's war ended on the morning of November 4, 1850, while he led a scouting party. Riding in advance, he spotted a lone Indian and started in pursuit. He called to the men with him to take the Indian alive, as he might be of use. As McKinney

---

34 This refers to Ebert. See Appendix B *The Known Dead and Wounded of the El Dorado Indian Wars of 1850-1851* for more details.

35 *Sacramento Transcript* November 6, 1850

rode after him, the Indian slid from his horse and attempted to make his escape into the brush. Deciding he would be unable to escape, the Indian stopped, drew his bow, and shot Lieutenant Colonel McKinney through the heart.

All the later accounts differ a little as to the details. However, a letter written that day and published by the *Sacramento Transcript* reported McKinney had sufficient strength to catch and hold the Indian until another of the soldiers, George Goodhill of Company C,[36] could come up and kill him. Other accounts say McKinney fired on his attacker at point blank range. Either way, McKinney lived for only three hours. His body was taken to the Rogers Hotel in Coloma. There Dr. Simmon extracted the arrow from McKinney's body, where he found it had passed through McKinney's lungs and into his heart. Later accounts embellished this to say the arrow penetrated his chest "up to the feathers."

The citizenry took the loss of McKinney, who had been serving a term as clerk of the district and county court at the time of his death, very hard. The officers of the court wore black crepe armbands for the next thirty days. The stores and businesses of Coloma closed for the day of his funeral. A large contingent of people, following a "shrouded banner and muffled drum"[37] escorted the body to the Coloma cemetery. Both the Masonic Fraternity and the Order of Odd Fellows (he belonged to both) took part in the funeral ceremonies. Many speeches extolling his character and what the loss his death represented to the community were made, both before and after his funeral. Finally, a resolution of respect was drawn up, published in the Sacramento newspapers, and sent to McKinney's family in Illinois.[38]

Sadly, El Dorado County has moved on, forgetting this brave and once well-liked young man. It is known he is buried in the Coloma Cemetery, but his grave is no longer marked, and its exact location has been lost.

---

36 *Sacramento Transcript* November 11 and 20, 1850

37 *Sacramento Daily Union* September 26, 1885 page 2 "Early Days in El Dorado". This is a colorful account of events, somewhat different from the contemporary accounts.

38 *Sacramento Transcript* November 11, 1850

Throughout the newspaper accounts of skirmishes and encounters, the count of both enemy combatants and enemy dead, given by the volunteer soldiers, is probably unreliable. In December of 1850 the *Sacramento Transcript* estimated that fifty-nine Indians had been killed in several skirmishes that year. Earlier, the same newspaper expressed the opinion that "in every skirmish yet the whites have been worsted," but did not sustain as many casualties.

Over and over again, as the militia encountered a village, they set fire to the dwellings and acorn granaries, guaranteeing that when the Indians returned, they would have no resources. That also increased the death toll, as starvation the following winter would result from the loss of their food supply.

To further confuse the issue, the *Placer Times* took a very different editorial posture toward the Indian Wars than that held by the *Sacramento Daily Union* or the *Sacramento Transcript*, making it even harder to know what to believe.

The editor of the *Sacramento Transcript* was scathing in his criticism of the editor of the *Placer Times* whom he referred to as "Don Quixote" Lawrence. Editor Lawrence apparently thought the threat not as great as the *Union's* editor did.

A member of the militia, Lieutenant Fyffe recorded that the *Placer Times* was "giving them knocks." When the men discovered the identity of the culprit among them who was sending the *Placer Times* information, they "hung him in effigy."[39] This division of opinion continues to this day among historians.

As the winter began to close the mountain passes, both sides seemed willing to take a break from hostilities, even though nothing

---

39 From the unpublished journal of James Perry Fyffe. Mr. Fyffe served with the Ohio Volunteers in 1848 in the Mexican War, and as a Colonel of the fifty-ninth Ohio Volunteer Infantry in the Civil War, where he distinguished himself in several battles. In civilian life he was both a judge and a newspaper editor.

had been decided by the battles fought so far. The troops were disbanded and everyone sought winter quarters.

Because so many of the skirmishes had taken place near Johnson's Ranch, it was natural that the ranch would become the headquarters. While the number of volunteers fluctuated, at one time there were two hundred and fifty. Some accounts say many more men were stationed on the ranch. As the last outpost of civilization on the western slope of the Sierra Nevada, it took courage to remain there once the volunteer militia disbanded for the winter.

In February of 1851, John Hancock Phillips, J. C. Johnson's partner, wrote this eloquent letter to Major Rogers to inform him of their circumstances:

> *In great haste I take up my pen to give you some information relative to the movements of the Indians in this vicinity. From the time your troops were disbanded until about ten days ago, [January 1851] we saw no sign of Indians; and were in hopes that they would not again molest us; but alas! We were mistaken. They have within the last ten days commenced a most fatal war upon our citizens. Several dead bodies have been found on the "South Fork" literally cut to pieces. No less than seven companies [of miners] have been attacked and driven from the upper bars, several of which were dangerously wounded.*
>
> *They made an attack on Taylor's Rancho a few days since, and fired some half dozen shots at him [Taylor] all without effect. They also made an attack on this place [Johnson's Ranch], on the miners three hundred yards from the house. Mr. J. C. Smith was dangerously wounded. All the miners on the "Upper Bars" of the South Fork have left, all the men have left this place except six.*
>
> *So this place is almost completely deserted.*

*Six men beside myself and lady yet remain. We are
determined to remain let the result be what it may.
There have been large lots of stock drove up on the
dividing ridge within the last ten days. It appears
that they are concentrating all their forces on "Silver
Fork"* [a branch of the South Fork that heads in Silver
Lake]. *What the result will be God alone knows. Now
will you be so kind as to make use of all honorable
means in your power to get the Executive to render us
some assistance.*[40]

One issue that might have caused the lack of attention that the
Indian problems were receiving from California's young government
was a change in executive leadership in early 1851.

Governor Peter H. Burnett had resigned, and was replaced by
Lieutenant Governor John McDougal on January 8, 1851. A month
prior to his resignation, Governor Burnett wrote to Colonel Rogers
informing him that in his opinion, one hundred men was a sufficient
force to protect the people of El Dorado, and that he should immediately
reduce his forces. Governor Burnett ended his report with a request
that "every effort should be made to terminate the difficulties as early
as possible, and at as little expense to the State as practicable."[41]

The legislature was also distracted by the relocation of the
seat of government from San Jose to Vallejo, a move that was "subject
to warm debate," as historians put it. In the end they succumbed to
the persuasive powers of General Vallejo and, following the close
of the 1851 session, moved the capital to Vallejo. In the light of this
upheaval, it is little wonder that those charged with the governance
of the state were too preoccupied to give the matter of frontier safety
much attention.

---

40 Adjutant General-Indian War Papers F3753:17 California State Archives
41 *Sacramento Transcript* November 20, 1850

Once in office, McDougal supported his predecessor's policies of Indian suppression. Governor Burnett had expressed this policy in his "Governor's Annual Message to the Legislature, January 7, 1851." In addressing the Indian Wars he opined, "That a war of extermination will continue to be waged between the races, until the Indian race becomes extinct, must be expected. While we cannot anticipate this result but with painful regret, the inevitable destiny of the race is beyond the power or wisdom of man to avert."[42]

J. C. Johnson didn't wait for the governor to act. As reported by the *Sacramento Transcript*, "Mr. Johnson, foreseeing that the Indians would return during the winter of 1850-51, has procured several Delawares and a number of whites to remain on his ranch, where he intends protecting himself, irrespective of any government assistance."[43]

He was wise to select the Delaware Indian scouts to protect his ranch and home. They had proven themselves to be fearless warriors and trustworthy. By offering them employment, Johnson also assured that the Delawares would stay in the neighborhood in case their services were still needed. A friendship formed between Johnson and one of the Delawares, Fall Leaf, that would have a lasting effect on Johnson's future, and a positive effect on the formation of El Dorado County.

---

42 *Journals of the Senate and Assembly of the State of California*, at the Second Session of the Legislature, 1851-1852
43 *Sacramento Transcript* December 5, 1850

ELLEN OSBORN

3

FALL LEAF
&
THE DELAWARE INDIAN SCOUTS

The Delaware Indian tribe, or Lenape, originated in what are now the states of New York, Pennsylvania, New Jersey, and Delaware. As the advance of Americans into their ancestral territory pressured them off their land, they were relocated several times. Currently, they live in western Oklahoma. During Fall Leaf's time, the Lenape lived in Kansas where they adapted to an agrarian lifestyle. Early on, they gave their allegiance to the newly formed United States government and ever after remained loyal.

The Delawares were famous for their skills as scouts. They have been described as tall, handsome, and muscular. Their skill in the wilderness was described poetically in an article from the *California Historical Society Quarterly*[44]:

> *A hundred years ago any westward bound*
> *caravan seemed incomplete without a Delaware scout*
> *in the background, to read the weather signs in clouds*

44 *California Historical Society Quarterly* volume 25 1946 "Tom Hill-Delaware Scout" by Francis Haines pages 139-147

and wind, trail-sign in the print of a moccasined foot or the gouge of a lodge pole drag. He found water holes in dry country, wood for fires and forage for horses in barren wastes, and game of all kinds to feed hungry men. On him, to a large extent, depended the safety, even the existence of the group.

What were they doing in California? John C. Fremont brought a few of them to California as part of his exploring party. They had traveled across the continent with him. Those scouts were definitely battle ready. In a report to headquarters Colonel Rogers mentioned the death of a Delaware, who was identified as Fremont's scout.[45]

Among the several Delawares that Johnson hired to defend his ranch were Fall Leaf and Jim Cook. Altogether five Delawares participated in the El Dorado Indian Wars. Delaware Ebert had died in that war, and he was considered to be the first casualty of the conflict when he took an arrow through the heart at close range on November 3, 1850.

In the tense and lonely days of winter in 1851, the only people brave enough to stay at Johnson's Ranch were the Delawares, hired as guards; J. C. Johnson; John Hancock Phillips and his plucky wife, Sophronia; her brother and his wife. Her brother had recently sustained a severe injury to his hip inflicted by an Indian arrow.

Even among the Delaware Indians, Fall Leaf stood out as a most fascinating man. As one of the army's Delaware Indian scouts, he was present for many of the most historic moments in western history.

The New York Times printed a colorful article on August 10, 1856, that included an interview with Fall Leaf. This interview was part of a longer series of articles entitled "Overland to the Pacific" written by "Jersey Blue," correspondent to the *New York Times*.

Fall Leaf was described as being fifty-five years old[46] at that

---

45 Adjutant General-Indian War Papers F3753:40 California State Archives
46 Fall Leaf's military records give his age in 1862 as forty. That would make his birth year 1822 and at the time of this article, he would have been thirty-six. Various sources give different dates of birth and age.

time. Since this interview took place just four years after he'd left California, the physical description would be similar to his appearance while in California: he stood five feet eleven inches in his moccasins, weighed one hundred ninety-six pounds, and was of a very athletic build—"the perfect Hercules of the forest."

At the time of the interview, he was mounted on a mule and stationed at the head of a military wagon train, clad as a wagon master, save for a solitary eagle feather trailing from his broad-brimmed black hat, as described by Jersey Blue. He was about to depart from Fort Leavenworth on an exploration of the interior in his capacity as guide with the army.

According to the *New York Times* correspondent, Fall Leaf could understand English, but did not speak it. He was able to elicit the information that Fall Leaf had a wife and eight children, and that he was born near the headwaters of the Delaware River. Fall Leaf claimed to be a friend of the white man, as history has proven him to be. Although best known to historians as Fall Leaf, his Lenape name was *Po-ne-pah-ko-wha*[47], which translates to "He who walks when leaves fall."

When Lieutenant John C. Fremont began his third expedition in his capacity as topographical engineer in 1845, he took with him as many as twelve Delaware Indian scouts. No single list of his Delaware scouts appears to be comprehensive, and none contains Fall Leaf's name. Fall Leaf would have been about twenty-three years old, so if he was among Fremont's scouts in 1845 this might have been his first major expedition as an army scout. This assignment would have introduced him to the vast interior of the United States, and taken him through many adventures with J. C. Fremont, including California's Bear Flag Revolt in 1846.

These adventures drew the Delawares into a number of skirmishes with the local California Indians and the Mexican *Californios*. History records their war-like behavior evidenced by the many scalps taken, each scalp represented by a feather in a warrior's

---

47 *Leavenworth Times* newspaper November 27, 1934. Fall Leaf's name is spelled differently in other sources, but all agree on its meaning.

hat band. One eyewitness to the Delaware scouts on the warpath described them as "savage and painted."[48]

In 1857 Fall Leaf was working as a guide for Major John Sedgwick in his campaign against hostile Indians on the United States frontier.[49] Along the way, Fall Leaf did some prospecting in the Colorado mountains. Later accounts said he got off his horse to drink from a small stream when he saw gold nuggets on the stream's gravel bottom and picked them up.

While he wasn't the first to find gold in Colorado, by paying for a purchase from a pouch full of gold nuggets at home in the town of Lawrence, Kansas, he started a gold rush from the town of Lawrence, one that he declined to join. From his experiences in California it can be assumed he would have quickly recognized the nuggets for what they were, realized their monetary value, and also knew how ruinous gold prospecting could be to a man's life.

Fall Leaf continued his career in the service of the United States Army. In 1858, he was working as a guide for Colonel Edwin V. Sumner, again pursuing warring and raiding tribes on the plains. In 1860, Fall Leaf's rifle accidentally discharged, causing an injury that disfigured his face[50]. However, this injury didn't keep him from continuing to work as a guide.

When the Civil War loomed, Fall Leaf was home in Kansas. He was given a command in the Union Army and the rank of captain. He even recruited and led Company D of the Second Kansas Indian Home Guard at the request of his respected old friend, John C. Fremont.[51]

---

48 *The Year of Decision 1846* by Bernard DeVoto page 272

49 *Men To Match My Mountains* by Irving Stone page 186. See also "The Pike's Peak Gold Rush" Chapter 3 *The Argonauts*, available on line.

50 *Warriors for the Union* by Deborah Nichols and Laurence M. Hauptman on historynet.com

51 *The Delaware Indians A Brief History* by Richard C. Adams pages 50-51 Page 50 also mentioned that Fall Leaf accompanied the Prince of Wales, later Edward VII of England in 1860 as he toured the United States.

Delaware Indians acting as scouts for the Federal Army in the West. Note the
feathers tucked ito their hatbands; each one represents an enemy killed.
From a woodcut in the "Soldier in Our civil War."

There is not a great deal written about the role of the Delawares
in the War Between The States, but what has been written shows them
to have been loyal and brave soldiers. Perhaps the best summary of
Fall Leaf's career with the army is found in a letter he dictated on
September 15, 1863 to Honorable W. P. Dole, Commissioner of Indian
Affairs, in Washington, D.C. In this letter he summarized four year's
of active military service, along with reminders of the promises of pay
to both himself and his men—promises of pay and land grants that had
not materialized.

Californians honor his memory with the name given to an
exquisite little lake that drains into Lake Tahoe: Fallen Leaf Lake. *The
Mountain Democrat* on October 26, 1861 ran an article about how the
lake got its name:

Fallen Leaf Lake on the southwest side of Lake Tahoe. An early view of the
exquisite mountain lake named for Fall Leaf.
Courtesy of the El Dorado County Historical Museum

*Mr. Bishop describes this lake (situated on
his new route over the Sierra Nevada,) as a most
beautiful body of clear, cold water. It is about two
miles long and one wide, very deep, and enclosed in
almost perpendicular walls of granite. It is named
after a Delaware Chief, who stood upon its walls, in
company with Col. Jack Johnson, and threw pebbles
in it, and as they buried themselves in its waters
delightedly exclaimed 'much deep.'*[52]

A letter commenting on Fall Leaf's name followed this article
to the editor:

52 F. A. Bishop, a well-known engineer of the time was in the Sierra
Nevada surveying for a possible railroad route through El Dorado County.

ELLEN OSBORN

Editors Democrat—Having noticed in several California newspapers an article from your paper in relation to a feasible route for a railroad to the Pacific Coast, in which you speak of 'Fallen Leaf Lake' as having been named after a Delaware Chief, I desire to make a correction in the name. It should be 'Fall Leaf Lake', as the only Delaware Indian whose name resembles the above is the one who acted as guide for Lieutenant F. T. Bryan of the Topographical Engineers, in 1855-56, and his name is 'Fall Leaf'. If I am wrong, there are many in California who can correct me. Very Respectfully, Samuel Dean[53]

These two men didn't share a common culture or language, but they shared a sense of adventure and purpose. Surely J. C. Johnson himself, in honor of the friendship and trust shared by them, had named the lake. As sometimes happens with place names a small change in the spelling took place, making it forever Fallen Leaf Lake.

---

53 *Mountain Democrat* newspaper December 7, 1861

4

Winding Down the War

As Johnson had feared, sporadic attacks continued through the winter of early 1851, with the militia responding. In the spring the militia formally took to the field again. After the winter lull, the spring of 1851 saw a resumption of hostilities. A seemingly unprovoked attack by Indians on a small group of prospectors in May of 1851, further fanned by the attention paid to it by the *Sacramento Daily Union,* is universally accepted as the triggering event, for the second and final round of the war:

> *On Friday night last a company of miners, on a prospecting tour, were encamped about six miles from Johnson's Ranch, above Hangtown, when they were fired upon by a party of Indians. A Mr. Wade, formerly of Rochester, Wisconsin, was shot dead. Another gentleman, whose name we have not learnt, received a very severe wound in the neck, but is likely to recover; while a third has not been found since the*

murder, and is supposed by his companions to have been killed at the same time.

This lamentable occurrence is justly calculated to incite the miners to take summary and terrible vengeance upon their merciless foe. And who can blame them? The hardships and privations of the miner's life are dreadful enough under the most favorable circumstances; but when is superadded to these, that of living in constant jeopardy of life, it assumes an aspect sufficiently appalling to deter the boldest spirits from the mines.

On Saturday, twenty-four men volunteered to go out for the purpose of obtaining the dead body of J. B. Wade. On repairing to the spot where the attack was made, they were unable to find anything save a few bones and a heap of ashes. Hence the presumption is, that the body was burned. About this time the Indians made an attack on this party, who had to cross the river, (the North Fork of the American),[54] *and keep up a fight while they were retreating. The Indians, supposed to number some two hundred and fifty, and mostly armed with rifles, followed the party about four miles.*

In this skirmish, a Mr. Clark, of Clay County Missouri, was wounded, supposed mortally. Four of the enemy are known to have been killed. Today some of the skirmishing party are in town, endeavoring to raise volunteers, with the intention to go out and give them "a little more grape."[55]

In pursuit of the Indians, the soldiers were compelled to

54 There appears to be an error here in the original report. The correct river is probably the North Fork of the Cosumnes River.

55 *Sacramento Daily Union* May 13, 1851

construct a bridge across the South Fork of the American River. The bridge only consisted of logs felled directly across the river, then crudely finished. It was the first bridge ever across that wild river, and it was not an easy or safe bridge to cross. Captain Graham reported losing one man of his command when the man fell into the frigid river, swollen with snow melt, and drowned.

Three days later they engaged the Indians in a fight that resulted in the loss of one man and several wounded soldiers. The Indians had anticipated the militia's approach and had devised a trap.

They tied three horses in a very rugged ravine, and then secreted themselves nearby, using boulders and trees for cover. Captain Tracy, coming upon the horses, sent three men down to retrieve them. As soon as they started to untie the horses, the Indians opened fire from every direction. The men attempted to retreat, but before they could scramble to safety, three were wounded and Edwin Jenks was killed.[56]

The Americans were forced to leave Jenks's body where it lay until Captain Graham took fifteen men to give covering fire, and ordered two of the Delaware Indian scouts, Fall Leaf and Jim Cook, to take the horses and four men to bring up the body of the dead man.

This battle is a good illustration of how the Indians could control the battlefield, yet they still lost the war.

It is important to consider the high caliber of the men who actually took part in the El Dorado Indian Wars before dismissing the entire event as a hoax. The roster of volunteers in the El Dorado Militia included such recognizable names as:

☐ J. Neely Johnson, the fourth Governor of California from 1856 to1858, and later Nevada Supreme Court judge, from 1867 to 1871.

☐ Gaven D. Hall, with the rank of major and judge advocate in the wars, who went on to serve two terms in the state assembly and two more in the state senate.

---

56 *Sacramento Daily Union* May 25, 1851

Other future statesmen who took part in the wars include:

☐ Dr. Obid Harvey, who practiced medicine in El Dorado County for several years before being elected to the state senate for three terms.

☐ Dr. Benjamin F. Keene who served four terms in the state senate.

☐ John Calhoun Johnson, adjutant and county treasurer during the war, was later elected to the state assembly.

☐ Albert Wilson Bee, quartermaster during the Indian Wars went on to be elected treasurer of Placerville in 1854, completing his term of office before his life was cut short in 1863 at the mines on the Reese River in Nevada.

☐ General Albert Maver Winn, the head of the California Militia, was one of the few with prior military experience. His first instruction in military matters was with the militia in Mississippi, where he rose through the ranks. He later was an officer in the Mexican War. Winn, who was always civic-minded, was the first mayor of Sacramento, active in many fraternal organizations, and worked for the betterment of both labor and business interests in California until his death in 1883.[57]

☐ William Rogers was sheriff of El Dorado County when the war broke out[58]. When he failed to be reelected in 1851 to the office of sheriff, he moved east to Utah territory, where he worked for a time as the Indian agent assigned to the Shoshones before settling on a farm in Elko County, Nevada, where he died in 1877. Rogers may have been the oldest man involved in the El Dorado Indian Wars, since he was fifty-seven years old at the time.

---

57 Sacramentoabout.com Albert Winn

58 El Dorado has had two sheriffs named William Rogers. The first, our subject here, served from 1850 to 1851. The second, William H. Rogers, originally from New York, served a term of office from 1864 to 1865. He was the sheriff in office at the time of the Bullion Bend Robbery. The two are sometimes confused.

☐ At least six medical doctors were on the roster.
☐ A nineteen-year-old boy, Marion Lamb, who was wounded during the war, recovered and went on to live his life quietly in El Dorado County, as did many other volunteers.
☐ Finally, a number of the men had either fought in the Mexican War, or would go on to distinguish themselves in the Civil War.

As to the dead and wounded, assembling a comprehensive list was challenging[59]. At least nine men were wounded seriously enough to have their injuries reported in the newspaper. Those killed in action were harder to identify, as at least four deaths were reported without giving a name, so they may be duplicates. However, the best guess is a dozen men were killed.

Of those reported killed, two are known to be buried in Coloma, and two are buried in Diamond Springs. It must be assumed, the rest were buried where they fell, (although there is some suggestion that the officers did not encourage this) or their bodies were transported to headquarters at Johnson's Ranch, and buried in the little cemetery Johnson established there. It is possible the first interments in Johnson's Cemetery were those fallen soldiers, although no evidence now exists.

The final activity of the militia took place east of the Sierra Nevada in Carson Valley. The troops circled around, covering a lot of miles, but failed to engage with the Indians, other than in skirmishes. They rode east over the summit of West Pass to Red Lake (in present day Alpine County), on into Carson Valley, then north to the southern shore of Lake Tahoe, and finally to Georgetown by way of the Georgetown Cutoff.

In an interesting entry, Lieutenant Fyffe recorded a vivid description of their evening camp on the shore of Lake Tahoe, where they had dined on venison and talked around the campfire:

59 See Appendix B *The Known Dead and Wounded of the El Dorado Indian Wars, 1850-1851* for the list of known dead and wounded.

The smell of the meat in conjunction with the effect on the inner man of some old rye loosened the tongue of the old hunters and to a deeply interesting auditory from personal reminiscences. The detailed tales of border wars, of Indian cruelty, and Mexican treachery and murder from the Rio Grande to the lakes of the north and suffering and starvation on the plains almost incredible. Old Peg Leg Smith[60] who for twenty years had been a denizen of the plains and old Jennings who accompanied Carson over them twenty-three years ago. I never saw a more attentive group of listeners.

Those scouting parties were active into the month of August, well after the Indian Agent and those in attendance at the Grand Council had signed the treaty. Probably no one east of the Sierra Nevada knew a treaty had been negotiated.

When orders to disband the militia arrived, some of men and officers refused to obey. In fact, based on several entries in Lieutenant Fyffe's diary, insubordination by the men and lack of direction from the officers was fairly common.

All good Indian wars end with a treaty, especially if there was an Indian agent on the job. California had three Indian commissioners at the time, including Dr. O. M. Wozencraft, a recent arrival from the East Coast. It fell to him to negotiate a peace with the Indians in the mining counties.

In June of 1851, the newspapers began to predict an early end to hostilities, and eagerly, even impatiently, anticipated the arrival of Dr. Wozencraft. The *Sacramento Daily Union* reported:

---

60 Peg Leg Smith was Thomas L. Smith from Kentucky. He lost his lower right leg when he was shot in the knee. Formerly with the Hudson Bay Company, Peg Leg was a notorious horse thief. Carson was Christopher "Kit" Carson from Kentucky, a well known mountain man and guide to John C. Fremont.

Dr. Wozencraft has sent out couriers through
the entire northern country, to assemble all the chiefs
with their tribes in "grand council," for the purpose
of completing a treaty with them, which shall secure
to them their rights and privileges, and at the same
time ensure the safety of the whites.

The editor went on to say, "God grant that this greatly to be
desired object may soon be effected, and that for the sake of humanity
this devastating and annihilating war may soon cease."

Dr. Wozencraft took his time getting there, as illustrated by
these snippets from *The Sacramento Daily Union*. The first Dragoons[61]
of the El Dorado Militia, commanded by Lieutenant Stoneman of the
regular army, were sent to escort Dr. Wozencraft on June 18, 1851. By
June 22, General Winn was on hand to greet the good doctor, waiting
in camp on Johnson's Ranch. On July 3, it was reported:

There will undoubtedly be a treaty concluded
between the whites and Indians next week, as couriers
have been dispatched to all important points for the
purpose of assembling the chiefs in council. The grand
'talk' is to come off at Norris's ranch on the American
River, about three miles from this city [Sacramento].

On July 11, Dr. Wozencraft was still enjoying the hospitality
of Sacramento where he was reported to be in attendance at the theater
"in company with the dragoons in full uniform and our beautiful
ladies to adorn the dress circle..." While Dr. Wozencraft enjoyed the
theater, the settlers and soldiers waited, and clashes with the Indians
continued. The residents of El Dorado County were reported to be
"greatly dissatisfied with the masterly inactivity" of the U. S. troops.

At last a time and place were agreed upon. The chiefs of
all the Indian tribes would assemble in general council at Weimar's
Ranch on the Yuba River. The distance from El Dorado County to this

---

61 A dragoon is a mounted infantryman.

general council makes it unlikely that any of the local Indians, who were combatants in the El Dorado Indian Wars, were present.

A correspondent of the *Sacramento Daily Union*, who chose to hide behind the *nom de plume* of "Jehu," gave an eyewitness account. [62] The alias gave him license to report what transpired as he chose, and he chose to do it with great humor.

On July 16, 1851, about two hundred Indian men assembled, but not with their wives and children in tow. Jehu opined that the bad character reputation of white men, made it necessary for the Indians to hide and protect their wives and children, something they had been trying to do throughout the conflict.

The conference began with a feast described by Jehu:

> *The Indian Commissioner has been honored by the presence at his hospitable board, of about two hundred half starved, root and bug eating red legs; who did ample justice to his splendid collation, consisting of four fine tough taroons, and a portion of the Indian supplies, brought from Norris's Rancho near Sacramento.*

The following day, with all the participants assembled, Jehu recorded that Dr. Wozencraft's speech commenced: "By telling them who he was and who they were; what was his mission and what they had to hope for or expect; and in fine, gave them to understand who *was* who, and what *was* what."

Dr. Wozencraft spoke in English, it can be assumed, so how much was understood can be left to conjecture. Jehu continued:

> *Everything arranged to the satisfaction of all parties concerned, the treaty, three yards, seven inches and three quarters long, was then signed; first by the Peacemaker, and then by chiefs and head men*

---

62 Jehu was a slang term for a teamster, a biblical reference to 2 Kings 9:20 "The driving is like that of Jehu son of Nimshi—he drives like a mad man."

in the order of rank. This having been done, jackets (of state) lined with scarlet, and trimmed with copper lace and buff cloth, were then presented with all due ceremony to the signers. After this, three fat bulls were immolated, when they all went their way rejoicing.

On July 27, 1851 this was followed with a letter to the editor that stated, "The troops engaged in the late Indian War, having been disbanded, and the war may be considered at an end, although they failed to 'conquer a peace'."

The volunteer soldiers, of course, claimed this as a victory. Celebrating somewhat prematurely, a meeting of the second battalion was held at Johnson's Ranch on June 21, 1851. General A. M. Winn presided, and John Hancock Phillips acted as secretary, preserving a record of the proceedings.

Several resolutions were presented and all passed unanimously. First, that in recognition of their bravery and volunteer services in the expeditions against the hostile Indians, Fall Leaf and his Delaware companions should be presented with metals, struck especially for them.

A further resolution was passed to approve the course of Major Rogers "in the defense of our frontier" and thank him for his service.

Finally, Brigadier General A. M. Winn was "to receive our heartfelt thanks for the bold, honest, and patriotic course pursued by him, in his several addresses to the battalion." Previously the men had surprised General Winn with a special pin of gold. For once, the men caught him without a prepared speech.[63]

The treaty was sent along its way, to pass through the usual bureaucratic channels to ratification. Instead, it joined with seventeen other treaties "of friendship and peace" that were negotiated with California Indian tribes by the three commissioners, O. M. Wozencraft, Redick McKee, and George W. Barbour, in the years 1851 and 1852.

---

63 *Sacramento Daily Union* June 22, 1851. Also the diary of James Fyffe June 22, 1851.

The United States Senate refused to ratify any of them. It has been suggested that powerful mining interests, concerned that proposed reservations for the Indians were, in part, located on gold-rich land that they wanted to mine, convinced the senate to take no action.

The treaties were ordered filed under an injunction of secrecy, where they remained until 1905. Therefore, there was no treaty, but no one seemed aware of that fact. Attacks on both sides continued, but no one suggested calling out the militia again.

What followed was a war of words, as the disbanded men tried to collect their pay and contractors to receive their payment. Lieutenant Fyffe noted that the "War Loans Bill" failed to pass because there were men who opposed the bill on account of alleged fraud on the part of contractors. Fyffe recorded in his diary that the bill passed just before the legislature adjourned. The pay, in any event, was not great, and anxious to return home, he did not wait to collect.

N. W. Kays, in a letter home, reported having served one month with the rank of private for five dollars per day in the form of state script. The official record gave the rate of pay as eight dollars per enlisted man, sixteen dollars for officers, and two dollars a day per man for supplies and incidentals. Some men never got paid because the proper paperwork had not been completed to enroll them as members of the militia.

From as early as November 1850, General A. M. Winn was appalled by the cost. He advised Rogers to reduce the number of men and advocated that he "wind the war down soon if you can't get the Indians to stand and fight."[64]

At one point Major Kelly wrote candidly to General Winn that "Colonel Rogers says he knows nothing of military life...reports... show plainly that he does not, and that great difficulty must grow out of such irregularity."[65]

---

64 Adjutant General-Indian War Papers F3753-:28 California State Archives

65 Adjutant General-Indian War Papers F3753-:30 California State Archives

When hostilities resumed in the spring of 1851, Albert Wilson Bee had replaced B. F. Ankeny as quartermaster of the militia. A. W. Bee was well positioned for the quartermaster's job. He and his brother, Frederick A. Bee, ran a store in Placerville. Albert's brother, F. A. could stay in town and run the store, while A. W. Bee took care of the militia's needs. The quartermaster was responsible for supplying all types of supplies, including arms and food, all items the store already had on hand to sell to the miners.

Stories about fraud and abuse began to surface. Author C. W. Haskins recorded the tale of the storekeeper substituting kegs of black sand for black powder. He went on to say, "In consequence of the great similarity of appearance, neither the grand army, the Indians, nor Uncle Sam, ever knew the difference."

An earlier account gives another, fuller version:[66]

> *During the campaign it is related that Quartermaster General A. M. Winn came on an official visit to honor and be honored by the "brave soger-boys." His coming was announced, and preparations made for his reception in true military style. In the woods among the Indians, no cannon were to be had, and a musketry salute was all that could be given. Muskets were heavily charged and the braves were drawn up in a line to do homage to the great chief. As he approached orders were given to fire, when to the astonishment and chagrin of officers and men, snap, snap, snap of percussion caps only were heard along the line. On an examination it was found that the Commissary had sent a powder keg containing black sand, and all the arms had been loaded from that keg. At this time it is susceptible of proof that three, four, and even five hundred per cent*

---

66 The Argonauts of California by C. W. Haskins, 1890 and Sacramento Daily Union March 27, 1875 page 3

profit was charged for supplies furnished the troops, and on powder and lead perhaps greater profit than the above. The name of the man who sold black sand for powder, and pickled sausages for corned beef, can be given. "Jay"

It is quite likely "Jay" was thinking of A. W. Bee. The Bee brothers did show signs of prosperity shortly after the war concluded.

In November of 1853, the *Empire County Argus* carried an ad announcing, "Messrs. Bee and Jackson are now offering an entire new stock of groceries, provisions, liquors and hardware in their new fire-proof building on the Plaza, opposite the Empire Hotel in Placerville."

Also, in October of 1853, A. W. Bee and his bride from New York hosted a large party at his recently built suburban residence;[67] a fine home that is now known as the Bee-Bennett House, although almost nothing of the original residence survives. F. A. Bee also built a large home close by. The brothers had done well financially. How much of that was due to the commerce of the government during the Indian Wars is unknown.

Finally, four years after the conclusion of the war, the California legislature appointed a committee to sort out the war claims, and attempted to balance the books. Among the quartermasters who had failed to make returns of public property, A. W. Bee stood out with $19,060 unaccounted for.

It appeared that this missing property arose from the purchase of animals for which Major Bee had given certificates of indebtedness, and which were subsequently paid for by the Board of Examiners of Military War Claims. Presumably, these animals were horses and mules.

At the end of the war Major Rogers sold forty animals at public auction. To his credit, A. W. Bee urged the senate to appoint a committee to investigate any alleged deficiency on his part. In all likelihood, inexperience with running a war, poor record keeping, and

---

67 *Placerville Herald* October 22, 1853

the very nature of the frontier were to blame, rather than any deliberate attempt to defraud.

Whatever the outcome of that committee's investigation, it is clear that A. W. Bee had not lost the confidence of the government. For many months following the war's conclusion, newspaper advertisements appeared similar to this one:

> *War Claims. The undersigned is prepared to act as agent in the adjustment of all unsettled claims against the State of California for services in the first and second Battalion California Volunteers. Persons holding discharges are invited to call upon the undersigned, Albert W. Bee.*[68]

Sometimes the war was called the "Johnson-Rogers War of 1851," especially in later accounts. Since William Rogers was the officer in charge, and the base of operations was Johnson's Ranch, it is easy to understand how this name came to be. However, some of these later accounts unfairly targeted both men with the excesses and failures of the whole operation.

For instance, *The History of El Dorado County* stated, "J. C. Johnson who kept a store and trading post on his ranch, had the undisputed revenue from the whole camp."[69]

It is true he kept a store stocked with items to sell to emigrants and miners in his vicinity. He probably did sell to the individual soldiers camped there, also. But later writers have continued to amplify Johnson's role, and portray him as avaricious and uncaring: "a perfect villain."

One nineteenth-century writer had the decency to, at least, mention that as many of the main actors in the affair had passed away,

---

68 *Mountain Democrat* February 25, 1854
69 *The History of El Dorado County* ed. by Paolo Sioli pages 157-159

he didn't want to revive the scandal. It is interesting how little the main actors had to say about the wars and their roles in them.

By the time Paolo Sioli, editor of *History of El Dorado California* had set his interviewers up in the Cary House Hotel in Placerville to carry out their task of collecting the historical memories of the locals for his history of El Dorado County, all the main figures for the Indian Wars were dead: Major McKinney in 1850, John Phillips in 1852, A. W. Bee in 1863, J. C. Johnson in 1876, William Rogers in 1877, and finally, A. M. Winn in 1883.

It is important to remember that Indian wars were going on during the 1850s in several locations throughout the state, not just El Dorado County. As the Sixth State Assembly of 1855 undertook to sort through the claims presented to them from the Indian Wars,[70] the board of examiners had a big job to do.

The statewide war debt was more than a million dollars, which exceeded the allowable limits by more than $100,000. El Dorado's share was $22,118.45, of which the board of examiners disallowed $10,442.44, leaving the "amount carried to Roger's credit" as $11,676.01.

Governor Bigler then dispatched Winslow S. Pierce to Washington to lobby for reimbursement from the federal government. The reaction of the United States Government to this request for repayment for the debt incurred by the several Indian wars fought in California prior to January 1854, was to request a full accounting—itemized, and supported by vouchers.

State officials found themselves in a difficult spot. Due to a lack of a state capitol building at that time, the public archives were stored in a rented space, and were in a general state of confusion. So, rather than present the claim of California under the provisions of the Act of August 5, 1854, they applied to Congress to change the rules. As an alternative, they offered settlement based on the value of bonds that the state had sold to finance the activities of the state militia.

---

70 *Journal of the Sixth State Assembly of the State of California* Sacramento State Printer 1855 exhibit C Claims Acted On And Claims Rejected by the Board of War Examiners

A California Indian war bond.

Military Department Adjutant General. Indian War Papers, F3753, Claifornia State Archives.

Congress agreed to this proposal. As the *Report of the Fifty-First Congress, First Session* stated, "It should therefore be conclusively presumed that the assumption of the bonds was in fact a full and complete equivalent to a direct reimbursement to the state;

and the matter of said expenses prior to January 1, 1854, should be regarded as an account fully liquidated and finally closed."

The bondholders were paid, with interest, but interest only until the date of the Act: January 1, 1854. This resulted in a financial loss to the bondholders, because an act assuming payment wasn't passed for another thirty-two months. The settlement of war debt in California was further confused by militia actions going on in several places throughout the state at the same time. War debt continued to accrue as Indian wars, especially in the far northern part of the state, continued for several more decades.

The war bonds themselves are also a convoluted topic. For an investment of one hundred dollars, the bondholder got a bond that paid twelve percent interest, some only paid seven percent, and apparently some did not pay interest at all.

There was a state bond roster that showed 1,564 bonds were sold prior to January 1, 1854. By 1856, when the bonds were finally paid, most were in the hands of a few Eastern speculators, many of whom had purchased the bonds from the original owners for very small amounts, some as low as twenty-five cents each.

In accordance with the agreement with congress, John Mullan, council, attorney, and agent for the State of California, signed off on a balance sheet where the war expenses equaled, dollar for dollar, the war bonds sold. Using this method of reimbursement, the United States Government never had a chance to review what they had paid for.

Perhaps a later attempt was made to secure further federal dollars, because the report went on to make this somewhat testy statement: "Certainly the State ought to be content to, and ought to be held to, abide by the programme [sic] of its own selection after rejecting the more exact one offered by the Government."[71]

The El Dorado Indian Wars concluded without a ratified treaty, without an end to attacks and counterattacks between the

71 *Report of the Fifty-First Congress, First Session 1890*

miners and Indians, and with a final balance sheet that was fantastical in nature. Everyone was relieved it was over, even if payment of the war bond interest continued to occupy legislative and judicial time until a decision by the California Supreme Court put this matter to rest in 1895 [72].

<hr>

72 *Sacramento Daily Union* October 10, 1895

5

INDIAN HATTIE

One consequence of the war was the displacement of Indians, who lost their homes and extended families. Because their traditional lifestyle was destroyed, the survivors often had to live in an unfamiliar place among unfamiliar people. The stories of the lives of Hattie Tom and her aunt Emma are good examples of how two individuals adapted and survived. While it may never be known with certainty that this was their circumstance, there is much evidence to suggest it was.

Two separate accounts, recalled later what may be the same incident. In 1875 the *Sacramento Daily Union*[73] ran a story about the El Dorado Indian War of 1851, in which the writer, while scoffing in general at the futility of the war, wrote that, "The trophies of the expedition were one Indian buck killed, one blind squaw and two pickaninnies captured, and the destruction of a few deserted wigwams."

The other similar story appeared in *The Argonauts of*

---

73 *Sacramento Daily Union* March 27, 1875 "Johnson-Rogers-Indian War of 1851

California.[74] This time the story changed a little to say that one old squaw, with her papoose, were found in a ditch asleep.

Compare those stories to the one told by Hattie herself many years later, as remembered and recounted by Mabel Rupley[75], who knew Hattie and to whom Hattie had told the story.

The white men and the Indians got to fighting, as Hattie recalled. Her mother put her down on the ground and put brush over her and shook her finger and said "White man! White Man!" Nobody came back for her until the morning. In was in fact, her aunt Emma, Hattie's mother's sister, who had hid her and who came back for her. Hattie recalled much later in her life that her mother never saw an American,[76] so she had probably been dead for some time, probably by 1849. Therefore, Emma's role in Hattie's life was like that of a godmother who must care for the child in the case of the death of the mother.[77]

While the little girl lay hidden, the rest of the village started to make their escape over an established trade trail that followed Peavine Ridge east, then across the main crest of the Sierra Nevada to Carson Valley, or perhaps to seek shelter among the people of Chief Washo Ben, whose village was near where the town of Meyers, California, is located today.

Captain Tom, Hattie's father and the leader of their village, was friendly with Washo Ben. Although Washo Ben was a Washoe and Captain Tom was a Nisenan, they had celebrated "big times" together in the past.[78] They may have become acquainted during the annual exchange of pine nuts from Nevada for acorns from California.

Throughout the El Dorado Indian Wars the natives sought the protection of the mountains where they had the advantage of knowing

---

74 *The Argonauts of California* by C. W. Haskins 1890 Chapter XI page 149
75 This story was related by Mabel Rupley on oral history tape #74 El Dorado County Museum
76 Ibid.
77 "A Collection of Maidu Indian Folklore of Northern California" unpublished compiled by Dorothy J. Hill 1969 page 224
78 *Ethnology of the Nisenan* by Ralph Beals 1933 page 366

the terrain, and where there were places to hide known only to them. The path Hattie's people travelled, took them by way of what is now called Desolation Valley.

According to Hattie, Desolation Valley got its name when a big snow had come some years ago, and all the people had frozen to death.[79]

The bleak windswept landscape of Desolation Valley
as it might have looked in Hattie's time.
Courtesy of the El Dorado County Historical Museum

As a side note and point of interest regarding this story, the Johnson family descendants have repeated an old story about Johnson, where he, with his Indian guide (Fall Leaf, the Delaware Indian) came upon some dead bodies in the high mountains and piled them up and burned them. The family story became a little garbled when, in trying

---

79 Desolation Valley was first known as Devil's Basin. In the early twentieth century the name Devil's Basin disappeared from maps. "Devil's Basin" was replaced with Desolation Valley, perhaps by the newly formed Forest Service. The first reference found to the new name was August 1903 in the *Mountain Democrat*. For a time, both names were used concurrently. Desolation Valley in turn gave its name to Desolation Wilderness when it was created in 1969. Desolation Valley is now partly covered by Lake Aloha.

pursuits of a civilized life. There is a high likelihood that both Emma, who died on December 3, 1908, and Hattie's son, who died "about 1900" are buried there. The exact location of their graves is unknown.

An ethnologist working in the area in the early twentieth century recorded:

"These two old squaws (Emma and Hattie?) live here alone on this mountain and are the most aboriginal in temper and hospitality I ever saw. They are Nician [sic] people and have seen very few whites at this place during the past thirty years."[81]

It isn't absolutely certain that the ethnologist referred to Emma and Hattie, but he was working in the part of El Dorado County where they lived at the time when he made this observation.

Many of the people in El Dorado County would be amused if an outsider, such as this researcher, found Hattie and Emma to be reclusive. Hattie had lived for extensive periods of time in the households of several of the old families of the county. She had spent quite a bit of time on the Rupley Ranch, where Indians were welcome. Hattie also cooked and washed for several families over the years, where she was always well liked by the children. She was a regular visitor at the home of Milt Morris, the United States Forest Service ranger assigned to Pacific Ranger Station. She became good friends with his wife and children, often joining them for lunch.

When Emma died in 1908, Hattie was her administrator and sole heir. The probate file[82] established the relationship between the two women, and confirmed that Emma had no family other than her niece, Hattie.

It also gives a better idea of Hattie's age. Hattie's obituary made the claim that she was a hundred years old at the time of her death in 1928. This information was provided by the county hospital, where she died. However, in her statement in the probate file of her aunt, Hattie gave her age as "about sixty." So eighteen years later when Hattie died, she would have been closer to eighty years of age.

---

81 Unpublished field notes of Dr. J. W. Hudson, original on file, Department of Anthropology, Field Museum of Natural History, Chicago
82 Probate File #1008A El Dorado County Historical Museum

The actual ages and birth dates, as well as the Nisenan names for both women, are lost to us. It was not the custom of the Nisenan to share their names with others. The use of the surname "Tom" comes from the belief that "Captain Tom" was the last name of "their father," even though it is known the two women did not share a father, but were aunt and niece.

The name Tom is fairly common among the names assigned to local Indians by Americans. "Emma" and "Hattie" were names that were popular among Americans at the time, and were undoubtedly given to them by some of the first Americans with whom they came in contact. Since there were so few settlers in the area in 1851, it is a good possibility that the soldiers brought Hattie and her aunt Emma back to headquarters at Johnson's Ranch where the wife of Johnson's partner, Sophronia Phillips, herself the mother of two little girls, may have taken them in.

A letter printed in the *Mountain Democrat* on January 11, 1929 entitled "About Hattie Tom" is valuable for the information it provides about Hattie as a young woman.

Eva C. Carmichael of Plymouth, the correspondent, said she had lived near Hattie in Camino. Eva wrote that Hattie married a white man by the name of Boles, who was originally from one of the southern states. Together they had a son, about whom little is known. She further stated that Hattie's son died at the age of sixteen. It is said he is buried on Emma's property.

Carmichael added, "She said her husband was kind to her, but left one day and never returned." Some time later, a stranger had sought Hattie out, and had questioned her closely. He told her that her husband had been his tent-mate through the last years of the Civil War, a soldier of the Confederate Army.

Hattie probably didn't understand why her husband would feel the need to leave her and risk his life to fight for a cause she didn't understand, in a place far away, a place she had never heard of.

In Carmichael's letter she said Shingle Springs was the last place Hattie knew him to be. He had gone there to begin the long journey home, to what was then a hostile nation. He must have spoken warmly of her to his tent-mate, for the man to take the time to look Hattie up after the war. While the letter doesn't say so, it is probable that Boles died before the end of the war and was unable to return home to her.

Hattie seated in a chair with tools in the background.
This photo possibly taken near the end of her life.
Courtesy of the El Dorado County Historical Museum

The recollections of Lloyd Morris, the son of Milt Morris, the ranger assigned to the Pacific Ranger Station, confirmed that Hattie was once married. He recalled her husband as a Dutchman whose last name was Tom.[83] It is more likely that Hattie never changed her name, but others might not have been aware that the man she called her husband had a different name, Boles.

In 1927 and again in 1928, ethnographers interviewed Hattie Tom. Both she and other informants described the place of her birth as "a small settlement near a spring on a rocky hillside on the north side of the South Fork of the American River." This description fits both the place Emma homesteaded, and the place on maps now known as "Indian Hattie's."[84]

In the days before the Americans arrived, the Nisenan would move their camps often, yet it has been said that most Nisenans would die within a mile of where they were born. Hattie followed that migratory pattern, at times staying at Fresh Pond at the Pacific Ranger Station where she had made a traditional cedar bark house, or at the place she inherited from Emma, or at times with families in the Camino area.

While she ate with the white families who befriended her, she also prepared the traditional Indian diet for herself. Hattie had a favorite rock where she ground acorns, a staple of the Nisenan diet, wearing several mortar holes. She was also known for her woven baskets made in the traditional fashion of her people.

On a blustery day in late September of 1925, Hattie's days living on her own came to an end. When Ranger Morris went to check on Hattie he found her badly injured by a fallen tree limb. Before he could render first aid to her, he had to cut away some of her long black hair—an act Hattie found outrageous and hard to forgive.

He took her to the hospital in Placerville where she was treated and where she stayed and lived until her death on December 26, 1928. While she was living at the hospital, another anthropologist tried to interview her about her early years, but noted that whenever Hattie reflected on her early days, she was so consumed by the despicable

---

83 Unpublished letter written by Lloyd Morris dated January 17, 1998. The original is in the possession of the USFS.
84 United States Department of the Interior Geological Survey Pollock Pines Quadrangle

actions of the whites against her people she had trouble concentrating on his questions.

When Hattie died, she was buried in the Indian cemetery on the Jack Johnson Ranch. Her passing was noted with an obituary and a ceremony attended by many citizens who had known her for most of their lives.

It was the well-meaning intent to lay her to rest with her family, but she would have been closer to them if she could have been buried with her Aunt Emma and son on the forested ridge where she had lived so many years. Perhaps, by then only Hattie knew where that was. If indeed she had started her life among Americans at the ranch of Jack Johnson, there is some sense of "coming home" to be buried there.

6

THE JOHNSON CUTOFF
EMIGRANT ROUTE

Following the conclusion of the El Dorado Indian Wars, John Calhoun Johnson began exploring, on his own, the part of the Sierra Nevada mountain range today called the Crystal Range[85], looking for a better route through the mountains to bring emigrants to Placerville.

All of the emerging communities in the gold mining districts desired to have their population increased by emigrants, and they actively promoted any route that would direct the emigration to their town. Marysville, for instance, hired James Beckwourth, an explorer and mountain man, to locate a passable route that would lead directly to their city[86]. Others satisfied themselves with hiring men to go out along the established trails to hand out waybills touting the advantages of their route over others.

---

85 See *Lake of the Sky Lake Tahoe* by George Wharton James for a description of the Crystal Range, which extends northwest from Pyramid Peak to Phipps Peak.
86 *Jim Beckwourth Black Mountain Man and Chief of the Crows* by Elinor Wilson

Since the Carson River Route was already directing the emigrant traffic to Placerville, there was no compelling need to look for another route. Nonetheless, Johnson must have had an idea that a better route was possible.

These trips into the mountains to explore came so soon after the El Dorado Indian Wars, it would have been prudent to take a number of men with him for protection, but only Fall Leaf, the Delaware Indian who he employed as his guide, was known to have accompanied Johnson. Riding through the mountains in pursuit of the local Indians during the El Dorado Indian Wars of 1850—1851, Fall Leaf must have become aware of the passes, the safest crossings of the South Fork of the American River, and perhaps more importantly, where the Indian trails were. Fall Leaf and Johnson had skills that complimented each other's.

Johnson had learned some surveying back home in Ohio, and had his own recent experience crossing the Sierra Nevada on the Carson River Route. This background gave him the skills to locate a new road. He was looking for terrain that could be navigated by wagons, with a minimum of improvements, with the goal of opening his new route as soon as possible.

They found what they were looking for. Some roadwork was required, and the people of Placerville paid for it. In the spring of 1852, a party of workmen under the direction of Johnson graded fourteen miles of road and constructed a bridge across Brush Canyon, and another across the South Fork of the American River[87]. The bridge, widely advertised as the only crossing of the South Fork, was first called Johnson's Bridge.

Before the close of the 1852 emigration season, the bridge had been taken over by William Bartlett who had established a way station nearby, one referred to as "Bartlett's House of Entertainment." So, as early as 1852, the people of Placerville had an investment in their road.

---

87 *Sacramento Daily Union* April 26, 1852

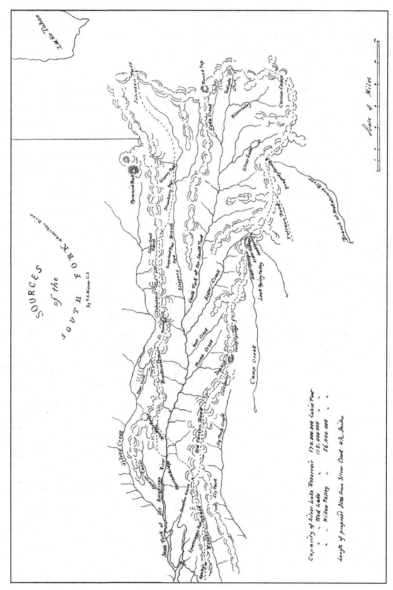

Sources of the South Fork of the American River
by surveyor F. A. Bishop, 1855.
Courtesy of the Bancroft Library University of California, Berkeley.

Johnson's explorations took place from 1851 through 1853.[88] Based on his thorough examination of the mountains west of Lake Tahoe, Johnson could be confident he had chosen the best possible route into El Dorado County from the east. With the improvements later suggested by government surveyors Sherman Day and George Goddard, it remains the eastern point of entry into the county. No better pass has been found than the one today called Echo Summit.

Woodcut of sketch of Lake Bigler by George H. Goddard, surveyor, 1854.
Printed in *Scenes of Wonder and Curiosity in California*
by James M. Hutchings, 1862.

There is evidence of some of his other explorations. In July of 1853, the *Placerville Herald* ran a front-page story about a trip to Lake

---

88 There are some sources that say he did his explorations as early as 1848. Based on reliable sources that prove he wasn't in California before 1849, that date is wrong. However, once something gets into print, it is nearly impossible to correct it.

Bigler[89] (as Lake Tahoe was then known) over what is today called the Rubicon Route. The actual trip took place in May.

Since Johnson was identified as the guide on that trip, he may have been there the previous season. This well-used Indian trade trail became popular in the late nineteenth century as a way for summer visitors to reach the shore of Lake Bigler and the resorts at Wentworth Springs and Rubicon Springs, but not as an emigrant route.

It is still popular today with Jeep enthusiasts. Worldwide, it is known as a premier four-wheel drive trail. Officially, it is a county road, but it has been left in its rustic condition for recreational use. It is the site of the annual "Jeepers Jamboree."

Another curious bit of evidence of Johnson's far ranging explorations of the region is the rock known as the Johnson's Monument.

Johnson's Monument on the side of Mount Mildred, Placer County.
Photo by Author

89 See Appendix A *The Origin of Lake Bigler* (Tahoe) as published in the Placerville Herald for the full text.

It is located in Placer County in the Tahoe National Forest. A ninety-one foot tall monolith of dark gray Andesite[90], it dominates the head of Grayhorse Valley. Of obvious volcanic origin, it is severely overhung, with the top larger than the base. It stands alone on the steep flanks of Mt. Mildred. A monument—in the surveyor's sense—it may be associated with the 1853 jaunt to Lake Bigler, although it is not visible from the popular Jeepers' route known as the Rubicon Trail, so the reason for association with Johnson still remains a mystery.

Finally, a mute piece of evidence of Johnson's ramblings near Lake Bigler is his so-called cane. This is one of only a few of his possessions still known to exist. It is in the collection of the California State Department of Parks and Recreation in Sacramento. The acquisition papers identify it as "a cane—decorative and sturdy." It was presented to Sutter's Fort along with a small tintype of Jack C. Johnson and his brother Nathan, probably taken in California.

The information given by Ann Johnson Butler, his daughter, was that Colonel Jack Johnson, and his father before him, had owned the cane. The physical description is an "object of untreated, light orange-brown, knobby wood." On examination, the curious duckbill-shaped handle appears to have been very roughly cut, looking like that spot is where the limb was broken or cut from the base of the plant. The end is pointed, not a typical characteristic of a walking stick or cane.

This history was accepted as correct until two more of these canes were found in old photographs. One photo appeared in the *Pony Express Courier*, January 1948. In it the cane is being held by John Willson Laird, and is identified as the "Staff of Relief." The Staff of Relief is a term used by the organization, E. Clampus Vitus.

There was an active chapter of E. Clampus Vitus in Placerville to which J. C. Johnson probably belonged. His walking stick may also have been used as a "Staff of Relief."

The more significant picture, in terms of identifying the original purpose of the stick, is a portrait of the famous Washoe Indian

---

90 See Geographical Map of the Granite Chief Wilderness Study Area and Adjacent Parts of the Sierra Nevada, CA by David S. Harwood 1981 USGS

basket maker, *Dat So La Lee*. She is posed with several of her baskets, a cooking stick, and is holding what is a twin to Johnson's cane.

This evidence strongly suggests Johnson's cane is actually a Washoe digging stick, an important tool in everyday Washoe life.

The unanswered question is: did Johnson receive this stick, which he so obviously prized, as a gift from the Indians he met on the shore of Lake Bigler? While the story in the *Placerville Herald* identifies the Indians as Diggers, they were very likely Washoe.

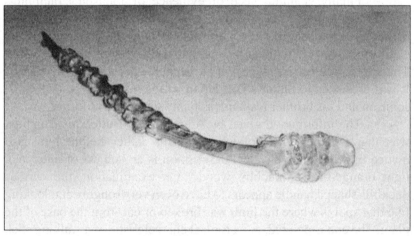

Johnson's walking stick, photographed at Sutter's Fort repository,
Sacramento, California.
Photo by Author

The advantages of the Johnson Cutoff over the older Carson River Route were that it was fifty miles shorter, two thousand feet lower in elevation than the highest point of the Carson River Route, and had only a single crossing of the South Fork of the American River.

Today, when modern day travelers look at the route Johnson laid out, they might wonder why he chose the route he did; it winds around, goes straight up in places, and follows a high ridge line. No better explanation can be given for this than a letter written in May of

1857, by Sherman Day,[91] who did the first full survey of the area and made the suggestion to place the route closer to the river where the modern highway is located today:

> *Dear Sir: By means of your daily paper, I have been enabled, although here in a retired spot, to keep pretty well posted in regard to the various wagon road movements. I notice that several writers and speakers allude to the road surveyed by me between Placerville and Carson Valley as the Johnson's Cut-Off road, and having, as some of them say, formerly passed over Johnson's Cut-Off, they proceed to draw a comparison between that route and their favorite route. I wish, through you, to protest this, and to inform such persons that the route surveyed by me is not Johnson's Cut-Off at all.*
>
> *The two roads do not pass either the eastern or western summit of the Sierra at the same point. It is true that, for about nine or ten miles on this side of the western summit, at and near Slippery Ford, the two roads touch or approach each other somewhat as two crooked sticks laid side by side might do. At each end of this ten miles they diverge, and are not again coincident except for a short distance near Placerville, among the permanent settlements.*

Mr. Day went on to make a point-by-point comparison of his route to Johnson's, then stated:

> *I do not intend, by this comparison, to reflect on Col. Johnson's skill as a road maker. He did the best he could with the limited means at his disposal, and deserves much credit for having opened*

---

91 *Sacramento Daily Union* May 19, 1857, "The Proposed Wagon Road Routes"

a road passable for wagons where before it was
scarcely passable for mules.

Echoing this sentiment, Dan Gelwicks, Chairman of the
National Road Meeting stated, "We, as citizens, appreciate the energy
and indomitable perseverance in its exploration."[92] Chairman Gelwicks
was voicing the gratitude of the citizens of El Dorado County to J. C.
Johnson for accomplishing, on their behalf, what every community
in the gold country wanted: a route to bring the emigrant directly to
their doorstep.

Today it is often assumed the responsibility for keeping
travelers connected by way of safe and modern roads is the
responsibility of our government. However, in the past that wasn't so.
Road building and maintenance was considered to be the prerogative
of private enterprise.

Roads and bridges were made profitable by means of the tolls
charged to those who passed over them. In this matter and in several
other important ways, J. C. Johnson's opinions ran counter to the
common wisdom of his time, and have proved closer to the popular
opinions of today. He argued for the county to provide free roads
to emigrants.

Proof of his stance was recorded in the May 14, 1853
Placerville Herald when he addressed a mass meeting advocating
keeping Bartlett's Bridge[93] toll-free, offering this resolution:

"Resolved: That said bridge having been constructed by the
citizens of Placerville at their own expense, they alone ought to have
a voice in determining whether said bridge shall become a toll bridge
or remain forever free."

---

92 Sioli, Paolo *The History of El Dorado County* page 120
93 Bartlett's Bridge is named for William Bartlett who operated a way
station near the bridge. He is the Bartlett of "Bartlett's Guide to California."
He probably paid for the survey and printing of the waybill designed to
bring more emigrants over the route. He took over what had previously been
known as Johnson's Bridge and began charging a toll. While disagreeing
on the issue of charging emigrants a toll to cross it, Bartlett and Johnson
remained friends. See Appendix C for the full text.

On August 6, 1853, El Dorado County declared Johnson
Cutoff a public road.[94]

Bartlett's Guide to California, printed in the *Placerville Herald* office, 1853.
Copies of this handbill were given to emigrants on the east side of the Sierra Nevada
to convince them to choose this route that would bring them to Placerville.
Courtesy of the Bancroft Library University of California, Berkeley

94 *El Dorado County Board of Supervisor's Minutes Book A* page 156

ELLEN OSBORN

Endless lines of print in the local newspapers, and hours of debate, were devoted to just which route was best and how to pay for the necessary improvements. Many people favored the government paying for the roads, but the public balked at picking up the bill, so private enterprise and toll roads were inevitable. Clearly, everyone recognized the need for a passable stage road, regular mail service, and a telegraph line to truly connect California with the eastern states.

The railroad was but a dream at that time. And, of course, each community championed the route that first reached them. The Johnson Cutoff enjoyed loyal support from the citizens of El Dorado County. It was common for the supporters of other routes throughout California to compare their route to the Johnson Cutoff.

On August 3, 1854 by Act of Congress, Johnson Cutoff was declared a post road.[95] J. C. Johnson, famously, carried the mail himself across the snowy Sierra even before Snowshoe Thompson.

The date of this trip was probably 1853. Johnson may be the messenger referred to in the July 23, 1853 *Placerville Herald* where a small note appeared saying the messenger from Carson Valley to Placerville made the trip in twenty-five hours with seven stops to rest. Snowshoe Thompson made his first trip with the mail in 1856.[96] In fact, there were several other men who tried to make mail carrying across the Sierra Nevada a regular and profitable business in the years from 1851 until Thompson became the regular—if unpaid—carrier.

The celebrated Pony Express used this route to carry mail.

Many years later, The *Mountain Democrat* ran the following article:

Vindication of History

In referring to the pending allowance by Congress to "Snowshoe Thompson" for carrying the mails across the Sierra Nevada, some of our

---

95 Act of Congress 10 USSL page 543
96 *Snowshoe Thompson* pub. by the Carson Valley Historical Society page 7

exchanges speak of Thompson as the pioneer in the business for which the allowance is proposed. While we do not wish to depreciate Thompson's services, and feel gratified that he is to be paid liberally, it is due to truth and justice to state that one of our old citizens—J. C. Johnson of Johnson's Ranch— preceded Thompson as a trans-montaine *mail carrier, opening up, marking out, and traversing the route subsequently traveled by Thompson, known as Johnson's Cut-Off and crossing the range through the depression laid down on all maps as Johnson's Pass. By this route and through this pass Johnson carried the mail from the present site of Carson to Placerville in twenty-six and one-half hours, previous to Thompson's first trip. Pay Thompson what you will, but let the truth of history be vindicated: Jack Johnson claims the nestorship of* trans-montaine *mail carrying on foot by the Placerville route.* [97]

Modern Americans are accustomed to mailing their letters with postage affixed at the post office or dropped in a box for delivery by the United States Postal Service. How is it, one might ask, that individuals would be allowed to legally carry mail?

On June 11, 1853 the *Placerville Herald* ran a story that gave an idea of how that was authorized: "Outside Letter Mail Carriage— Congress has provided by a late law a system of letter-carrying outside the mails... [Those with] suitable envelopes with prepayment of postage can hand their packages to whoever they choose to trust."

Johnson's July mail run may have been one of the first authorized by this new law, and was perhaps done to publicize the new law.

---

97 *Mountain Democrat* January 4, 1873

In May of 1857, Johnson was elected to serve on the Three County Wagon Road Convention held in Sacramento. The purpose of the convention was to select the best possible route and raise money to pay for it through El Dorado, Sacramento, and Yolo Counties.

Johnson's Route was adopted, and work begun to make the improvements suggested by surveyor, Sherman Day. This began a long-term evolution of improvements and changes, which continued until just before World War II, when the road finally settled into the current route of Highway 50. Along the way it acquired several new names: "The Placerville Carson Valley Road," the "County Road," and the "Road to Washoe" when silver was discovered in 1859 in Nevada. In 1895, when the Department of Highways was formed, Highway 50 became California's first highway. The improved route is an official part of the Lincoln Highway.

An interesting note is that the Placerville and Humboldt Telegraph Company, when it finally came through, followed the old Johnson route, with the lines crossing Brockliss Bridge[98] and strung along Peavine Ridge. It was called "Bee's Grapevine," because, in the rush to get in the seventy-five miles of line between Sacramento and Fort Churchill, Nevada, it was sometimes draped over brush, not unlike a wild grapevine.

The telegraph put the Pony Express out of business. In fact, F. A. Bee, one of the originators of the Pony Express,[99] had intended the Pony Express only to demonstrate the usefulness of regular and rapid communication with the East. He was president of the Placerville and Humboldt Telegraph Company. Communications across those lines began as early as September of 1858.

---

98 Brockliss Bridge, named for its builder, Anthony Brockliss, replaced Bartlett's Bridge with a sturdier, less flood prone bridge in 1854. After it's opening, Bartlett's Bridge was abandoned.

99 Bancroft. Hubert Howe *The Works of Hubert Howe Bancroft volume XXV History of Nevada, Colorado, and Wyoming* page 228

This route has been called one of the most storied and romantic roads in the history of the United States.[100] Over the years, it has seen many famous travelers, some of whom recorded their experience. Among those travelers were Mark Twain, Horace Greeley, Kit Carson, Collis P. Huntington, Thomas Starr King, Adolph Sutro, Susan B. Anthony, a pre-presidential Ulysses S. Grant, and Colonel Albert Sidney Johnston.

The U.S. Army Sixth Infantry, on one of the longest continuous marches of any regiment of infantry in the history of the frontier, marched from Fort Leavenworth, Kansas, to Benicia, California, a total of 2,147 miles.[101] Add to that scene the colorful dash of the Pony Express rider, Snowshoe Thompson on his long skis, shoulder to shoulder with the trudging emigrant on his way to make his fortune—in many ways, its history reads like a great Western novel.

Among the throngs following this route were also a few notorious criminals. For a time Johnson's Hill (now called Echo Summit) was also referred to as "Mickey Free Point" because a notorious robber and murderer carried out an especially bloody attack on one of the way stations nearby. In 1855, his crime spree ended with a very public hanging in Coloma, with Mickey Free singing and dancing his way to the gallows.

The Bullion Bend Robbery took place on June 30, 1864, near what is now Pollock Pines, California. The robbers were Southern sympathizers looking to finance their cause with some of the silver bars and the contents of the treasure box Wells Fargo regularly shipped by stagecoach from Genoa to Placerville. The silver bars were recovered, although it is rumored that the bags were a couple of bars short. The robbers were pursued and eventually all were captured, but not before a blazing gun battle in which Deputy Sheriff Staples was killed.

Later, during the trial, Alban Glasby, one of the robbers, testified that the night before the robbery they had stayed at the Six Mile House. Unfortunately, Glasby wasn't able to give the location

100 Cross, Ralph Herbert *The Early Inns of California 1844—1869*
101 Swanson, Clifford L. *The Sixth United States Infantry Regiment, 1855 to Reconstruction*

of the Six Mile House, so today it is not possible to determine if J. C. Johnson, whose home and hotel had been known as the Six Mile House since 1849, had been the unknowing host to the soon-to-be notorious Bullion Bend robbers.

In 1864, another house six miles east of Placerville was also known as the Six Mile House. According to a Reiber family history, they often hosted teamsters overnight, so it's possible it was that location where the robbers stayed.[102]

It is equally possible it was at the Johnson residence, since it is known from the Larsen family history that their family stayed with the Johnsons in the 1860s when they first arrived in the county, evidence that the Johnsons still housed travelers.

Travel by stagecoach over the Sierra Nevada was not for the faint-hearted. The stagecoaches were crammed as full as possible with passengers, the freight and luggage loaded on top, and perhaps a few daring passengers on top of the luggage. The coach then took off at breakneck speed over steep and stony roads. One mistake and all would end up at the bottom of one of the many deep canyons.

Some the stagecoach drivers, or "knights of the whip" as they were known, gained fame for their daring. Hank Monk, one of the best known, was the subject of this famous story told by Mark Twain:

> *Horace Greeley went over this road once. When he was leaving Carson City he told the driver, Hank Monk, that he had an engagement to lecture in Placerville and was very anxious to go through quick. Hank Monk cracked the whip and started off at an awful pace. The coach bounced up and down in such a terrific way that it jolted the buttons all off Horace's coat, and finally shot his head clean through the roof of the stage, and then he yelled at Hank Monk and*

---

102 Rieber, Joralemon Dorothy. *To Live Strivingly 1849—1942.*

*begged him to go easier—said he warn't in as much
of a hurry as he was a while ago. But Hank Monk
said, Keep you seat, Horace, and I'll get you there
on time and you bet he did, too, what was left of him.*

This anecdote, which first appeared in *Roughing It*, may or
may not have any basis in fact, but it is too entertaining to let die.

Although Monk's trip with Mr. Greeley was recorded as one
of the faster trips, making the journey of 112 miles in twelve hours,
Hank Monk himself would probably have chosen a different dash
down the mountains as the scariest.

It was a winter night in 1862, with the road frozen and icy.
To counter those conditions, an iron shoe was placed under one of the
wheels, as the brake would have been of little use on the steep run from
the summit of Johnson's Hill to Van Sickle's Station on the southern
shore of Lake Tahoe. Almost immediately the iron shoe failed. The
coach crowded the horses and frightened them into running away.
Hank's arms quickly became so fatigued that he couldn't control the
horses. The horses, frightened as they were, instinctively kept to the
track and covered the distance of five and one-half miles in sixteen
minutes, without even waking the sleeping passengers.[103]

J. Ross Browne wrote this vivid description of the road's
condition in 1859: "The road is five feet deep by one hundred and
thirty miles long and is composed chiefly of mountains, snow
and mud."[104]

He was not alone in that opinion. Nor did the situation improve
in the next decade. In September of 1869, the *Mountain Democrat*
wrote: "Great complaints are being made at this time about the rough
state of our roads, and yet we have to pay our regular two dollars and
fifty cents cash every year, and can hardly get out of town, east or
west, without paying extra at a toll gate, and still the roads are bad."

---

103 One of the many great stories about stagecoach drivers in *First Baby in
Camp*.
104 J. Ross Browne. *A Peep at Washoe and Washoe Revisited*. Balboa,
California: Paisano Press, 1959, page 105

As early as 1851, the county supervisors had divided up all the roads within El Dorado County into twenty-two road districts and appointed a supervisor for each. Failure to accept this dubious honor could result in a fine of twenty dollars. In 1854, and probably for a longer time, J. C. Johnson was the supervisor of district eighteen, which was the road from Spring Garden House eastward to the county line.[105]

Road crews were comprised of local men between the ages of eighteen and fifty years old, who were conscripted to work with their own tools for the number of days set by the Court of Sessions for a given year, usually two days. A man could send a substitute to work in his place or shirk, although shirkers could be fined.

An El Dorado County road crew ready to do one of their obligatory days of work near White Rock Springs.
Courtesy of the El Dorado County Historical Museum

---

105 California county boundaries in the 1850s were not all the same as they are today. Land originally in El Dorado County is now in Placer, Alpine, and Amador Counties and also the State of Nevada. See *California County Boundaries* by Owen Coy for a further explanation.

George Johnson, who lived in Coloma, remembered it this way:

> *The roads in sidling land had to be supplied with water breaks or little levees, which were made cater-cornered. In wet weather, a heavy wagon with wheels locked was very apt to cut through water breaks and would have two streams of water following in wheel tracks much to the grief of the road overseer. Sometimes he, when repairing water breaks and filling ruts, would find gold in the gutters, although no one ever got rich from the gold picked up. Everybody had a chronic grudge against the road overseers or supervisors for allowing such roads.*[106]

No history of the road would be complete without the story of Henry Hooker's turkey drive of 1866. Hooker was one of Placerville's Main Street merchants who lost almost everything in a fire in 1866.

Casting around for an idea of how he could recoup his losses, he came up with the idea that if he could get turkeys to the silver miners in Nevada for the holidays, where it was rumored that item was not available, he could name his own price. He bought five hundred turkeys in California, hired a helper, and made plans to drive them over the Sierra Nevada. Concerned about the turkey's ability to walk seventy miles over rough and snowy terrain, he had them first walk through warm tar, then sand, to create a protective covering. They made it to the summit when something caused them to take flight. Hooker looked on in horror, thinking he had now really lost everything. Imagine his joy when upon reaching the valley below, he found the turkeys alive and well, ready to resume their journey. [107]

---

106 George is no relation to the family of J. C. Johnson. This George's father Charles, an emigrant from Sweden, learned English grammar from J. C. Johnson's brother Nathan.

107 *Sierra Heritage* December 1999 "Get Along Little Turkeys" by Craig MacDonald

Hooker's gamble paid off, providing him the stake to purchase a cattle ranch in Arizona, where he became well known and wealthy. Later, Henry Clay Hooker and his brother Cassius Hooker would cross paths with J. C. Johnson one more time in Arizona, in a fateful way.

Less entertaining, but more important, much valuable freight was shipped over this route, both to and from the silver mines of Nevada. It has been opined that the traffic during the 1860s was possibly the greatest movement of men, materials, and animals ever known. For the first few years of Nevada's silver boom, everything built or used had to be freighted over the Sierra Nevada.

Traffic was described as nose to tailgate for the entire length of the road. Not an easy job, teamsters needed to be tough to deal with the difficult working conditions. One teamster wrote home to his parents saying, "The roads is [sic] terrible dusty—part of the time can't see the team for the dust." As an interesting side note, in that throng of wagons and teamsters were two of Johnson's brothers-in-law: Eber Adam Hagerdon and James Knox Hagerdon.

While in the planning stage of the Central Pacific Railroad, Theodore Judah sent a man out to count the traffic over El Dorado's county road. For eight weeks during the busiest season for travel over the Sierra Nevada, a count was kept. Knowing a railroad would be able to attract this traffic away from the county road, Mr. Judah wanted to estimate its potential revenue to the railroad. This count was included in his report as Chief Engineer dated October 10, 1862.

He recorded during that time 5,868 people, on foot and in vehicles, with 46,538 animals, including the teams pulling 9,053 vehicles of various sorts passed over the route in both directions. While the counter failed to record the weight of freight traveling west, he did count 19,386,200 pounds of freight of all kinds carried east into Nevada. Ultimately, the railroad was built in Placer County and did attract the valuable commercial traffic away from El Dorado's county road.

The local Indians found the stream of traffic over the mountains entertaining to watch. Not knowing what to call wagons, they came up with the word "wohah" based on the constant shouts of "whoa" and "haw" from the men driving the teams. An early ethnographer noted that when an Indian would see an American coming up the road, he would cry out, "Here comes a wohah!" at the same time swinging his arms as if driving oxen. This performance would produce convulsive laughter from his companions.[108] Unfortunately, the Indians also saw much that they would appropriate for themselves, especially livestock, creating a great deal of animosity.

Much has been written about the way stations that were located on the route, there to provide needed supplies to the emigrants, and sometimes a place to spend the night and eat a hot meal. Proprietors moved their stations to follow the customers as the road was improved and rerouted.

A few of the historic roadhouses still exist and can be visited, such as Strawberry Lodge on Highway 50, and Sportsman's Hall located in Camino on Pony Express Trail, old Highway 50.

Johnson's own house served as a hotel and small store in the early years. Many emigrants recorded in their diaries that they stopped at Johnson's Rancho, or passed it, as it was often the last stop before they reached Placerville.

The way stations close to Placerville and below the winter snow line would stay open the year around. Those farther up the mountain would leave their station at the end of the season's emigration to winter elsewhere. Those stations were often just brush shelters or the back of a wagon filled with those items the owners knew they could sell to emigrants. The prices were, of course, inflated. Prices usually rose in proportion to the distance from Placerville.

The original Johnson Cutoff continued to be popular with the ranchers who drove their cattle to summer range in the Sierra Nevada every year. This practice began very early in the history of El Dorado County. George Goddard, one of the government surveyors, while

---

108 *Tribes of California* by Stephen Powers 1976 reprinted from Contributions to North American Ethnology, volume III 1877

making his survey in 1853, reported seeing much stock grazing on Peavine Ridge. That the mountains can still, in present day, sustain cattle all summer, provides evidence that there was ample feed for the emigrant's cattle, a vital requirement for any emigrant route.

The huge old growth trees that so captured the imagination of the early emigrants soon fell to the woodsman's axe to satisfy the demand for lumber to build gold rush communities and shore up mine shafts. Sawmills followed the timber harvest up the mountainside. Logging continues to this day, as does the practice of pasturing range cattle. Both represent lifestyles beloved by those who live them.

The ice business was another commercial endeavor that began very early. Emigrant diaries mentioned sharing the road with wagons hauling ice out of the mountains. In September of 1856, J. Robert Brown, while looking for his strayed cattle came upon an ice house[109]. He briefly described how artificial ponds had been created to gather ice during the winter, later harvested in blocks and kept in ice houses, until the ice was shipped to Placerville and beyond in the warmer months. Anthony Brockliss, owner of Brockliss Bridge was engaged in the ice business. It was his ice house that is remembered in the name of Ice House Reservoir.

Today, in some places the old road is dotted with summer homes and campgrounds. Most of the original route of the Johnson Cutoff is on the Eldorado National Forest. Recreational users keep the forest alive with activity. Places where the solitude is complete can still be found along the original route of the Johnson Cutoff. In a landscape crowned by impressively large granite outcroppings, surrounded by brush and trees, only wind interrupts the silence. There it is possible to imagine the experience of the first gold seekers braving their way through, following the ancient paths started by the animals of the forest, and widened by Indians' use. These abandoned portions of trail are again the dominion of wildlife.

---

109 J. Robert Brown diary This was very near present day Ice House Reservoir.

A segment of the Johnson Cutoff near Wright's Road, found in pristine condition.
Verified by artifacts and the General Land Office surveyor's notes, 1875.
Courtesy: Dee Owens

As routes were abandoned and soon forgotten in favor of better ones, so apparently, were the men who discovered them. On July 24, 1869, the *Mountain Democrat* ran this story:

> *Recovering—The many friends of J. C. Johnson will be pleased to hear that he is fast recovering from the injuries received by walking out of a window in the third story of the Cary House in this city. Col. Johnson is an old mountaineer—has sought out and opened for public use many trails through the mountains—but this last act, performed while in a somnambulistic state, caps the climax for discovering and taking cutoffs. Not one man in 500 could take the same trip and escape with his life. Col.*

*Johnson is being waited upon by Dr. Worthen of this
city, who says he will soon have him out again.*

An old timer who was present, picked up a piece of chalk and
wrote on a board, "The Johnson Cutoff" placing the board beneath
the French window from which Johnson had fallen. Later on, the old
timers were saddened to hear how many passersby did not know what
the "Johnson Cutoff" was.[110]

The Johnson Cutoff research group working in the field, September, 2010.
Courtesy: Dee Owens

While many locals and descendants of J. C. Johnson
maintained an interest in the route, it wasn't until 2005 that volunteers,
under the auspices of the Eldorado National Forest and the Oregon
California Trails Association (OCTA), formed a volunteer research
group to go out into the woods and find it.

Besides wanting to find the remnants of this historic trail,
they also wanted to qualify it for inclusion and protection under the

110 *The Argonauts of California*, pages 111 & 112, Haskins repeated this
story with some added details and embellishments. He stated the injury was
a broken arm.

Omnibus Public Lands Management Act of 2009, which includes sixty-four individual routes in more than a dozen states from the Mississippi River to the Pacific Coast, adding those to the trails already under the protection of the National Trails System Act of 1968. Inclusion under this Act would qualify the Johnson Cutoff for designation as a National Historic Trail, which will help to preserve it for future generations to learn from and enjoy. The National Park Service manages the National Historic Trail System.

The question might be asked, why would it be so hard to confirm the location of this historic route that once carried so much traffic? The answers can be found in the many subsequent uses described above, and how activities, such as timber harvests and recreational uses have obscured the original trail. This is a fire-prone area, so fire and fire suppression activities have also erased traces.

To accomplish this task required special knowledge, techniques, and equipment. It also took thousands of volunteer hours. To begin with, the researchers built on the earlier work of others. Members of OCTA who had experience on other trails shared their knowledge. OCTA also provided established standards to follow, referred to as MET standards (Mapping Emigrant Trails). These standards are published and accepted throughout the nation.

There is a surviving copy of *Bartlett's Guide to California*[111] that describes it in detail, and serves as a guide.

The Eldorado National Forest historian and archaeologists did valuable earlier work. The Forest Service provided one of the most helpful tools: typed copies of the original General Land Office surveyor's notes from the 1870s. The maps produced from this survey are also available and were also used, but the notes contained more information than would ever made it onto the maps.

It became a standing joke among the group that the width of a pencil line on the map could cover many feet on the ground. The notes

---

111 The complete text of *Bartlett's Guide to California* is in Appendix C.

contained the original surveyor's latitude and longitude measurements that could be programmed into a hand-held Global Positioning System (GPS), which directed the researchers—no matter what the current conditions on the ground were—to the exact spot.

It was helpful that the surveyor made many references to the "old emigrant route" or the "Johnson's Route" or even "old trail." These then could be pinpointed, providing the confidence of where the route would be found. This information was then confirmed with physical evidence, and mapped.

On occasion, when working an area where the surveyor had failed to provide clues to the historic trail's location, mapping programs available on the Web were used to model the terrain so it could be visualized in different ways to locate a likely route through the mountains.

It may sound easy, but it was far from easy. The volunteers had to combat weather, heavy brush, steep terrain, and hike long distances from the present day road just to get to the area where they wanted to

One of the markers placed on the Johnson Cutoff by Trails West, Inc. This one is located on Pony Express Trail in Pollock Pines California.
Photo by Author

work. Some segments, at the time of this writing, still elude discovery as to their exact location.

In 2011, another volunteer group, Trails West, Inc. put their signature markers, made of railroad rail, along the Johnson Cutoff, so that anyone interested can now find the route. Each marker carries a quotation from an emigrant diary so that some of the thoughts and impressions those nineteenth century travelers experienced, when passing that spot, can be known.

It is a great loss to history that Johnson didn't record his experiences and thoughts about exploring the Sierra Nevada's Crystal Range. It would be interesting to know what he thought of all the subsequent activity along this route. It is hard to imagine, in later years, that he didn't look to the peaks of the Crystal Range, so visible from points on and near his ranch, so dazzling white with winter snow against the bluest of skies, and not call to mind his adventures.

ELLEN OSBORN

7

JOHNSON'S RANCHO

The Pioneer Association of Sacramento recorded J. C. Johnson's date of arrival in California as July 27, 1849. A few days later, as he made his way down the mountains to Placerville, Johnson happened upon the lush meadows and gentle wooded hills where he would make his ranch and home for the next twenty-six years. He had found what he was looking for: rich soil to farm.

In a letter to the editor of the *Mountain Democrat* dated September 13, 1862, Judge O. Russell stated, "J. C. Johnson and his partner settled on this place in August or September 1849, and used it exclusively for agricultural purposes. It is well known that this is the first spot ever cultivated in El Dorado County."

Johnson filed on his ranch on December 25, 1849, in the General Land Office at Sacramento, California. His statement number is 1974, and it can be seen today in the ledger entitled *Abstract of Declaratory Statements*, which is housed in the National Archives in San Bruno, California. The legal description of the ranch is: *Placerville*

Township, El Dorado County, Township 11 North, Range 11 East, section 35, and also lot two of section 1 Township 10 North Range 11 East, for a total of one-hundred and sixty acres.

Today, Apple Mountain Golf Resort occupies the ranch site. Johnson and his house are memorialized at hole four with the words "Cock-eye's Cabin" carved on a nearby rock. The farms of Apple Hill surround the golf course.

Hole Four on Apple Mountain Golf Resort called "Cock Eyes Cabin."
The site of the ranch house and emigrant hotel known as the Six Mile House is on the low knoll behind hole four.
Photy by Author

The Apple Hill Growers Association was formed in the 1960s, and it helps to keep Johnson's vision of an agricultural district alive.

The mission of the association, which represents small farmers, is to save their way of life. They do this by opening their farms to the public. Every fall, visitors from surrounding communities flock to Apple Hill to buy produce and baked goods, and teach their children about farm life.

According to the 1861 *Webster's Dictionary*, published in New York, there was no such word as "ranch," although Westerners were using the word freely and all understood it to mean what it means today. The word "rancho" did appear in the dictionary, described as a Spanish word meaning, "A small hamlet, or large farming establishment for rearing cattle or horses." Since Johnson referred to his ranch as a "rancho,"[112] perhaps a small community is what he intended to create.

According to the *Mountain Democrat*, in 1855 Johnson's Rancho precinct saw fifty-seven voters, and in 1856 sixty-five persons turned out to vote. On October 15, 1859 the paper gave a census of children at Johnson's Rancho with fifty-four children living in the vicinity, twenty of whom had been born in California. Johnson's Rancho met the definition of a hamlet long before the nearby town of Camino came into existence.

Camino had a population of three hundred at the time the post office was established in 1904. Before it took the name of Camino, it was called The Seven Mile House, a reference to the way station located there as a rest spot for emigrants, and later for teamsters hauling freight over the Sierra Nevada to the silver mines in Nevada.

Johnson's contemporaries gave descriptions of what the ranch looked like to some of them. Since so many emigrants stopped at Johnson's ranch in 1850, by reading their diaries a fairly complete picture of both the house and life at the ranch is given. The first house was described in the journal of Silas Newcomb, an arriving emigrant, as a double log cabin. It didn't survive the snows of the winter of 1849-50. A house built of shake quickly replaced it[113].

It has been described as the first cultivated spot reached in

---

112 In the 1850 U. S. Census both Johnson and his partner, John Phillips, gave their occupations as "rancheros."
113 Shake was understood to mean hand cut boards.

California by the *Traveler's Guide to California*, and as the first settlement reached by emigrant J. J. Scheller on August 12, 1850 at the end of his journey west.

On August 4, 1850 Seth Lewelling described the dust at Johnson's Ranch as "red chalkolet [sic] six inches deep."

The Diary of George Shepard recorded that Johnson was "selling meals, liker [sic], and provisions to travelers." He observed that Johnson "has quite a house" and called him rich. That was on the 13th of August 1850.

Two days later another emigrant, J. S. Shepherd, passed through and commented that the house was "rather rough, but welcome to the eyes of men who had roamed in the wilderness as long as we had." [114]

A particularly colorful entry was found in an anonymous journal where the writer described a Sunday in September of 1850:

> *The first house we came to is called Johnson's Ranch; here we found a preacher giving the miners a sermon of the scorching kind. The landlord had packed the bottles all to one end of the table, to make room for the Bible and hymnbook. This arrangement played the duce with the miners, for the old man was pretty windy, and the miners became very dry, but the landlord would not let them have a darned drop till the service was over.*

In 1850 there were many references to Johnson's Ranch in emigrant diaries, but after 1850 there were only a few. The probable explanation is that improvements to the road allowed travelers to reach Placerville sooner and there was less need to stop so close to town.

The 1850 United States Census gives this glimpse of the activity at Johnson's Ranch. There were seventeen people listed as

---

114 The author has collected diaries, letters or reminiscences of emigrants who mention Johnson's Ranch between 1850 and 1853. See the bibliography for a list.

members of the household. All were engaged in mining except Johnson and his partner John Phillips, who gave their occupation as rancheros. With three exceptions, all were from Johnson's home state of Ohio. The real property was valued at ten thousand dollars.

Johnson had become quite comfortable, financially, by providing services to emigrants at the hotel and store on his ranch. He also would buy their worn out teams and wagons, recruit the cattle on his pasture, and then drive the revived animals to Sacramento's auction yard where he would sell them for a good profit.

A poetic description contained in a letter from General A.M. Winn written during the El Dorado Indian Wars, can be found in the *Sacramento Daily Union* on June 22, 1851:

> *Johnson's Ranch where the camp is located is a beautiful spot; finely covered with pine trees of immense size, and in the most beautiful valley, with fine grass and limpid springs of good water. The barley and garden vegetation looks well; while several hundred head of sheep and cattle in view, brings back to us thoughts of other days. This ranche [sic] is owned by Capt. J. C. Johnson, the former Adjutant of Maj. Rogers First Battalion. It is a lovely and comfortable heritage. May he long live to enjoy the fruits of his industry and enterprise.*

The 1853 emigrant diary of David Shaw described stopping at Johnson's ranch, "which consisted of a double log and shake house, kept as a trading post chiefly to supply the miners with tools and provisions. It also had, in addition, a dining room and sleeping accommodations that consisted of bunks arranged against the wall one above the other."

This described the scene that Johnson's future wife, Emily Hagerdon and her family saw when they arrived in California that same year and took up residence at Johnson's Ranch.

From the July 9, 1855 *Sacramento Daily Union* comes this

description of the ranch, which offers a clear answer to the confusion between the two ranches known as Johnson's:

> There are two ranches in the State known as Johnson's; one on Bear river, in Placer county, and one in El Dorado, about five miles above Placerville, on the Johnson's Cut-off route over the Sierra Nevada[115]. The latter is owned and cultivated by J. C. Johnson, Esq., who was a prominent member of the past legislature, from that county.
>
> His ranch is located but a short distance from the South Fork of the American River, and about forty miles[116] from the snow line, in a pleasant valley, which contains now some eighty acres of very productive meadow land, and about as much more which can be cultivated. Mr. Johnson has wheat, barley, rye, oats and corn growing. Rye, wheat, oats and barley grow finely. He has also sowed clover and herds grass[117], which are growing very rank and luxuriant. In a few years, with cultivation, Mr. Johnson may be able to cut clover and herds grass equal to any in the Atlantic States. Every species of vegetable, particularly potatoes, grow in rich abundance. From an examination of this ranch, as well as others situated in its neighborhood, we are quite well satisfied that farming may be pursued successfully to a much greater extent in the mountains than is generally supposed. In addition to the grains named

---

115 These two ranches are often mistaken, but have very different histories. The ranch on the Bear River is located at the end of the Truckee Trail emigrant route.

116 This is an obvious typographical error. The correct distance is closer to four miles.

117 Herds grass is another name for Timothy grass, a perennial grass considered to be nutritious fodder.

we saw buckwheat growing. **For fruit raising we
are convinced that these mountain ranches may
become famous, particularly for apples.**[118]

*Mr. Johnson cuts this year eighty tons of hay,
which sells at forty dollars per ton. There are but few
points in that region where hay can be cut, which
renders it more valuable. A stream of living water
runs through the valley, and the land lies so that every
acre of it can be irrigated.*

*Mr. Johnson has built him a large two story
dwelling house, and has, everything considered, one
of the most desirable farms we have visited in the
country.*

This is the only known photograph of the Six Mile House.
The identities of the three people in the picture are unknown.
Courtesy of the Oakland Library, Oakland, California

This accompanying photo shows the house. The identity of
the persons on the porch is unknown, although it is likely Johnson is

---

118 The emphasis is the author's. This is an important and prophetic
statement.

one of them. Since the location of the original photograph is unknown, it is not possible to get a better copy.

The architectural style of the house is Greek revival, popular between 1820 and 1850 in the East, and continuing in popularity in the West until the 1870s. The style of gable front and wing is a subtype common in Johnson's home state of Ohio. The six by six-paned windows were common to 1850. One sash appears to be partially open, which indicates construction after 1850, if the upper sash is movable. The roof may be of tin. Cut nails and locally made brick were found at the site. The cellar measured fifteen feet by thirty-five feet.

In 1976, Mrs. Rose Larsen Corbell, born at the turn of the century on her family's farm near Camino, California, gave this recollection of the Johnson house when she was interviewed for *I Remember...,* which is a collection of reminiscences of long time residents in the county:

> *The* [Larsen] *family arrived in El Dorado County in July 1860, at what was known as "Johnson's Meadows," a few miles east of Placerville. As I remember, there was a large house on the place. It had at least three stories and fireplaces in every room, and of course it was a Mecca for our pilgrimages as children. The house was in a bad state of disrepair. The story went it was haunted, and I believe sincerely that it was.*[119]

Irene Larsen, who moved to Camino with her family in 1921 and married into the Larsen family, was an early supporter of Apple Hill. In 1986 she recounted similar memories of the Johnson residence:
> *Johnson Meadows is near my home. Yes, it used to have a three-story frame building on top of the hill. We used to call it the "old haunted house" and ramble through the buildings back in the 1920s. We had church picnics in the meadows. There is a*

119 *I Remember. . .* page 117

*graveyard there fenced. Our Larsen family arrived in
1860 and stayed at this building until they staked out
their homestead near by.*[120]

A member of the Johnson family, Edna McBride, described the
final end of the house by saying it didn't burn down; it "walked away."
She also recalled family members participating in its final destruction
by helping themselves to bits that interested them. She remembered
going up there on a picnic for that purpose. Mrs. McBride also recalled
the house as having three stories with the top story devoted to use as
a ballroom. She described its location as "on the other side of the
reservoir" and its condition as "deserted and falling to ruin."[121]

The final house was consistently described as having three
stories. However, the only known surviving photograph shows a house
with only two stories. The photo is of the second house, built by 1853.
No picture of the final house has been located.

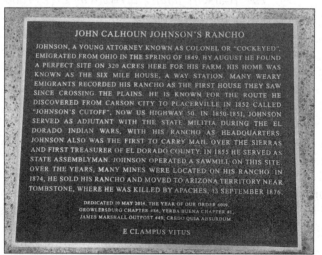

Historic marker placed at Apple Mountain Golf Resort, May 2014,
by E. Clampus Vitus.
Photo by Author

---

120 Letter to author from Irene Larsen January 27, 1986
121 Personal communication with Edna McBride November 29, 1985

The deed of the Vallejo Mining Company, executed on September 20, 1867, mentioned distance measured from "the old site of the former residence of J. C. Johnson," suggesting a prior residence was no longer in existence by 1867.

That was a sad and silent end to what was once one of the gems of El Dorado County's early history. It must indeed have been haunted with the echoes of shouts of hopeful young men, giddy with the realization that they had survived their long journey and had arrived safely in the gold fields, expecting they would quickly become rich. Later, it must have been haunted with the sounds of ordinary family life as Johnson's children grew up on his farm.

It can only be speculated why this was allowed to happen. What is certain is that the glory days of Johnson's Rancho, as a local landmark, ended with the sale of the ranch to A. J. Blakeley.

The pine trees of immense size, mentioned in the 1851 newspaper article, are absent in the later accounts, because as early as 1851 a sawmill, known as Predmore and Company, was logging and milling the pine trees, along with the equally impressive cedar trees, on the ranch.

James Predmore, owner of Predmore and Company, moved his operation into Placerville by1852, but his sawmill was followed in succession by Curtis & Company Lower Mill located in Johnson's North Canyon[122] in 1853-54; Bartlett's Sawmill in 1855; the Mountain Mill; and Johnson's Steam Mill in 1859; all located on Johnson's Ranch.

Logging and milling activity probably continued until the source of logs became too distant to make operating a sawmill there practical and profitable. Sawmills were prevalent in El Dorado County at the time. Records show between 1855 and 1861 there were always forty or more sawmills in operation.[123]

---

122 Places named for Johnson now lost: Johnson's Canyon, Johnson's North and South Canyons, and Johnson's Hill.
123Binder 6 *Bibliography of Early California Forestry El Dorado County* part 2 El Dorado County Historical Museum

Steam sawmill in the early 1860s. Original caption was: "near Sportsman's Hall."
It is similar to the sawmill operting on Johnson's Ranch near Sportsman's Hall.
*Courtesy of Library of Congress, Prints and Photographs Division,
Lawrence & Houseworth collection*

Mining activity was always present on Johnson's Ranch, from the very earliest days. Johnson himself was one of those miners. Over time, quartz mines, and finally hydraulic mines joined surface placer mines. None of these mines was among the most productive mines of El Dorado County, but apparently several showed promise.

In September of 1855, Johnson showed the editor of the *Mountain Democrat* a piece of quartz literally covered in gold, taken from a newly discovered vein near his house, which was one of several veins opened that year in his neighborhood.

Then in December of 1855, the *Mountain Democrat* reported that bank diggings on Johnson's North and South Canyons were paying well. By February of the following year, the newspaper reported that Townsend, Clark & Co. was averaging seventy-two dollars per day, with gold selling for eighteen dollars per ounce.

A young Johnson engaged in mining gold
with a long tom, pick and shovel.
Courtesy of Johnson descendant, Mark Rayner

Initially, the miners and Johnson coexisted peacefully enough. Johnson's position was they could mine there as long as they did not disturb his agricultural pursuits. By 1858, however, there began to be conflict, both over the destructiveness of mining to established crops, and infringement of water rights.

Some of these conflicts played out on the pages of the *Mountain Democrat* and are recorded in the county records. Thus began a long struggle for Johnson to keep his ranch and livelihood intact against continual efforts to encroach on the ranch and on his established water rights. Johnson's reservoir, in particular, came under frequent assault as miners cut into it to get the water they wanted and needed to work their claims.

Not only did Johnson have to deal with escalating incursions by miners causing damage to his reservoir and system of ditches intended to carry water to his crops, but litigation as well. Johnson, as the first resident in the area, created a system of water delivery to his ranch to adequately irrigate his crops through the dry summer months. A delinquent tax list gave a good idea of the extent of his irrigating ditches: he claimed the waters of Brush, Iowa, and Johnson's North and South Canyons for a total of eight miles of ditches.[124]

As neighbors arrived, there was pressure to share water. Indeed, Johnson's ditches crossed several ranches that now belonged to others. One of these neighbors, Michael Maxwell, entered into an agreement with J. C. Johnson for a share of the water flowing through these ditches. This agreement was officially recorded on January 11, 1864.[125] These shared water rights were specifically to be used for agricultural purposes only.

This amicable agreement between neighbors, unfortunately, later became the basis for litigation that lasted well into the twentieth century. As time rolled on, mining activity and its demand for water diminished, and the properties that once were Johnson's Ranch and Maxwell's Ranch were sold and subdivided.

The earlier agreement was either ignored or not known by the subsequent owners, spawning the litigation. Case number 2537 *Charles Hand and Sarah Celio versus John Cleese and Guiseppe and Amelia Gasparini*[126] reached the California Supreme Court, who rendered their judgment in bank on August 29, 1927.

Supreme Court Presiding Judge W. A. Anderson wrote this about the initial disposition of waters rights:

---

124 *Mountain Democrat* January 30, 1875

125 *El Dorado County Book A Leases* pages 131 et seq.

126 These are well known people in El Dorado County. Charles Hand was sheriff and tax collector of El Dorado County from 1912-1922. He was an admired and respected man. Sarah Celio was the wife of Charles Celio, a member of an early cattle ranching family in Lake Valley. John Cleese was a farmer who is remembered today in the name of a road in Apple Hill. Guiseppe Gasparini was a Swiss emigrant who worked as a logger and rancher. He is best known for an incident where he had to defend himself from a mountain lion with only a knife, earning him the nickname "Butcher Knife Joe."

In considering the main case, without attempting to set forth the extensive evidence in relation thereto, the Court may say there is nothing more clearly established in the case than that 'Johnson' was the moving spirit in the construction of the water ditch in controversy here; it bears his name, and this name seems to have been in the mouths of every witness who testified. Johnson Canyon, the main source of the water supply for this ditch, likewise bears his name, and it seems inconceivable that the project which seems almost monotonously connected with his name would not have been instigated and pioneered by him. Indeed, the very instrument between Johnson and the party from whom the defendant Cleese deraigns title speaks of the water ditch as 'the Johnson ditch' and 'his ditch.' Certainly a solemnly executed instrument conveying important property rights to one who did not own the land would not have been permitted to have been couched in such terms as are contained in the Maxwell-Johnson agreement if Johnson's rights in the ditch were not entirely beyond controversy. [127]

Even with this clear-cut decision, litigation commenced again in 1931, and again as recently as 1961, as new owners tried to obtain a larger share of the water. Even though the original ditches were simply cut into the soil or made of logs, remains of these old ditches can be seen today.

Less than a month after entering into an agreement with Maxwell over distribution of water rights, Johnson sold his reservoir to the South Fork Canal Company for one dollar, with the provision that should the South Fork Canal Company abandon it or fail to maintain it, it would revert back to Johnson. The deed further stated Johnson still retained the right to all the water he needed to irrigate his ranch.[128]

---

127 *California Decisions Volume 74* page 259
128 *El Dorado County Deeds Book I* page 249

This appears to be an attempt to quell further conflict and litigation. Since the reservoir is not mentioned in the deed of sale to Blakeley, it can be assumed that the South Fork Canal Company was continuing to maintain it at the time. Johnson's Reservoir is not in existence today.

Johnson might well have been wise to distance himself from these coveted sources of water, especially with tensions over water rights running so high.

On May 25, 1870, Jesse Hendricks, a ditch tender in the employ of the South Fork Canal Company, was murdered on the Johnson ranch. His remains were not discovered until December 19, 1876, when a deer hunter stumbled upon his bones, scattered down a hillside next to a flume. Since his pocketbook containing money and his pocketknife were found along with weathered scraps of his clothing, robbery didn't appear to be the motive.

The local authority, Sheriff Hume, had made a vigilant search at the time of Hendricks's disappearance. So Hendricks's body had probably been buried in a shallow grave then was later disturbed by animals and weather. Had he happened onto a miner cutting into one of the South Fork Canal Company's ditches? Was he murdered to keep it quiet?

Johnson wasn't the only one feeling intense pressure on his lifestyle as a farmer. On March 3, 1866, a public meeting was held at the Placerville courthouse for the purpose of drafting an appeal to the Congress of the United States. California was a long way from Washington, D.C., but the men of California kept a careful eye on what congress proposed to do, especially in ways that affected them economically.

Congress at that very time was crafting what would be the Congressional Act of July 26, 1866. This Act established a method for obtaining a mineral patent from the United States. This was followed by the Congressional Mining Act of May 10, 1872. There was concern that congress would protect mining rights at the expense of farmers, a fear that was justified. A lengthy and impassioned description of the issues appeared in the *Mountain Democrat*. Here is an excerpt:

> *For, as the matter now stands, there is no security for the farmer, the ditch owner NOR THE MINER, in the possession even of the soil each cultivates, occupies or works. The farmer plows his field, sows his grain, plants his crops, puts out fruit trees, sets out, and with great pains and at large outlay of capital and labor, covers the hills and valleys with vineyards, and gathers about him by unremitting toil, all the comforts and conveniences of life, and when he would realize the rewards of all this labor, he suddenly finds that it is not his, but that it is liable to, and may be completely destroyed in a few weeks time, by the incursions of, too often, lawless and irresponsible men, who under the pretense of mining, or searching the ground for precious metals, work irreparable ruin to his lands, and utterly destroy his labor of years, and he is without the ability to prevent the invasion of his home, and without means of redress when havoc and destruction have been completed.*
>
> *This results from the want of TITLE to the soil, for the present status of interest in the soil affords him no basis for preventing the injuries complained of, and redress when perpetrated. It is true that by the law of this State, passed in 1855, it is provided that the miner shall give to the party upon whose premises he desires to enter and mine, PROVIDED THEY CONTAIN VALUABLE IMPROVEMENTS, a bond of indemnity for damages occasioned thereby; but this amounts to practically nothing. It is difficult to estimate in dollars and cents, the value placed upon a farm that the farmer holds and regards as his home, and but few are willing to be subjected to the necessity*

of holding their homes under an ever impending invasion of some party or parties, who may utterly destroy the value of the same. It is moreover a fact, that the parties giving, or liable to give the bond, are generally men utterly without means; the bond, if one is given, is one of straw, and experience attests that none, or very few, have ever proved good or available, or has money, to the knowledge of the undersigned, in any instance, ever been collected thereon. "

The "undersigned" is a list of names—one hundred and twenty-two in all—a veritable who's who of El Dorado County at the time. It included, besides Johnson, many names still known in the county today.

The public meeting took place as scheduled at the courthouse on March 3, 1866. Following the usual oratory, the minutes reported that, "Mr. Johnson moved that a committee of seven be appointed to draft a Memorial to Congress expressive of the sense of the meeting. The motion was adopted and the chair appointed Messrs. J. C. Johnson, G. W. Swan, A. Litten, E. C. Day, Ogden Squires, D. Brooke, and A. J. Christie, as such a committee. A recess of half an hour was taken."

After the break, the memorial was presented in final form.[129] It appears likely that Johnson had previously written the memorial, which was reviewed and perhaps edited by the whole committee given the short time the committee had to complete their work.

On the motion of N. A. Hamilton the appreciation of the Association were tendered to Mr. Johnson for his "able address," and it was accepted by the Organization of the Agricultural and Mining Association of El Dorado County. The memorial was forwarded on to congress in Washington, D.C.

The importance of this issue cannot be overestimated. It is hard to say how much this memorial moved congress to act. Based on the years of rancor and costly litigation that followed, it appears not much. This is a dark chapter in the history of our developing nation.

---

129 See complete Memorial to Congress in Appendix D.

There were other events going during this period of history, which had an impact on El Dorado County.

The years of the Civil War and Reconstruction weren't good ones for anyone as the nation struggled to get back on its feet. One bright spot was the advancement of the transcontinental railroad, completed in 1869 with the driving of the golden spike in Promontory, Utah, connecting California with the eastern states.

Early on, hopes were high among the residents of El Dorado County that they would be beneficiaries of this great transcontinental railroad. People living along the chosen route, wherever it was located, stood to gain financially. It was certain two railroads would not be built.

The survey by F. A. Bishop favored Johnson's Pass over the Truckee route in Placer County. Even more exciting to Johnson was the possibility the proposed route might pass directly over his ranch! If it did, his property would greatly increase in value.

It was not to be. The Truckee route was the one chosen.[130] Toll road operators on the Placerville Carson Valley Road did not want to give up their lucrative businesses without major concessions on the part of Collis P. Huntington, Mark Hopkins, Leland Stanford, and Charles Crocker[131], but there were other considerations as well.

The city fathers of Placerville were delighted to think they might have a railroad reach their city. In 1863 they voted for the City of Placerville to purchase $100,000 in capital stock in the Placerville and Sacramento Valley Railroad. The County of El Dorado also purchased stock, along with many of the leading citizens. The results were disastrous when the Big Four worked to put El Dorado's competing railroad out of business. Ten years later the editor of the *Mountain Democrat* had this to say about the debacle:

---

130 Read *High Road to Promontory* by George Kraus for more details.
131 Known as the Big Four, they were the primary backers of the transcontinental railroad.

A locomotive belonging to the Sacramento Valley Railroad.
The citizens of Placerville so dearly wanted the SVRR to build a line to their city.
Author's collection

Our people were, once upon a time, for El Dorado to give a quarter of a million and for Placerville to give one-hundred thousand dollars to our little rattleteebang Shingle Springs railroad. As a result, our people have been compelled to resort to one dodge after another, not daring to have a board of supervisors, compelled to disband our city government, hiding like a guilty debtor from our creditors, squirming under the infliction of a fifty cent tax on each one-hundred dollars, whereas fifteen dollars on the hundred would hardly meet our probable legal liabilities resulting from a railroad fever.[132]

To avoid individual lawsuits and possible financial ruin, the city officers resigned, effectively ending city government, a

132 *Mountain Democrat* November 4, 1876 page 3

condition that continued from 1873 to 1900. Payment on the bonds was pursued, adding more than thirty years interest to the debt. This created a condition that had "so far affected the fair name of the city and depreciated her property valuations." To end the stalemate, one hundred citizens issued a promissory note in 1899. The city redeemed them by the issue of new bonds. Municipal officers were then elected and took office in April of 1900, restoring Placerville's government[133].

Even more disappointing was all the money Johnson—along with many other El Dorado County residents—lost by buying stock in the Placerville and Sacramento Valley Railroad before it went bankrupt. Johnson had originally put up five hundred dollars for stock in the railroad. Apparently, he, along with sixteen other men, had refused to make good on their pledges to the bankrupt railroad.

The railroad sued, and all seventeen cases were heard on February 20, 1866. The judge found in favor of the railroad, resulting in losses considerably larger than the original pledges. This became one among several financial setbacks that made it harder and harder for Johnson to meet his financial obligations, especially as it was followed so closely by the suit brought by his neighbor, A. J. Blakeley.

As a promoter of the railroad, Johnson was probably looking at life as a farmer might. When he bought stock in the Placerville and Sacramento Valley Railroad, he was undoubtedly thinking of the markets that El Dorado produce could reach with the help of a railroad.

As might be expected of Colonel Jack Johnson, he joined other community leaders making speeches promoting the Placerville and Sacramento Valley Railroad[134]. A railroad did finally reach Placerville in 1888, and later was extended to the town of Camino to carry lumber from the mills. And indeed, as Johnson envisioned it would, it mostly carried agricultural products and lumber.

---

133 The *Mountain Democrat* ran a series of articles by Doug Noble, beginning on January 5, 2007, that provide the full story of the Placerville and Sacramento Valley Railroad.
134 *Mountain Democrat* May 3, 1862

8

BLAKELEY VERSUS JOHNSON

As a family man, Johnson concentrated on his ranch and growing family. He intended to live out his life there in pastoral peace. However, even though his property was thought by many to have been thoroughly mined out as long ago as 1860, he and four other men formed the Vallejo Mining Company[135] on his ranch in 1867. Johnson's willingness to be involved with this mining venture was probably so he could keep an eye on what was happening on his property.

Predictably, the mine was never a good producer of gold. Everyone lost interest in it except one man: Alburn J. Blakeley, Johnson's neighbor and one of the partners. Blakeley wanted the mine, so under the laws of the time, which favored mineral rights over agricultural rights, in 1871 he filed to take the mine and ranch away from Johnson—the very thing Johnson had feared and had worked for years to prevent.

---

135 Apparently the mine was named Vallejo because several of the partners lived in the town of Vallejo, California.

This was not Blakeley's first foray into litigation against a neighbor for the purpose of taking away his mine, property, and source of support. He had been successful in filing on and acquiring the placer mining claim of an elderly bachelor, Isaac Yoakum in 1869. Mr. Yoakum died penniless in a Placerville boarding house two years later.

Johnson proved to be a more tenacious adversary.[136] Perhaps that is why Blakeley first took his belligerent aggression against Johnson to an unlikely place: the Masonic Lodge, of which they were both members.

Alburn James Blakeley, Johnson's neighbor
and adversary over the right to mine Johnson's property.
Courtesy of the El Dorado County Historical Museum

---

136 See complete text of Johnson's Brief in Appendix E.

ELLEN OSBORN

Fraternal organizations were very important in the lives of nineteenth century men and their families. Membership in a fraternal organization provided a place to socialize and a promise of financial relief to members and their families, including a Christian burial. (Today, these needs are provided for by insurance policies.) A list of fraternal organizations, made in 1886, showed seventeen active fraternities in El Dorado County. Examination of their rosters revealed that many people belonged to more than one.

From the earliest days of the gold rush, Masons helped fellow Masons and their families who arrived destitute at the end of their arduous journey overland. In accordance with Masonic teaching, they were supplied with food and clothing at no cost. At times this Masonic charity almost overburdened the lodge members of Placerville.

On August 21, 1854 Johnson was initiated into El Dorado Lodge Number 26, Free and Accepted Masons in Placerville. He was raised to Master Mason in the lodge. El Dorado Lodge was started with a dispensation from the Grand Lodge of California on June 26, 1852 by Master Masons from the eastern states. Initially without a lodge building, they met on a nearby hilltop.

In 1861, several of the members started a new lodge in Upper Placerville, known as Palmyra Lodge number 151.[137] According to the records of the Grand Lodge, the reason nine members of El Dorado Lodge wanted to start their own lodge was there were, in their opinion, too many Jews[138] in their old lodge.

Johnson was one of the organizing members. He served as Palmyra Lodge's first Tiler or doorkeeper of the lodge room, preventing non-Masons from entering or eavesdropping. Later, in the ebbing days of the gold rush, Palmyra merged back into El Dorado Lodge, which is known today as Placerville Lodge.

On August 13, 1868 Johnson's troublesome neighbor, Alburn J. Blakeley joined Palmyra Lodge.

---

137 Records of the California Masonic Grand Lodge

138 There was a small but thriving Jewish community in Placerville at the time. Isaac Sutvene Titus M.D., Master of El Dorado Lodge, went on to become Grand Master of California, the first of three Grand Masters produced by El Dorado Lodge.

A LOVELY & COMFORTABLE HERITAGE LOST

There is a darker side to Masonry. Although members are encouraged to leave their "petty piques and quarrels" outside the lodge, if a member of a lodge feels another member has acted toward him in an un-Masonic manner or failed to act in accordance with Masonic law, charges of un-Masonic conduct may be brought, which can result in a Masonic trial. If a member is found guilty, he can be suspended for a period of time, or permanently banned from membership.

On February 27, 1872 Alburn J. Blakeley chose to bring charges against Johnson, charges arising out of their escalating animosity over their mutual involvement in the Vallejo Mining Company. The charges Blakeley brought against Johnson were:

1. Being habitually intemperate during the years 1869 through part of 1872.

2. Vilifying and traducing the character of Master Masons.

3. Having threatened Mr. Blakeley with personal violence, stating, "I am getting so I can pull a trigger." This was taken as a threat to shoot Blakeley.

4. A second threat to shoot Blakeley.

5. Blakeley characterized Johnson as dishonest [Blakeley accused him of stealing the records of the Vallejo Mining Company from his house] and threatening to injure him [Blakeley] and his property.

6. Using vile and disgraceful and overbearing epithets towards other Masons.

Seven commissioners were elected to examine the charges brought against Johnson. The commission met and took testimony with both Blakeley and Johnson present. When evidence was closed, the commissioners voted by ballot. The outcome was: guilty on all charges except charge number six. Johnson's punishment was suspension, effective June 20, 1872.

At this point the record becomes a little fuzzy. Apparently, Johnson could have asked for reinstatement thirty days later, but failed to do so in a timely manner, so the suspension was renewed and eventually became permanent, consigning his name forever to the *Black Book of Masonry*.

Johnson had good reason to be angry with Blakeley. Blakeley had filed on 146 acres of Johnson's ranch and sent J. M. Anderson out to survey the land Blakeley planned to take. When Anderson tramped right through Johnson's vegetable garden to complete the survey, Johnson began swearing at Anderson and making threats against Blakeley. Furthermore, Blakeley posted the legally required "Notice of Intent to File" inside a locked cabin, rather than in a public place as was required by law. Johnson offered this as evidence of his "rascally" behavior.

Several witnesses upheld the charge of Johnson being intemperate. One lodge brother candidly stated Johnson was in the habit of leaving intoxicated whenever he came to town. He did go on to say he never knew Johnson to be drunk at home.

Caroline Blakeley, Alburn Blakeley's wife, gave testimony during the Masonic trial that on one occasion Johnson forced his way into their carriage when he had been drinking. Caroline, perhaps understanding Johnson's wife, Emily's disapproval of drinking, compassionately gave Johnson supper at the Blakeley home and put him to bed to sleep it off, even though their houses were only about one mile apart.

There is other evidence that Emily did not tolerate drunkenness in the house around herself or her young children, either on the part of her husband or their adult son, George. (In 1875-76, George's name appeared regularly on the registers of the Cary House and the Central Hotel in Placerville, even though the Johnson home at that time was a short stroll away on Cedar Ravine Street. Perhaps after a night of revelry with his friends, George was in no shape to go home.)

Johnson's fall from the Cary House hotel third story window, resulting in a broken arm, in 1869, could easily have been due to inebriation. It does appear that his drinking stopped in 1872, but the damage had already been done.

The Masonic trial was quickly followed by the real threat to Johnson, the possibility that he might lose his home and ranch in the litigation that Blakeley now initiated through the General Land Office.

A long and expensive legal battle followed as Blakeley appealed every decision adverse to him. Finally, after the appeals took the case all the way to the office of the United States Secretary of the Interior, where the original decision favorable to Johnson was reaffirmed for the final time, Johnson had reason to feel elated.

In a rare expression of emotion he told the editor of the *Mountain Democrat,*[139] he "felt as though the weight of 160 acres, extending to the center of the earth, had been lifted from his shoulders. Although," he quipped, "it would have been heavier if it had contained valuable minerals."

Johnson's elation was cooled shortly thereafter when Blakeley made queries about reopening the case, and offered to pay the expenses. Prior to this, in addition to being under the threat of losing his home and livelihood, Johnson was paying all the expenses, as well as his attorney's fees.

Knowing Blakeley would not give up, Johnson finally agreed to sell Blakeley his ranch. He did so only because that was the only way he could remove the thorn in his side that Blakeley had become. Once he decided to offer his ranch for sale, Johnson seized the upper hand. He insisted that Blakeley must buy the whole ranch, increased in size over the years to more than three hundred acres, not just the choice piece he coveted. Even the actual sale was acrimonious, as was evident in the deed itself.

Undoubtedly other mining men in the county were watching this case proceed, wondering how the outcome might affect their future plans. Apparently this method of acquiring mining property didn't tempt them, as Blakeley was only one of the few to try it.

Johnson, a rancher now without a ranch, moved his family of six (soon to be seven) children to Placerville where he briefly tried his hand at shop keeping.

---

139 In this story that appeared in January 31, 1874 a comment was made that the actual decision in Washington was given by Assistant Secretary of the Interior Benjamin Rush Cowan, an old classmate of Johnson's. A diligent search was made by the author to connect the two, but except for both men growing up in the same part of Ohio, no connection was found..

A. J. Blakeley carefully filed all the proper patents[140] on the ranch to prevent himself from losing it. It is notable in his filing that he waited out the five-year statute to do so, so he could reply truthfully "No" to the question, "Has there been any litigation on this property in the past five years?" Once in possession, Blakeley commenced to reopen the Vallejo Mine, renaming it the Blakeley Mine. Under Blakeley's ownership, the agricultural potential of the ranch was neglected.

Losing their property to Blakeley forced Johnson to seek other means of supporting his family. Staying only long enough to put his affairs in order, Johnson opted to leave the state entirely, seeking his fortune in the newly emerging mining districts in the territory of Arizona.

A. J. Blakeley showed off a heavy bag of gold containing old-fashioned shot gold (fine gold dust) worth $2,300 to a *Mountain Democrat* reporter, claiming he took it from the mine on the old Johnson Ranch. Blakeley also had with him about thirty nuggets worth about four hundred dollars at that time, which he also claimed came from that mine.

The newspaper reporter went on to muse, "Where did all that gold come from? It is heavy, much of it coarse and rough, indicating that the source of it cannot be far from its present [placer] deposit. Where is that quartz ledge?"

There was the suggestion that all of that gold did not come from the same mine, even though Blakeley claimed it did. Perhaps Blakeley was hoping for vindication when he restated his case that the mine could potentially pay in excess of $100,000. The paper ran the story,[141] but it is doubtful if it helped to change people's opinions of his past actions.

A government mining report[142] printed in 1883, gave an idea of

---

140 Mineral entry file #5273 Alburn J. Blakeley for the Blakeley Placer Mine, National Archives

141 *Mountain Democrat* May 4, 1878

142 *Report of the Director of the Mint Upon the Statistics of the Production of the Precious Metals in the United States*, 1883 pages 43-44

how the mine fared once the ranch was wholly Blakeley's. According to the report, where Blakeley himself was undoubtedly the source of information, some very fine large nuggets of gold were mined there, and placed on exhibition at both the county and state fairs. Blakeley claimed to have taken no less than $200,000 worth of gold from this mine.

The report provided a description of how Blakeley extracted gold by the use of placer hydraulic mining techniques, a method that washed away the soil, which was then passed through a sluice where the gold particles were extracted. The mud and tailings produced by the technique were then discarded, often into nearby streams or rivers.

That destructive method was outlawed by a federal court decision issued in 1884. While the original decision applied only to

An example of the destructive force of hydraulic mining.
This mine is located at French Corral in Nevada County, circa 1866.
Courtesy: Library of Congress, Prints and Photographs Division, Lawrence & Houseworth Collection

the mines near Marysville, California, it was quickly cited and applied to legal cases filed throughout the gold bearing counties of California, ending the practice of hydraulic mining that the ruling judge called "a public nuisance." As practiced by Blakeley—according to the report in an almost boastful tone—the act of hydraulic mining annihilated "what was once one of the most fertile meadows to be found."

Here is revealed the essence—the very heart of Johnson's vigorous objection to the Blakeley Mine. He had seen the aftermath of hydraulic mining. He could not bear to see that happen on his ranch. Once the ranch was sold, Johnson would have to go so far away that he would never have to see this disfiguring wound on the bosom of his beloved ranch. Could it be said of him that he was an early environmentalist? Among his so-called eccentric ideas was the belief that we should care for the earth so that in turn, it would provide for us.

Before leaving the unsavory topic of A. J. Blakeley's tendency to take what he wanted without regard to the rights of others, his relationship with his wife, Mary Carolina Flethesicer Thaler, needs to be considered.

Caroline's past is nothing if not murky. She consistently stated she was born on March 24, 1824 in Bremen, Germany. The Blakeley family story was that she came to California by ship in 1850, which may be substantiated by the passenger list of the steamer *Gold Hunter*[143] that arrived on November 22, 1850, and lists a M. Fleshener. There is no one else on the list with the same surname, nor anyone named Thaler.

She was said to have married John Thaler in California. According to the family, their first child, Mary California Thaler, was born in Placerville on January 14, 1853.

John Thaler was in the hotel business, owning first the Dutch House in White Rock, later selling it to buy the Five Mile House from A. J. Blakeley.

---

143 *Sacramento Transcript* November 22, 1850

Why Blakeley wanted to sell a piece of property that he later bought back and owned for the rest of his life, is unknown. What is known from the county records is that Thaler only owned it for six months before Blakeley bought it back.

Based on the flurry of litigation that accompanied the sale, there were apparent bitter feelings. The last known date that John Thaler was seen in El Dorado County was the day the sale was completed, July 11, 1854. John Thaler disappeared.

One month later, John and Caroline's second child, James Henry was born.

Mary Carolina Blakeley
Courtesy of the El Dorado County Historical Museum

Caroline, with her young children and A. J. Blakeley, occupied and operated the Five Mile House together. Blakeley family tradition holds that they were married on February 14, 1855.

However, a diligent search of available public records failed to find evidence of a marriage between Caroline and John Thaler, nor a divorce for them, nor a subsequent remarriage of Caroline to Blakeley. This raises plenty of questions, such as what was the cause of Blakeley's anger toward Thaler? Did Thaler fear for his life? Where did he go? Was Blakeley trying to eliminate a romantic competitor from Caroline's life?

Caroline and A. J. Blakeley lived together as husband and wife, raising five children of their own in addition to Caroline's first two, until Caroline's death many years later.

Despite its active history, the place once called Johnson's Rancho is still a place of great natural beauty, looking much as it must have looked when Johnson first set eyes upon it.

The evidence of rancor, of litigation, and heedless mining practices has been erased by time. Its slopes again carry tall pine, cedar, and fir trees, and the stream of living water still sparkles as it flows through it. The meadows fill each spring with grass, and in the far distance the mountains Johnson explored are now part of a designated wilderness, preserving their wild beauty for all to enjoy.

9

THE JOHNSONS IN PLACERVILLE

In 1874, after the ranch was sold to Blakeley to end their personal conflict, Johnson moved his family to Placerville and started keeping a store in town. The store was variously referred to as a feed and grain store, or as a grocery store. It was located in the building attached to the western end of the county courthouse.

Johnson opened his store for business on October 20, 1874, where both he and his son, George worked. While changing careers from farmer to storekeeper may have seemed an odd choice, during the days of the emigration Johnson had kept a store at his ranch. So rather than a change of occupations, it was a return to an old one.

When the wildly popular new national fraternal organization, the Patrons of Husbandry, or the Grange, as it is more commonly known, reached Placerville, Johnson's store became the Grange store.

The El Dorado County Courthouse on Main Street, Placerville, California, with the attached building that housed Johnson's store as it appeared before the fire in 1910.
Courtesy of the El Dorado County Historical Museum

The Placerville Grange was organized on February 1, 1875.[144] The object of the Grange was to promote agricultural interests, so it is easy to envision Johnson taking an active part. A characteristic of Granges is that they have a meeting hall. The meeting hall of the Placerville Grange was on the second floor of Johnson's store.

Continuing his pattern of hospitality, Johnson's store was also the location where the El Dorado County Pioneers Society held their meetings. Johnson had joined the Pioneer Society in Sacramento, years before a Placerville society was formed.

Johnson sold the store in February of 1876. When the courthouse burned in 1910, so did the store. The courthouse was rebuilt on the same spot and expanded to include the space where Johnson's store had stood.

Some early day photographs of Main Street in Placerville give an opportunity to glimpse the building as it was before it was

144 *The History of El Dorado County* published by Paolo Sioli

destroyed by fire. Although long gone, this store had an interesting history of its own. In a souvenir edition published on January 24, 1898, the *Mountain Democrat* published this history of the store:

> *Schiff & Limpinsel: The store was originally known as the Old Grange Store, and was kept by Jack Johnson. Then Mr. Dixon joined and turned in the store for stock in the Grange from whence it obtained its name. The store was afterwards sold to Scott & Larne who were succeeded by Mr. Sandfoss, who took in Mr. Olmstead. This firm was succeeded by Hardy & Schiff upon August 20, 1889. Mr. Limpinsel bought in December 1890. The store was first in the upper building,*[145] *but moved to its present quarters in the Odd Fellow Building.*

The Cary House Hotel on Main Street in Placerville, California, circa 1880.
It was from one of the third-story windows that Johnson took a fall.
Courtesy of the El Dorado County Historical Museum

---

145 "Upper" here means the location further east, the old building next to the courthouse that burned.

ELLEN OSBORN

Johnson owned several lots and buildings in Placerville at various times during his life in El Dorado County, beginning as early as 1851. The one located on Cedar Ravine Street was where the family lived after the ranch was sold. Unfortunately, for those who seek to visit it, the house is no longer there. The lot was divided up over the years and the buildings there now are of twentieth century origin. There is nothing tangible left in Placerville as reminders of the Johnson family.

The last known picture of Johnson (left) with his brother Nathan (right), probably taken shortly before J. C. Johnson left for Arizona Territory.
Author's Collection

A Lovely & Comfortable Heritage Lost

Apparently there was little left to tie J. C. Johnson to El Dorado County after his ranch was sold. The lure of frontier life again appealed to him. He began to plan a move to Arizona Territory and perhaps that had been his plan all along. The dates of operation of Johnson's store correspond almost exactly with Blakeley's due dates of payments for the ranch. Johnson may have been concerned that Blakeley might not meet his obligation if Johnson wasn't there to enforce it. The final payment was made January 1, 1876.

It would have been quite in character for J. C. Johnson to put his affairs in order before he and his son, George, departed for Arizona. Aware of the risks of frontier life, he knew there was a possibility he would not return.

His wife Emily and the other children, ranging in age from not quite a year to fifteen years old, would stay in Placerville until a home could be prepared for them.

Since there was neither a probate nor a decree of distribution for his will, it must be assumed that he transferred his assets to his wife before his departure. His personal papers were probably stored somewhere and have either been lost, destroyed, or forgotten in someone's attic. In their absence, the public record will have to suffice. It does give a clear picture of a decisive and active man, one who left his mark on the young state of California.

10

ARIZONA TERRITORY & THE APACHES

Why Johnson chose to move to Arizona Territory is unknown. Perhaps he was influenced by the success of his friend and fellow forty-niner, Henry Clay Hooker, a former hardware merchant in Placerville, who had moved to Arizona and acquired a ranch of amazing size— four hundred square miles, boasting the Galluro Mountain Range as its western boundary. Hooker had become the "Cattle King" of Arizona.[146]

Or perhaps, Johnson felt the need to give his twenty-two year old son, George Pen Johnson, a start in life. Unlike his father, George had shown no interest in farming or the law. Maybe his father thought Arizona Territory would be a better place for a young man of George's temperament than the increasingly sedate village of Placerville. Having been born in 1854 during the wild, freewheeling days of the gold rush, George never gave up looking for that lost world.

---

146 *Mt Democrat* May 28, 1881 Description of Hooker's ranch

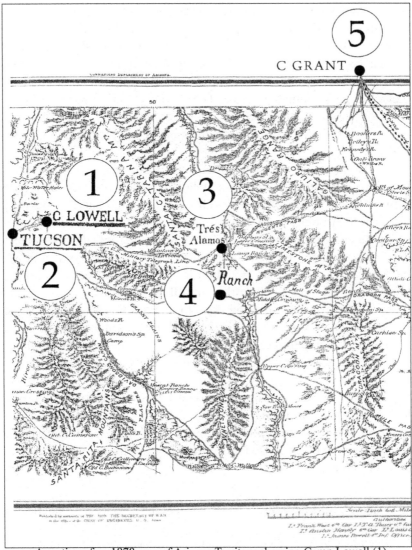

A portion of an 1878 map of Arizona Territory showing Camp Lowell (1),
Tucson (2), Hooker's Station and Tres Alamos (3), ranch site (4),
and Old Camp Grant (5). Off the map to the east (on right)
are New Camp Grant and Camp Bowie. Map by authority of
Brevet Major-General O. B. Willcox Commanding Department of Arizona.
Courtesy National Archives Record Group 77

Whatever their reasons, George and his father left Placerville in March of 1876, following the receipt of the final payment from Alburn J. Blakeley for the purchase of Johnson's cherished ranch two months before. They traveled by rail to the terminus of the railroad, which was then in San Bernardino County, California. From there they used pack animals to reach Tres Alamos[147] in Arizona Territory. Arriving in April, they settled on government land that appeared well suited for agriculture, about thirty miles upstream along the San Pedro River.[148]

John chose the place where the Babacomari Creek empties into the San Pedro River opposite where the town of Fairbank would later be located. The place was well watered by the San Pedro River, which ran through it. At the time, the country was covered with mesquite and timber, and was full of game: antelope, deer, and bear. When Lieutenant Colonel Philip St. George Cooke passed through the area with the Mormon Battalion in 1846, he had recorded seeing "troops of wild horses and cattle" as well.[149]

Tres Alamos, thirty miles to the north, was the nearest community and was where they traded for supplies with Cassius M. (Little Cash) Hooker, the station keeper. The nearest neighbor was William Onesorgen who kept the stage station twenty miles to the south.

Before the Johnson men could occupy their land, they first had to bury the former occupants, men by the names of Brown and Lewis[150] who had been murdered by Indians. The deaths must have been recent, as no one else had come along to find them lying where they had fallen.

---

147 Named for the three huge cottonwood trees that shaded the main ranch house.

148 Beginning here, much of this information is taken directly from the deposition of George Johnson, given in Indian Depredation Claim #8317.

149 *The Conquest of New Mexico and California in Historical and Personal Narrative* by Lieutenant Colonel Philip St. George Cooke page 76

150 *Arizona Citizen* September 23, 1876, some accounts say Brown survived.

Since John liked the location, they proceeded to settle on it, and moved into the cabin of split lumber that the two murdered men had built. They had only a squatter's right to be there.[151] However, John posted notices around the place showing he had entered it with the intention of making the proper filings, which was the first step to acquiring title. When established, they expected to bring the rest of the family to this new home, along with any neighbors from Placerville who wished to join them.

The planting season was upon them when they arrived, so immediately the Johnsons, father and son, began to break ground. To help with this backbreaking labor, they had six horses, a mule, and farm implements. They also had the help of Calvin Mowry, a partner they had acquired along the way. They broke, plowed, and planted about twenty-five acres, principally in corn with some vegetables.

They expected to market the harvest at the government posts located at New Camp Grant, Lowell, and Bowie. There were soldiers at each of these camps eager for fresh food, and equally hungry miners at the Santa Rita mines. The farm was located about fifty miles south and a little west of New Camp Grant, about thirty-five or forty miles west of Bowie, and about forty-five miles southeast of Lowell.

By September they had already sold a wagon load of corn, melons, and vegetables to the soldiers at New Camp Grant. They sold directly to the soldiers who wanted to augment the government issued beef and beans.

Mr. Mowry gave a prophetic interview to the *Arizona Citizen* newspaper, which appeared on August 19, 1876. He extolled the success of their crops, praised the boundless natural grazing, and encouraged other settlers to join them. He went on to reassure them that he had not seen an Indian in that neighborhood and did not fear any.

---

151 The term squatter has a fairly negative connotation today, but it has a long history in the United States. (See *Land in California* for an expanded explanation of the term and its role in our history.) What George meant here is that they had entered land that was not yet available for preemption. Their right would be one of possession only.

Mowry might have been wiser had he exercised a little more caution. Surely, everyone in the West had heard about the Battle of Little Bighorn that had taken place two months earlier, on June 25, 1876.

General George Armstrong Custer, who met his death in that infamous battle, was, interestingly enough, a Harrison County Ohio native, the same as J. C. Johnson. While the difference in age meant they were probably not acquainted, Johnson would have known who he was. Custer's death should have instilled some caution in Mowry and Johnson, and even in young George. After all, weren't they acutely aware that it had been the Apaches who killed Brown and Lewis?

On the morning of September 13, 1876, George and a companion, George Woolfalk, left the farm to ride up the San Pedro River[152] looking for home sites for the people from Placerville they expected would join them. On the third day they found a number of campfires, vacated only recently by the Indians. Fearing the trail was becoming too "hot" for them, they turned around and hurried home.

When they got to the cabin, they found no one had been there since they left three days before. Everything was just as they had left it; even the dishes from their last day were still on the table.

George and his companion hurried to the place about a mile away where John and Mr. Mowry had planned to work the day the younger men left them. Johnson and Mowry had been working on the riverbank, cutting a ford through the steep banks and across the San Pedro River, to reach the better road on the opposite side.

George and Woolfalk found the place where the two had built a fire to warm their noontime coffee. Alarmed, they hurried on to the riverbank. There they found Johnson, lying dead.

Apparently a band of Apaches, returning from a raid in Mexico to the San Carlos Reservation had happened upon the men and killed them. The ten-to-fifteen foot high banks of the river would have hidden their approach, giving their victims no warning. If Calvin Mowry had finally seen an Indian, his glimpse was a brief one. John C. Johnson was shot three times through the heart, and his head was

---

152 The San Pedro flows north out of Mexico.

smashed with his own shovel. Moccasin tracks of various sizes were around the body, also the tracks of between sixteen and eighteen unshod ponies. The Indians had also stolen all their other horses.

Geronimo and Chiricahua Apache warriors during the Indian wars in southeastern Arizona, circa 1885. Photo by C. S. Fly
Courtesy Arizona State Library, Archives and Public Records, History and Archives Division, Phoenix 97-2652

Dr. O. P. Ingram, who had happened to come along, had joined the search and was with George Woolfalk and George Johnson when they made this grisly discovery. Dr. Ingram described the scene: "Mr. J. lying on his face, stripped, with bloody matter oozing from a gunshot wound opposite the region of the heart, with shovel by his side and pick at his feet."[153]

For the first time in his life, George was on his own. Nearly every day before, his father had been there, to guide and counsel him.

---

153 *Arizona Citizen* September 23, 1876, a letter from O. P. Ingram

His father's sudden death left George unprepared. Decisions had to be made, actions taken; it was now all up to him.

Unable to leave his father's body, George hitched up the wagon to the two spent horses he and Woolfalk had ridden. He wrapped the body in some blankets and drove to Tres Alamos where there was a small burying ground. He drove directly to Cassius M. Hooker's store, where the Johnsons had bought their supplies.

Although time and temperature had taken their toll, Johnson's body was briefly taken into the store while two Mexican workers, Leandro Tautimez and Juan Borquez, dug a grave at Hooker's request. The workers then carefully placed the body into the grave, still wrapped in the blankets.

A small crowd of people had gathered to hear George tell his story, and they formed the funeral party, along with Hooker's household. They huddled under a hot September sun around the hastily dug grave to hear the familiar and soothing words of the last rites read for a man they hardly knew. As they silently listened, no one could fail to reflect that they might also one day share his fate.

Many of the up-river settlers were so frightened by this unprovoked attack on Johnson and Mowry that they chose to stay at Hooker's Station for protection.[154]

Hooker raised a party of twelve men to go back with George the next day to look for his father's partner, Calvin Mowry. Neither George Woolfalk nor Dr. Ingram was willing to return to the murder site. They found Mowry's body about a hundred yards from where Johnson's body had been found. He had been shot three times in the back. Mowry was so badly decomposed that he was buried right there.

As they were riding back, the party encountered two groups of mounted army men: one under the command of Sergeant George H. Eldridge[155], Company C Sixth Cavalry from New Camp Grant, and a second party under the command of Sergeant J. Dorman, Company D

---

154 *Arizona Citizen* September 23, 1876

155 George H. Eldridge was a veteran of the Civil War. He was also a recipient of the Congressional Medal of Honor for "gallantry in action" during the Texas Indian Wars with the Kiowa in 1870.

Sixth Cavalry, all of whom had volunteered to join the search.[156] The burial party went up to New Camp Grant to notify the soldiers at the post of the deaths of Johnson and Mowry.

Members of a cavalry unit at Fort Grant, Arizona Territory in 1876.
Very likely some of the men who rode out looking for Johnson's killers.
Survey of U. S. Army Uniforms, Weapons and Accoutrements,
page 30 by David Cole.

Then came the hardest part for George. He sent a telegram, addressed to the Rev. Newell in Placerville, asking him to give the news to his mother. It read "Father killed by Indians on the 13th. Break news easy."

The trail of prints led away from the murder scene toward the San Carlos Reservation. Some of the volunteers followed it a mile or more, and concluded it was Indians from the reservation who had committed the attack.

---

156 Records of New Camp Grant Arizona Historical Society Tucson, Arizona

ELLEN OSBORN

According to a War Department report, about four hundred of the most renegade Chiricahua Apaches, led by Juh, Geronimo, and Nolgee, had fled to Sonora, Mexico to carry on their raids there and in the United States. During the year 1876, the official report listed more than twenty settlers killed, and much stock stolen. Perhaps those Apache men had been trying to secretly visit their families at the San Carlos Reservation, and had encountered Johnson and Mowry along the way.

On September 19, 1876 Captain Tupper of New Camp Grant was ordered to take thirty-six men to join the search for the murderers, and to protect the citizenry. While a real effort was made, no arrests followed. Certain individual Indians were known to be renegades and dangerous, but the army was unable to connect them with that particular crime.

At that time, the Apache nation was a major concern of the United States Army and neutralizing the Apache threat to settlers was a primary focus. To accomplish this "five-thousand troops, or roughly twenty percent of the entire U. S. Army in Arizona, were in pursuit of fewer than forty hostile Apache."[157]

A contributing factor was the United States government's failure to keep its promise to provide beef to the Apaches in exchange for their promise to stay on the reservation. The beef supply ended early that year, forcing the local Indian agency to direct the Indians to hunt in the mountains for food, a situation that almost guaranteed raiding.[158]

At the time they buried Mowry, the corn had not been touched. When George returned in about a week to salvage the crop, he found it trampled down and plundered or eaten. At the same time other property, provisions, and household goods had been taken or destroyed. There were fresh tracks around. He saw where the Indians had been camping in the field and had turned their stock loose to feed. The Indians had built fires along the creek and cooked the corn. They had dug up the

---

157 *Arizona* by Marshall Trimble page 199
158 Report of The Commissioner of Indian Affairs, Report of the Secretary of the Interior, 44th Congress Second Session 1876

vegetables. What they could not use they had cut down and spoiled. Two-dozen chickens were missing, and were presumed roasted. The looters cut a double set of harness, taking pieces they wanted, and cutting the rest to useless shreds. They did not damage the cabin, but ransacked its contents. They took bedding, clothing, guns, and other supplies, and as a final touch, scattered flour over everything.

The economic loss of the corn was overwhelming to George. They had about twenty acres in Missouri Dent corn. It was a splendid stand with large, well-eared stalks reaching sixteen-feet in height[159]. George later recalled, "We could lie there in the cabin two-hundred yards from the field and hear the blades of the corn crack they grew so fast." It was fully mature at the time, and in that climate, it was as valuable on the stalk as gathered. He estimated the yield to be fifty bushels to the acre.

The Johnsons owed money to Cassius Hooker, who kept the trading post at Tres Alamos. He had advanced them supplies against this crop. Because he wanted to recover as much of his loss as possible, Hooker sent a couple of Mexican workers back with George to salvage what they could. They were able to haul four small wagon loads back, all of which went to Hooker.

George stayed in the area until December to work off the remainder of the debt. Penniless, he left to make his way back to California as best he could, his dreams of pioneering a successful life for himself in Arizona Territory permanently shattered.

During those last months in Arizona, it is unknown if George, dissatisfied with the lack of punishment of the Apaches for his father's murder, had tried to exact justice himself. If a lone Indian crossed his path, it would not have gone well for that Indian. A true child of the West, he was a believer in frontier justice, as other events in his life would demonstrate. All his life, he maintained the rough demeanor of

159 In his deposition George Johnson stated the corn stalks were sixteen-feet high.

a frontiersman. He was a hard drinker, and bragged about the number of men he had killed.

The scene when George arrived home in Placerville, alone, at his mother's door, to face her grief, can well be imagined. Emily may have asked George the same question that has remained an open question for family members all these years: Why were two healthy young men out riding around the countryside while two older men (Johnson was fifty-four) were doing the hard physical work of cutting a road through a high riverbank in the September heat of Arizona?

For years following this tragedy, it was a matter of local history that Apaches at that place had killed Lewis, Johnson, and Mowry in 1876. It was often recounted as a curiosity to strangers passing through. For a long time Mowry's grave was visible on the riverbank just across from the town of Fairbank, until a flood washed his remains away.

It was never doubted that the murders were the work of Indians—specifically, the Chiricahua Apaches—as it was that section of the country that they frequented and where they harassed settlers. According to the settlers, the Indians at that time were known to kill people, drive away stock, to steal everything they wanted, and then destroy the rest.[160]

Perhaps J. C. Johnson simply underestimated the Apache threat. Accustomed as he was to the gentler "Digger" Indians he had lived among for twenty-six years in El Dorado County, he might truly have believed a statement made during the El Dorado Indian Wars of 1850-1851 that said, "One white man is worth ten Indians in battle."[161] Perhaps he didn't realize that, where Apaches were concerned, those numbers could easily be reversed.

It was during those El Dorado Indian Wars that he had served as Adjutant in the El Dorado County militia, offering his house and ranch for use as the headquarters. He had affectionately been called "colonel" by his friends forever after.

Some people in Placerville began to publicly express

---

160 Onesorgen deposition in the Indian Depredation Claim file #8317
161 El Dorado Indian Wars records, California State Archives

doubts about the demise of the "Colonel" John C. Johnson. It was inconceivable that this hardy pioneer was dead. He was, after all, the man who had walked away from a fall from a third story window with only a broken arm. This was the trailblazer who had carried the mail across the snowy Sierra Nevada alone and on foot. This was the man who had surveyed an emigrant route through grizzly country.

Was this a practical joke on a grand scale? Who might have been made uncomfortable by the news of his death? Did Alburn J. Blakeley feel the need to deny this tragedy because it compounded his guilt over forcing Johnson off his ranch in El Dorado County?

Wherever the doubts were coming from, the Johnson family felt compelled to lay those doubts to rest. They asked a friend, D. J. White, who happened to be traveling in Arizona, to confirm the facts of his death. White was a practicing attorney in Placerville who had known Johnson for years. After attorney White did so, the Johnson family published the facts of Johnson's death in the *Mountain Democrat*, February 23, 1878:

> *The following letter, in answer to one written by the daughter of the late Col. J. C. Johnson, we have been requested, by the members of the family, to publish:*

> *Oak Grove Ranch Arizona Territory*
> *Miss Harriet A. Johnson:*
> *Your request of January 21ˢᵗ, in reference to your father's death, is received. I regret to inform you that his decease is well known by those here who were acquainted with him in life, and who identified his body and assisted at his burial. That he was killed at or near his ranch location, on the Upper San Pedro River, in the Autumn of 1876, is undisputed; and that he and Mowry were murdered at the same time and place, by Apache Indians, is about as certain.*
> *Having known your father some sixteen*

years, and being aware that the doubt you mention was expressed by a few people in Placerville at the time I left in March last, I felt considerable interest in ascertaining particulars connected with his fate.

I have talked with several persons directly cognizant of the matter, among them C. M. Hooker and Thomas Dunbar, of Tres Alamos—the former, with others, attended to the burial, and can give you the exact date—also with H. C. Hooker, long acquainted with your father in El Dorado County, and here.

I trust that you have been long informed of these unquestioned facts, and therefore could not cherish the hope of an uncertainty. As it appears the "public" still entertains a doubt, you are at liberty to use this reply as may be deemed proper.

Respectfully,
D. J. White

This investigation of the facts by a respected Placerville attorney appears to have quelled the rumors. The insistence that Johnson was not dead may have stalled settlement of his estate. The proof of Johnson's death helped Emily and the children move on with their lives.

On March 3, 1891, by act of Congress, the United States government assumed financial responsibility for the depredations of Indians upon the property of settlers. Johnson's widow, Emily, filed her claim within the year. Time passed with little progress in proving their claim. Finally, George returned to Arizona in 1913 to look for witnesses who could provide the needed evidence. He felt he owed his mother this. It is possible he carried a lifetime of guilt that he was not at his father's side when danger arrived.

In returning to Arizona, George found the place much changed since he had last been there. Arizona had become the forty-eighth state, admitted to the Union in 1912. The town of Benson had replaced Tres Alamos, by then a ghost town. The railroad passed near

Emily Johnson holding Mary, their last child. This photograph was taken at
J. C. Kemp's Great Flying Gallery in Sacramento.
Taken the January before Mary's father left for Arizona Territory
Courtesy: Ancientfaces.com

their old home site. Still, he was able to locate several individuals to give depositions: William Onesorgen, Leandro Tautimez, who had dug the grave, and Severano Bonillas, another of Hooker's Mexican workers. C. M. Hooker, it was rumored, had returned to his native New Hampshire years before [162].

George, then older than his father had been at the time of his death, visited his father's grave. Although almost forty years had passed, he was able to locate the grave from the marker. At the time of burial, using the materials at hand, he had caused a stone "too large for a man to move" to be placed on his father's grave.

---

162 Other sources say C. M. Hooker moved to Southern California.

In later years, various members of the Johnson family have traveled to Arizona to look for his grave. While the faint traces of a cemetery can be seen on a mesa near the site of Tres Alamos, no individual graves can be identified. The ground is overgrown with mesquite, catclaw acacia, and other dry country brush. There is no sign even identifying it as a cemetery. Careful examination of the ground shows grave-sized rectangles outlined with small rocks, but no stone "too large for a man to move" is anywhere nearby. Identification of Johnson's final resting place remains an unsolved mystery.

Site of the cabin occupied by John and George Johnson near the San Pedro River as it looked in the 1980s. Artifacts dating circa 1876 were seen on the surface, as well as a stone threshhold.
Photo by Author

Not far to the south, the mining town of Tombstone had sprung up. According to legend, it takes its name from a story its first settler, Ed Schieffelin, used to tell. When in 1877 he would go out on prospecting trips, the soldiers stationed at Fort Huachuca warned him that he would only "find his tombstone" there in Apache domain. Surely the deaths of Johnson and Mowry were among the murders that the soldiers had in mind when they made this statement.

The site of the cabin that the Johnsons occupied for so short a time in 1876 can still be found today. It is located within the San Pedro Riparian National Conservation Area and is, therefore, accessible to the public. It is not marked, so the best guide is the description of it in the Indian Depredation claim, which says it is near the confluence of the Babacomari Creek and the San Pedro River. This area is also heavily covered by brush. It is possible to walk along the bed of the San Pedro River to reach the area where Johnson and Mowry were working at the time of their deaths.

Widow Emily Johnson was successful in pursuing her claim. In January 1914, the Court of Claims found claim #8317 compensable and awarded $385 for the loss of the horses and mule. There was, of course, no compensation for the loss of husband and father. Many settlers never even filed claims, assuming it would cost more to prove their claim than they would ever get. This was probably the case for the Johnson family. Still, it was recognition that the events, which took place on September 13, 1876, had altered the destiny of an entire family.

11

THE JOHNSON FAMILY
IN OHIO

John Calhoun Johnson and his descendants can trace their lineage to Captain Griffith Johnson of Maryland, a Revolutionary soldier.[163] He was J. C. Johnson's great grandfather. Drawn into the stream of Americans pressing the western frontier forward, J. C. Johnson's father and grandfather were among the first settlers of Nottingham Township, Harrison County, Ohio.

John was born there on the family farm, March 18, 1822, the eldest child of Nathan and Jane Marie Auld Johnson. His brothers and sisters were: William Hamilton Johnson, Elizabeth Perrin Johnson Moore, Margaret Jane Johnson Hazelet, and Nathan Johnson. Their mother died shortly after Nathan's birth.

John's father, Nathan Johnson Sr. was quickly remarried to Jeminah Howard, a widow with one son. Together they had five daughters: Emeline, Nancy, Rachael, Cynthia, and Harriet. The youngest, Harriet, was nine years old when John left Ohio for good.

---

163 Several descendants of Griffith Johnson are members of the Daughters of the Revolution.

A painting of the Johnson home in Harrison County, Ohio. Built in 1819, it is
John C. Johnson's birthplace. In 1886 Emma Canfield made this painting from a
photograph as a birthday gift for Margaret Johnson Hazlet, John's sister.
Author's collection

While he never returned, it is quite likely he maintained a
regular correspondence with family members. His closeness with
his brother Nathan is well known. Later, whether by coincidence or
design, John would give two of his daughters the names of two of his
half-sisters, Cynthia and Harriet.

John's sister, Elizabeth Johnson, and her husband Alexander
Moore named one of their sons, born in 1855, after her brother, John
Calhoun Moore.

All three of the Johnson brothers read law in Ohio and passed
the bar there. While neither John nor Nathan made a career of law,
their brother William Hamilton did. He was a practicing attorney in
Floyd County, Iowa, from 1854 until his death in 1879. He was elected
to the position of county judge in 1862.

One of Johnson's half-sisters, Nancy, took a photograph of the Johnson family farmhouse about 1857, after the family had left the farm. In 1886, artist Emma Canfield made an oil painting from the photograph as a gift for Margaret Johnson Hazelet. The oil painting depicts a spacious prosperous two-story farmhouse, built in 1819.

The probate file for Nathan, Sr. described a comfortable farm, prosperous, and typical of the time. As the eldest son, John might have reasonably expected to inherit his father's farm. However, between the years of 1856 and 1858 John and his full sisters and brother (all the children of Nathan's first wife), for a financial consideration, quitclaimed their interest in the farm to their youngest brother, Nathan. It is unclear why they did this, as there is no evidence that Nathan ever chose the life of a farmer, or lived there as an adult.

Nathan Johnson, Sr. died in 1844. He, and both of his wives, are buried in the Sharon Cemetery, sometimes called Seceder Cemetery, just outside of Deersville, Ohio. The curious name of Seceder refers to the small group of families who seceded from the local Presbyterian Church to establish one of their own. His will enumerated a number of pieces of property, including a lot in the town of Deersville, which he bequeathed to the Wesleyan Church to build a church sanctuary.

While John C. Johnson's great grandfather, Griffith Johnson lived out his life on one of the several land bounties he received as payment for his participation in the Revolutionary War, his children, thirteen in all, followed the frontier West, prospering and contributing to their communities. Seven sons of Griffith Johnson went to Ohio in the early days of settlement of the state, including John Calhoun's grandfather, John. Their land patents in Ohio were recorded in 1810.

Some stories about the descendants of Griffith Johnson are included here to illustrate the strong heritage into which J. C. Johnson was born. These are stories about his family that he grew up with, ones that shaped his attitudes and expectations of himself.

The early and middle 1800s were dangerous days in Ohio.

A well-known story in eastern Ohio is of two boys who were John Calhoun Johnson's cousins, James Johnson's two sons, John, age thirteen, and Henry, age eleven. In October of 1788, Indians captured the pair of them as they gathered nuts in the woods. While their captors slept, the boys took the Indians' rifle and tomahawk and killed them, then found their way home.

Their father, James, had spent a much longer period of time as a captive of the local natives in Jefferson County, Ohio, prior to 1800, with his release secured by English traders.[164]

Another fatal brush with Indians happened to J. C.'s granduncle on his mother's side, John Perrin, Jr. In 1755, he lost his first wife and son in an Indian raid on their settlement in Pennsylvania[165].

Nathan

Nathan Johnson, John's youngest brother also went to California, but he followed a very different path. Nathan's great passion was teaching. While in California, he taught grammar school and adult learning classes.

From his obituary it is known that he arrived in California in 1850. Born on January 21, 1830, Nathan was about twenty when he departed for the West, probably inspired by the exciting stories his brother must have written in his letters home.

While his means of travel are unknown, he might have opted to travel by ship since he was never as skilled an outdoorsman as his brother. It is also possible his brother warned him of the hazards of travel by horseback across the plains. It is clear his brother's ranch was not his destination. Nathan wanted to have his own adventures. Not interested in farming, and not planning to settle in California, he seems to have lived in boarding houses for the whole of his stay in the state.

---

164 *Biographical Record, Harrison County, Ohio*
165 *Bedford Gazette* March 29, 1907 "Early Local History"

John on the right with his younger brother Nathan. This photograph was probably taken during Nathan's time in California.
Coutesy: CA State Parks Sutter's Fort Collection

Although his obituary claimed he held high offices within the Masonic Lodge of California in the years 1854-55, queries into the records of the Grand Lodge of California do not support this. However, it may have been so, since early records of the lodge are spotty.

The first documented evidence of his activities in California was the election of September 1858, when he was narrowly defeated for the office of superintendent of schools in El Dorado County. In that same year he was installed as secretary of Acacia Lodge #92 Free and Accepted Masons in Coloma. He also joined the El Dorado Commandery #4 Knights Templar of Placerville in October 1858, where he was also an officer. The nature of these activities indicates he had been in El Dorado County for some time prior.

The editor of the *Mountain Democrat* newspaper appears to have liked Nathan. He certainly gave Nathan's activities plenty of coverage. On the last day of 1859, the *Mountain Democrat* devoted a large amount of space covering the recent school examinations at the Diamond Springs School, where Nathan was the teacher. There were between fifty and sixty students of all ages and over one hundred visitors present. Here are a few excerpts:

> *This examination showed, particularly among the smaller scholars, a proficiency far beyond their years.... The teacher seems to possess, in an eminent degree, those peculiar qualifications which are indispensably requisite to constitute a good teacher.... The great secret of his success as a teacher, aside from his natural capacity, may be attributable, in no small degree, to his extensive experience in the business, as he has been continually engaged in teaching ever since he arrived at the age of maturity, embracing a period of more than twenty years.*[166]

Added to the end of the article was a curious statement by the correspondent, who chose Veritas as his pen name:

> *In conclusion, Messrs. Editors, we may be pardoned for stating that Mr.* [Nathan] *Johnson has, during his residence here, acquired, among those*

---

[166] Twenty years of teaching sounds like an error or his first teaching credential was earned at a very young age. According to his obituary, he held teaching credentials in Ohio, California, and Michigan.

*whose good opinion is worth having, a reputation
for honesty, morality, and gentlemanly deportment,
equaled by few and surpassed by none in our
community. Notwithstanding he has been assailed and
vilified by some here, who, resorting to weapons of
falsehood and deception, have manifested a desire to
sub serve their own dark and selfish purposes rather
than to promote the public good, yet Mr. Johnson,
treating their viperous attacks as unworthy of notice,
has pursued the even tenor of his way and acquired
a reputation in his profession truly enviable and
not surpassed by that of any other teacher in the State
of California.*

This raises questions as to who "Veritas" was, and why he felt compelled to write a defense of Nathan. What was the reason? Could Veritas have been his brother, John? In other articles, the *Mountain Democrat* described Nathan as a man of strong temperance ideals and fascinating manners. Did some of the miners found him a little effeminate?

Years later a former student presented a "Catalogue of Pupils" who had been enrolled from March 7, 1859 to October 1, 1859"[167] at the Diamond Springs School. It listed over one hundred names of the boys and girls who were Nathan's students that year. [168]

Prior to becoming the headmaster of the Diamond Springs School, Nathan worked in the same capacity in Coloma where the school was called the Select School. He taught night school for adults in Coloma in about 1860 according to the biography of Charles J. Johnson (no relation), who had come to the United States from Sweden and wanted to study English grammar and spelling.

Nathan continued to teach in Diamond Springs until the spring

---

167 *Pony Express Courier* November 1934 page seven
168 The schoolhouse was located on the hill north of the Independent Order of Odd Fellows hall in Diamond Springs. The IOOF building is still standing, but not the schoolhouse.

of 1861, when he changed positions and took over the El Dorado Public School where he taught until a severe bout of rheumatism caused him to temporarily close the school.

Nathan did not return to teaching until January of 1862, when he assumed the schoolmaster's tasks in Johnson's District. At last he had joined his brother, and probably lived with John and his family until May, when Nathan returned to the East.

Before departing, Nathan showed the newspaper editor a letter that was offering him a teaching position "on the eastern slope," which he apparently did not accept. The position was likely in one of the silver mining boomtowns. Nathan may have left California, but he carried it with him in his nickname, "California." Nathan California Johnson is how he was thereafter known.

His next stop was the Ohio State Law School where, following his graduation in 1863, he was admitted to the Ohio State Bar. Nathan's career as a lawyer was short—if he ever practiced law at all—before he returned to his real love: teaching.

In 1865, the thirty-five year old bachelor, Nathan married Samantha E. McGowan, who was only seventeen at the time, many years his junior. Could she have been a former student? They had two sons, Jertha John Johnson,[169] born in 1868, and Nathan C. Johnson born in 1875. Both sons became pharmacists.

Nathan and Samantha lived in Berrien County, Michigan, where he taught school. From 1878 to 1879 he served as Superintendent of Schools, fulfilling an ambition he'd had since his California days. He had run for Superintendent of Public Schools in El Dorado County in 1858, but lost.

Nathan died at the age of sixty-three on August 8, 1893. He was buried in Oakridge Cemetery in Berrien.

Over the years, Nathan and his brother John continued their close relationship that had started when they were boys. At some time just before John left for Arizona, Nathan visited him for what would be the last time.

---

169 Even within the family his name was spelled variously Jertha, Jether, Jetha. He often went by J. J.

ELLEN OSBORN

Hagerdon Family

It is interesting to speculate why Luther Hagerdon chose to uproot his family from their comfortable home in Green Bay, Wisconsin, to travel to California in 1853. According to his daughter, Emily, it was for economic opportunity. It is likely that Placerville was their destination from the start. Prior to their arrival in El Dorado County, letters addressed to Adam, Luther, and J. O. Hagerdon awaited them at the Placerville post office.

Using Emily's reminiscence[170] as a guide, a little is known about their journey. In some ways, that document was as remarkable for what it didn't say as for what it did. She didn't give enough geographical detail to be able to tell if they came over the Johnson Cutoff, or took the older Carson River Route into California, since they both ended at the same place. But, based on the popularity of the Johnson Cutoff in 1853, it was the probable choice.

Emily never mentioned that their overland party was one comprised largely of children. Emily, herself, had turned twenty shortly after their journey began. Zilpha, Emily's stepmother, was Luther's second wife. She was in her mid-twenties and carried her infant son, Frances Leroy in her arms. An old family story tells that Zilpha and Luther were also the parents of twins who died tragically soon after arriving in California.

Based on the ages of her other children, those twins must have been older than Frances Leroy. It could be they died of one of the prevalent diseases of the time. Contemporary accounts of living conditions at the time tell of much sickness in the mines, such as dysentery and cholera, contracted by drinking unclean water— sometimes drinking the water that came directly from mining ditches. The twins were the first of what would become Johnson's extended family to be buried on his ranch.

Emily's father, Luther was much older than the typical

---

170 See the complete text of *The Life of Emily Hagerdon Johnson* in Appendix F.

emigrant; he was around fifty years of age. The eldest of the children, John O., had just reached manhood. Emily's brothers, Eber Adam and Charles Luther were teenage boys, and James Knox was about ten. Her sister, Harriet Ann was about seven or eight.

Emily's story suggested there was still another brother, but nothing is known about him. Just prior to her mother's death, Emily clearly stated that, "our family increased until there were eight of us: five boys and three girls." According to Emily, their maternal grandmother took her middle sister, Mary, to rear; therefore, Mary stayed behind when the rest of the family journeyed to California.

The available historical records give us no idea what Luther did during his short stay in California, or even how long he stayed. However, since Zilpha was back home in Ohio in time for the birth of her fifth child, Albert Edward in 1856, their stay was a short one.

Family tradition says their daughter, Ella Mariah, was born in California in 1854. Luther's name appears only on the 1854 Poll Tax Assessment Rolls in El Dorado County.

It is known that when Luther and Zilpha left California, they left Luther's entire first family behind. Emily became the surrogate mother to them all, including her brothers, John O., Eber Adam, Charles Luther, and James Knox, and her sister, Harriet Ann. When John married Emily, he opened his home and his heart to a complete family.

John O., the eldest, seemed to have struck out on his own, as his name appears in the official record of El Dorado County only once, where he paid his Poll Tax Assessment in 1854.

Both Eber Adam and James Knox Hagerdon were registered voters in El Dorado County in 1867. Both gave their occupation as teamster. That was during the boom years in the silver mines of Nevada, which generated a great deal of freighting business over the county road from Placerville to Carson City.

Eber enlisted in the Union Army on November 15, 1864, in Company D, 8th Regiment of the Infantry. Many young men from Placerville were in that unit. As of July 21, 1865, he was listed as a deserter from Fort Point in San Francisco, California. Since he was registered to vote subsequent to that date, and worked openly as a teamster, it appears the army wasn't interested in pursuing him.

It is known that many soldiers stationed at Fort Point contracted consumption (tuberculosis), and Eber may have been one of them. He may have wanted to get out of that foggy cold environment and receive care from his sister, Emily.

Eber married Martha Penter on March 12, 1870, in El Dorado County. Martha was so young the marriage required her father's consent. Their short marriage produced no children. He died at Johnson's Ranch on November 10, 1871, at the young age of thirty-five. The cause of his death is unknown. He is buried in the cemetery on the Johnson Ranch.

Charles Luther also drifted away to the city of San Jose, where he'd made his living as a painter, married, and had a family. Charles spent his declining years in the Masonic Home in Union City, California. He is buried in Alameda County, California.

James Knox lived in El Dorado County until at least 1872 when his name appeared on the ledger of the Vallejo Mining Company as an employee. He was living in Iowa in 1930 at the age of 86, according to the U. S. Census.

Emily's sister, Harriet seems to have stayed near her sister. On January 19, 1860, she married James Leslie, a teamster, in the nearby town of El Dorado. She was seventeen. On August 6, 1862, John sold his new brother-in-law, James, ninety acres of his ranch so they could settle nearby. Leslie was also for a time the proprietor of the Nine Mile House, a way station on the emigrant road, only a few miles from Johnson's Ranch. Then tragedy struck. First Harriet died, on July 19, 1863, and then James died in 1874. They are both buried in the family cemetery on Johnson's Ranch.

The cemetery on Johnson's Ranch goes by many names. In addition to its original name of Johnson's Cemetery, over the years it has also been called Old Fruitridge Cemetery, or Blair/Winkleman Cemetery. While today the cemetery appears much smaller, according to family tradition, Johnson's original donation to the county was three acres for a cemetery at that place. There are no Johnson headstones, despite the seven or more Johnson family members buried there. They probably had wooden grave markers that have fallen victim to time, or to a wildfire called the Cleese Road Fire, which swept through there in October of 1929.

It is thought that the earliest burials there are associated with the El Dorado Indian Wars of 1850-1851. Use of this cemetery has been continuous. While the exact number of burials may never be known, the total of documented burials is forty-nine. The cemetery is under the jurisdiction of the County of El Dorado. More details about its history and occupants are available in the archives of the El Dorado County Historical Museum in Placerville.

John and Emily's Children

John and Emily were married on New Year's Day, 1854, three months after John spotted Emily in the stream of arriving emigrants and induced her family to come stay with him, in hopes that he could get to know Emily better.

For the next twenty-two years they would live together on the ranch and raise their family of nine children there. The children were: George, Clara Belle, Cynthia, Anna Harriet, Nathan (named for his uncle), John Calhoun, Jr., William Henry, Charles Luther, and Mary Emily.

After the home place was sold, and John died in Arizona, it was up to Emily to finish the job of raising their children. She held the family together by the considerable force of her personality.

Their first born, George Pen arrived on December 5, 1854.

171

Emily Johnson in her later years in San Jose, California
Author's collection

As mentioned earlier, George was most probably named for an Ohio statesman of the era, George Hunt Pendleton, who along with George's father, John, had attended Cincinnati College. George's middle name appears variously as Pen or Penn. It is noteworthy that he signed his marriage license George Pen Johnson, but it well may have been Pendleton, although no document has appeared to confirm that.

George's arrival was followed by the births of Clara Belle and Cynthia, both of whom died in infancy. Almost nothing is known about Cynthia. Little Clara Belle died on the day of her sister Anna's birth.

Anna herself wrote the sad story in her prayer book, stating that Clara died from eating something she found in the cellar, possibly the heads of phosphorus matches. That was a common cause of death for small children in those days. Clara's short existence was recorded for all time by the 1860 U. S. Census taker who happened to arrive at the ranch just prior to the sad event. Anna wrote in her prayer book that Clara died in the morning of June 22, 1860 and she, Anna Harriet, was born that evening. Clara Belle's obituary confirmed that date[171].

Following Anna's birth, the family welcomed in succession: Nathan on February 22, 1865; John Calhoun, Jr. on November 24, 1867; William Henry on July 13, 1869; Charles Luther on February 1, 1872; and Mary Emily on April 6, 1876.

There is some confusion over the exact year Mary was born. The 1876 date would have her born just after her father left for Arizona Territory, which may explain why the family stayed behind.

However, The *Mountain Democrat* announced the birth of a daughter to John C. Johnson and wife on April 8, 1875, in Placerville. Newspapers make a lot of errors but they rarely announce a birth a year before it happens. Mary was the only child not born on the ranch.

Of their nine children, Emily and John raised seven to adulthood, with the youngest children raised by their widowed mother. All of them, except Nathan and John Jr. married and produced families.

George worked as a laborer at times, but preferred mining, first in El Dorado County, then in Placer County. About 1882 he went to work briefly as a groundskeeper at Agnews State Hospital in San Jose where he met and married Fredericka Persson,[172] a Swedish emigrant who was also working there. Together they had seven children. As he settled into family life, he relocated the family to Auburn, California.

He still preferred the solitary life of a miner, and often spent long periods of time away from his family at his mine. In Placer County his first claim was at Rich Flat, located at the head of Rich Gulch in "Old Auburn," south of the fairgrounds. In later years, he

---

171 *Sacramento Daily Union* July 28 1860 page 2 column 1
172 The author's great grandparents.

had a mine on the old Madden Ranch. A member of the family still has the little ore cart he used at his mine. Older family members recalled seeing it on a short length of rail at the entrance to his mine.

George Pen Johnson
Photo from Author's collection

Another activity he carried on at the mine got him thrown into jail. He operated a still there, even when he was advanced in years. What attracted the attention of the law was the discharge of a gun. This resulted in a visit from the colorful Placer County sheriff, Elmer Gum, who put George in the county jail for operating a still and being in possession of alcohol. The incident took place in 1928, during Prohibition.[173] While the seventy-four year old George maintained he only made whiskey for himself and a few friends, his product was well enough known in the area to go by the name of "Squirrel Tree" whiskey.

In his teen-aged years in Placerville, George was an enthusiastic member of the Placerville City Guards, one of El Dorado County's militia units. He took honors for his marksmanship. George's Navy Colt pistol is still owned by one of his descendants. He was active in the Native Sons of the Golden West. George died on July 3, 1932, and was buried in the Odd Fellows Cemetery in Auburn.

Anna Harriet was married three times. Her first marriage to Milo Hamilton Oldfield, a member of a well-known pioneer family of El Dorado County, ended in divorce in 1882, but not before their daughter, Viola was born.

Anna Harriet Johnson
Author's collection

---

173 *Placer Herald* February 4, 1928 page three

Milo and Anna's brother George were working together on a mining venture at Spanish Hill in 1881 shortly before the break up.[174] Whatever caused the marriage to end is not known. Milo deserted his family and moved to Modesto.[175] His name later showed up on the Tulare County 1886 voter's registration with his occupation listed as carpenter.

Anna took her maiden name back and supported herself and daughter by working as a seamstress. She went on to marry Peter Felix Goley, a miner living in the Kelsey District, with whom she had two daughters. Peter Goley was much older than Anna. Born in France, he arrived in the United States in time to fight for the Union cause in the Civil War. He was a survivor of the battle of Gettysburg.

Nathan Johnson
Author's collection

John Calhoun Johnson, Jr.
Author's collection

174 *Mountain Democrat* July 30, 1881
175 El Dorado County Civil Case #236 H. A. Oldfield Plaintiff vs Milo Oldfield Defendant

After this marriage also ended in divorce Anna's final marriage was to Alburtus Butler who worked for Southern Pacific Railroad. She lived most of her adult life in Sacramento. She was a member of the Native Daughters of the Golden West. Anna died on May 28, 1937, and was buried in the Odd Fellows Cemetery in Sacramento.

Nathan made his living as a butcher in San Jose. He died on November 17, 1922, and is buried in Oak Hill Cemetery in San Jose, California, next to his mother.

John Jr., who went by "Jack," was known as "Foghorn" among his cronies. John followed his brother into the vocation of butcher, but also worked gold claims in Placer County.[176] He died in San Jose, California on September 3, 1933. He is also buried in Oak Hill Cemetery.

William Henry Johnson
Author's collection

---

176 *Sacramento Bee* September 1933

ELLEN OSBORN

William Henry was the most successful of all the children. Because of his prominence, his life story was published in the *History of the State of California and Biographical Record of Coast Counties of California*. These county histories were popular toward the end of the nineteenth century and into the early twentieth century.

It is important to take into consideration that a person paid to have his biography included. People submitted what they wanted printed. Therefore, factual errors could make it into print. The information about William, specifically, should be reliable, while trust should not be given to what was written about other family members and events before his birth. In the biography was the only reference to "the history of the early days of California, written up and left him by his father," a document that has eluded discovery in recent years.

William had a very interesting life. Raised by his widowed mother, he was deprived of the influence of a father from the time he was seven years old. He received a public education, first in Placerville and then in San Jose, where he moved with his family at the age of twelve.

By William's account, his first career was as a jockey. He recalled riding racehorses for Lucky Baldwin on all the principal tracks in California, Hawaii, and Australia. He then learned the trade of a barber, but influenced by the story of his father's life, he turned to the study of law and was admitted to the bar in 1897. He established a successful law practice in San Jose, where he was known for his courtesy in the courtroom. He was city attorney for the City of San Jose from 1910 to 1912. His marriage to Belle Ziegler produced three children. His died on February 7, 1933.

Charles Luther married Caroline Foesterling, a member of a pioneer family. They had three children. They lived in San Jose, California, where they raised their family, and where he had a shoe store. Charles was living in Sacramento when he died on July 9, 1943.

This line of the family has used the surname "Johnston" rather than Johnson. The 1880 U.S. Census showed the whole family, while still in Placerville, with the surname Johnston, not Johnson.

The Johnson's youngest daughter, Mary Emily, or Mamie, as

she was known, grew up in a single parent household, but with plenty of family around her. She married Albert Robb with whom she had two children. The Robbs lived both in Oakland and San Jose, California.

Charles Luther Johnston with wife Caroline
Author's collection

Mary Emily Johnson (left) with mother, Emily (right)
and daughter, Gladys (front)
Author's collection

Mary died January 3, 1953, and was buried next to her mother in Oak Hill Cemetery in San Jose.

Before she died, mindful of the heritage she had from the lives of her parents and their mark on the history of early California, she gave a family history to the California State Library in 1950. Unfortunately, she made some errors, which, since they reside in such a venerable repository, have been, and continue to be, picked up and repeated by researchers.

For instance, she gave her father's date of arrival in California as 1846, a date that is contradicted by the record in several places. He did not have a ranch on the Bear River. She had his ranch confused with the other Johnson's Ranch that was the base for the Donner Party rescue.

It is hoped that this work will serve to correct these errors for future historians.

After her husband John's death in Arizona, Emily stayed a few years in Placerville before moving to San Jose to be near her brother, Charles. She ran a boarding house in her home on Coe Street. It was there that she met and married her second husband, John H. Jacobs. Emily died in San Jose on March 3, 1917.

The Santa Clara County Pioneer Society conducted her funeral. Alexander Philip Murgotten, pioneer newspaper editor and an old friend from her days in El Dorado County, gave the eulogy. Emily is buried in Oak Hill Cemetery, alongside three of her children.

EPILOGUE

This history, built on fragments of information about the life of John Calhoun Johnson is in some ways surprising in how clear a window into the past it provides. On the other hand, it is disappointing that so little tangible evidence is left: his ranch is a golf course, his home in Placerville has been torn down and the lot divided, the store burned long ago, his emigrant route is no longer in use and is visible to the casual observer in only a few places, his papers lost or destroyed, and his grave never found. The Old Johnson Cemetery is still known by that name, but there are no Johnson family headstones to visit and care for.

There is a sign on Highway 50 pointing to a short section of side road still called Johnson's Pass Road. However, Johnson's Hill is now Echo Summit. Apple Mountain Golf Resort has named Hole Four "Cock-Eye's Cabin" because it is near where Johnson's house stood. Old maps identified North and South Canyons on his ranch as Johnson's North and South Canyons, but current maps have dropped the "Johnson." Not only can his grave not be located, but books about Arizona's ghost towns frequently don't even mention Tres Alamos or Hooker's Station. Calvin Mowry's bones are said to have washed away many years ago when the San Pedro River flooded over its banks.

This was not just the fate of Johnson. For most of the men and women mentioned in this book, the same is true. Where is the grave marker for Lieutenant Leslie McKinney? For that matter, there are no grave markers for any of the dead from the El Dorado Indian Wars. Even though John Phillips was buried in Placerville, the location of his grave has been lost. There are no memorials, plaques, or markers for any of the persons mentioned here, at least not in El Dorado County. The exception is the marker recently placed by E. Clampus Vitus on the grounds of the Apple Mountain Golf Resort, commemorating J. C. Johnson and his ranch.

Those were risky days. As we saw with Johnson's partners, John and Sophronia Phillips, the specter of disease and premature death was always present.[177] Financial ruin was also waiting to catch the unwary, the overly optimistic, the too trusting, and the just plain unlucky. In their rush to make their individual fortunes, the people of El Dorado didn't have time for sentimentality.

The Blakeleys do have their family plot in Union Cemetery, right inside the Bee Street gate. Alburn and Caroline have impressive headstones, the first one sees as one enters. The Bee family is remembered by the name of Bee Street, which runs past the Bee-Bennett House, now a restaurant. Only the cellar dates from the days of the Bee family occupancy.

The gem of a lake named for Fall Leaf will always recall the memory of Johnson's Delaware Indian friend. That is perhaps the only place in California that can be said with certainty that Johnson named. The spot on the map known as "Indian Hattie's" keeps Hattie Tom's name and memory alive.

As early as 1855 Johnson recognized that the hills around his ranch were capable of producing apples, and would someday make that district famous. For a half-century the hospitable farmers of Apple Hill have been opening their farms to the public, while the reputation for the fine quality of their products has spread throughout California,

---

177 See details of the lives of John and Sophronia Phillips in Appendix G.

Nevada, and beyond. Johnson would undoubtedly be pleased to see Apple Hill's annual celebration of agricultural life, with their farms clustered around what was his beloved ranch.

Johnson's descendants can be proud to claim him as an ancestor. He always stood for the rule of law. He loved his country. His capacity for hard work was impressive. His devotion to family never wavered. His contemporaries may have called him eccentric, but the ideas he promoted, such as toll-free roads and the belief that every property owner deserved a path to obtain clear title to his land, were simply a little ahead of his time.

Johnson's legacy is his many descendants. Most of them still live in California. They have made their contributions to society in many ways, and continue to do so.

I am proud, and a little humbled, to count myself as one of them.

A Lovely & Comfortable Heritage Lost

ELLEN OSBORN

ACKNOWLEDGMENTS

I thank the following individuals and groups for their help. Without them, I never would have completed this work. I owe so many people so much.

First, I am indebted to my husband, Ford Osborn, who encouraged and helped me from the very beginning.

For their patience and able assistance with research, my thanks go to the staff of the National Archives in San Bruno, the staff of the El Dorado County Library, especially research librarian and friend, Bonnie Battaglia, fellow researchers Hazel Schubbe and Beverly Cola.

I also thank employees of the U. S. Forest Service on the Eldorado National Forest past and present: District Archaeologists Krista Deal, Karin Klemic, Judy Rood, and Jordan Serin, Historic Resources Program Managers Katy Parr, and Denise McLemoore, and Dana Supernowicz, Historian. I give a special word of thanks to all my fellow Oregon California Trails Association members.

For reading early versions of my manuscript and offering helpful suggestions that made it better, I thank Mary Cory, Director, El Dorado County Historical Museum, historian Don Buck, and my cousin, Miles Johnson. I am grateful for the encouragement all my Johnson relatives gave me, with special gratitude to cousins Thelma

ELLEN OSBORN

Knudsen, Hugh Thomas, and Edna McBride, and my mother Lillian Parmley, all of whom are no longer with us.

For encouragement and guidance with the craft of writing, my thanks go to the El Dorado Writers Guild and Northern California Publishers and Authors. Finally, I doubt this work would have ever been published without the able editing of Jo Johnston and publisher Annette Chaudet of Pronghorn Press.

ABOUT THE AUTHOR

Ellen Osborn has a passion for history. This passion led her, along with her husband Ford, to move to Pollock Pines, California when they retired. Located right on the old emigrant trail, they could easily research the emigrant routes, especially the Johnson Cutoff.

As a direct descendant of John Calhoun Johnson, she has always been fascinated by his life, and by how little historians have written about him and his many contributions to the fledging state of California. This led Ellen to years of research and finally, to write this book.

Along the way she has written articles for Sierra Heritage and the Overland Journal on related historical topics. As a member of the Placerville Shakespeare Club, Ellen helped research and write El Dorado's True Gold, Notable Women's Stories in 2013. In this popular dramatic production, Ellen portrays Etta Farmer, El Dorado's first woman doctor.

Ellen was honored by the Daughters of the American Revolution in 2013 with their prestigious Historic Preservation Recognition Award for her many contributions to the preservation of El Dorado County history. In 2011, Ellen and her husband were

ELLEN OSBORN

presented with OCTA's Senior Trail Boss Award for tireless dedication to the location and preservation of the Johnson Cutoff.

As a volunteer researcher for the last sixteen years at the El Dorado County Historical Museum she has helped countless visitors find answers to their questions about the Gold Rush Days.

A Lovely & Comfortable Heritage Lost

An early view of Lake Tahoe while it was still offically Lake Bigler, taken at Glenbrook. #8687.
Courtesy of the El Dorado County Historical Museum

APPENDIXES

Appendix A
The Origin of Lake Bigler (Tahoe) as published in the *Placerville Herald*
(footnotes 15 & 89)

Appendix B
El Dorado Indian Wars Dead and Wounded
(footnotes 34 & 59)

Appendix C
Bartlett's Guide to California
(footnote 111)

Appendix D
Agricultural and Mining Association of El Dorado County/ Memorial to the Congress of the United States
(footnote 129)

Appendix E
Brief of John C. Johnson, Contestant, Patent No. 199
(footnote 136)

Appendix F
The Life of Emily Hagerdon Johnson, her story
(footnote 170)

Appendix G
John and Sophronia Phillips
(footnote 177)

ELLEN OSBORN

APPENDIX A
The Origin of Lake Bigler (Tahoe)

(As transcribed from the *Placerville Herald*, July 1853)

Lake Bigler is the largest of those mountain lakes that characterize the summit of the Nevada mountains, and generally lying in and usually surrounded by valleys of greater or less extent, but at great heights between the Sierras of California's eastern range. This lake is supposed to be about sixty miles in length, and is from ten to twenty in width; it is nearly surrounded by high and inaccessible barriers of rock, that in many places are nearly perpendicular for more than two hundred feet. Upon the eastern side, about midway from north to south, is a singularly arched cavity or entrance that leads to dark and hitherto unexplored recesses, and the fact that strange sounds, at certain seasons of the year are emitted from its gloomy caverns, has given rise to the following singular legend, transmitted from sire to son, from a greatly remote period to the present, and is one of the very few in possession of the Digger Indian.

Directly opposite the "Spirit's Lodge," or cavern, (for so it is called) is the only spot where nature, in her last great convulsions, left a deep gorge in the mountains, lying east to west; this holds true for a great distance either north or south from this particular locality. But here for more than half a mile in width upon the lake, and running westwardly and upward from it for nearly two miles, is a beautiful slope of fertile ground, covered with the most luxuriant growth of mountain clover, with here and there a beautiful copse of the fir tree and quaking asp. It is a perfectly elliptical amphitheater opening into the lake upon a clean sandy beach; not a blade of coarse grass is seen, but the green clover, like a closely shaved lawn, reaches to the little belt of sand that separates it from the waters.

Immediately back, or to the west end of this beautiful vale, is a mountain peak, rising high above the surrounding ones, in the top of which is the yawning crater of an extinct volcano, that strange as it may appear, has no immediate connection with the legend of the spirit cave. This little gem among mountain vales, is the summer resort of the "Digger," and as the lake abounds with fish, 'tis there he luxuriates till the next winter's snows drive him to the valleys. The vale is accessible from the lake, and by a single pass only through the mountains a little to the north of the old crater; it was at this pass that we, with our guide and interpreter, Col. J. C. Johnson, entered the "spirit vale."

There were but about seventy Indians in the valley, though it might be made as well the happy home of thousands, for the waters of the lake at this place are literally alive with fishes, among which the speckled trout of great size and the real salmon predominate. It was nearly night when we reached the lodge of the grand chief, but a few rods from the water's edge. He received us kindly, at the same time remarking that we were the first white men that ever trod the shores of the lake at this point, though the south end is frequently visited, being but about two miles from the immigrant road, from Carson Valley to Placerville by Johnson's Cut-Off. The sun nearly setting, threw a dazzling light upon the opposite side of the lake, distinctly revealing the entrance to the great grotto, though nearly ten miles distant. It appeared an immense opening surmounted by a nearly perfect, Gothic or pointed arch, and either our imagination or the truth led us to believe that we could see a great distance within along its rugged sides, and the smooth tapering sheet of water that extended like the point of a spear still further on, convinced us of the truth of the existence at least of the heretofore much doubted cavern of the Genii. We were much pleased at finding some two or three very good canoes that had been made from the pines that grow upon the extreme northern border of the lake, and from thence taken to the spirit shore. In one of these it was our intention to embark the coming morning for the spirit's cave, having made an arrangement with the chief, by paying its full value, so certain was he that we would never return, if once we passed the entrance to the cavern. For more that half the night, did a poor and totally blind, old, yes more than *centenarian* Digger, pour forth from his shriveled lips, the ancient legend of his tribe, relating to what he termed "the rock and water prison of the demons," and as it possesses something of interest, as connected with the ancient geological formation, and subsequent changes that have been wrought by great natural causes and at a greatly remote period, upon this portion of the American Continent, we are constrained to give it entire as it fell from his lips, though in our language. He said:

"Long before these mountains were lifted up so very high as they now are, the Digger Indian possessed the whole earth, and were a great people. Then this little valley and lake made a part of the grand river *Tro-ko-nene*, (or Humboldt) which at that time poured its waters into the great sea in which the sun sets; then were our people happy, for the whole country was more level than now, and far more beautiful, besides the great fish, (meaning salmon) now only numerous in the lake, were plentiful, even to the head waters of the Trokenene and the whole country was filled with trees and vines that bore sweet fruit.

"But the time arrived when a new people, unlike our fathers, only in being more warlike and powerful, though speaking a different language, came down from the north and began a terrible war, destroying our homes, our wives and our children. And though unaccustomed to war, our fathers made a long and determined resistance; but after years on years of terrible warfare, were at length all driven away, or made the slaves of their conquerors for life."

"Yes," said he, his sightless eyes streaming with tears, "Our fathers and our mothers were made slaves, and for ages did they and their children toil on and serve their terrible masters; and so hard was their lot, so deep and abject their servitude, they became *fools* and lost all record of the moon or time, and like trees, knew nothing. But at length the Great Spirit put a stop to this by destroying alike our people and their oppressors. A great wave like a mountain came up from the sea, and swept them all away, that they were seen no more; all but a *few* poor Digger slaves and their masters that were the great spirits or teachers of their people; and as there were no mountains then, they assembled upon the top of a great temple that our people had been compelled to rear, and where they worshipped the sun and kept alive a perpetual fire. And thus were a few of our fathers and mothers saved, with a remnant of their hard taskmasters.

"But no sooner had the waters all gone back, the earth once more become green, and the *Trokenene* flowed within its banks as before, that the earth convulsed, and rolled from side to side, that then the first thunderings ever known beneath the ground were heard and they were terrible. At length however, all was still again; but before half a moon had passed away, terrific fires burst forth from out of the ground, and showers of hot and sulfurous ashes fell around, and our masters sought safety within the great temple we had reared, *but they shut the poor fools out!* The Great Spirit saw it and was displeased, for now the heavy thunderings were heard again, the earth shook and trembled, deep chasms were formed, that throwing up vast volumes of smoke for a few moments, as suddenly closed again. And then it was that these great mountains, never before seen, *were lifted up.* The *Trokenene* was stopped, or lost in the new great sea, then for the first time seen in the east, and which continued to exist for many years but at length dried up and was lost, as the waters of the eastern *Trokenene* now are, by the sands that lie under the rising sun."

On being asked what became of the "Great Spirits" their masters, that had sought refuge in the temple, he replied:

"First let us follow the fortunes of my people. No sooner had their hated masters closed the doors against them, than our people, to escape the fires that were bursting out around them hurried to the *Trokenene*, and in their canoes hastened down its now rapidly increasing current towards the sea, and had barely made good their escape, before these great mountains by an awful convulsion that shook the whole earth, were lifted up, and all the beautiful groves, the home alike of our ancient fathers and their subsequent conquerors, were wrapped in one awful chaos of fire and smoke and ashes.

"The *Trokenene*, no longer the greatest river of the western sea, coursing its entire length through fields and forests of perpetual green, now reduced to a mere mountain torrent, came hissing and boiling down along the bottoms of deep volcanic gorges.

"But the paleface would feign know what became of the remnant of the oppressors of our people. For more than twenty moons were the mountains entirely hid from our view—by day obscured in a canopy of smoke and ashes, and at night great fires streamed up until they reached the stars, many of which were melted away and fell to the earth like raindrops, and these made the ore that the white man seeks.

"At last when all was still again, and the great rains had put the fires all out, and a wind, greater than ever before was felt, had driven the smoke away, our fathers saw how terrible had been the anger of the Great Spirit. Instead of green fields and trees teeming with sweet fruits, every vestige of vegetation had been swept away, and in place of a plain so gentle in its descent towards the sea, as hardly to be perceived, all was one vast, broken, sterile mountain traversed by rocky precipices and deep gorges, as you now see them, and on which the first snows ever seen by our fathers fell, and from which they have never entirely disappeared, nor never will, until the children of the Great Spirit shall again displease him, at which time the whole earth will be burned and its ashes thrown into the sea.

"It was a long time before the spot, on which has stood the great fire temple, could be recognized, for though the mountains had ceased to tremble and the great fires that had so completely consumed all, had gone out, yet were there a few great volcanoes that continued to burn, and which neither the great rains nor yet the winter's snows could extinguish. One of these, and the last and greatest of them all, is the one at the head of this little vale; but even this one has long since gone out, for when I was a boy, small volumes of smoke rose upward from deep fissures in the rocks; but while it did burn, so say our fathers, it cast forth a river of fire that ran along the ground, filling up deep fissures and yawning caverns that lay around it, and but for this little lake freezing the fiery river in its course, the spirit home of the fire-worshipers would have been leveled up, and every trace of their prison home lost forever."

"But," said our interpreter, "how came they *there*, when your fathers left them locked within their temple walls?"

He replied, "The temple stood upon the banks of the *Trokenene*, but all trace of that deep and ancient river is lost except this lake, this valley and a deep ravine beyond yonder cave, on the eastern slope of the mountains. But here, where now sleeps the lake, once stood the temple groves of the ancient conquerors of our fathers; but when the mountains all around, by mighty lifting from beneath, were raised so very high, the temple and its groves were lifted up too, but its foundations were the substance that fed the burning volcano beneath.

"At length a vast chasm was formed, that when the mountain ceased to burn and throw up its fiery torrents from below, became filled with water from the melting of the mountain snows, but its great foundations had been weakened, and down it sank, with all its altars and its burned up groves, deep beneath the level of the lake, all but the dome of the great temple, around which were gathered and still clinging the last remnant of that hated race; and because they would thus cling to life, the Great Spirit became enraged, and descending to the earth, walked upon the water as though on solid land, and taking them one by one, hurled them, as the child hurls the pebble upon the water, far into the deep recesses of the cavern, and watched them there till the waters of the lake rose to their present height and shut them in. And from that day to this, have their wailings and pent-up moanings been heard, increasing in terror and intensity at that season of the year when the waters of the lake are increased by the rapid melting of the winter's snows; and there they must ever remain till the Great Spirit releases them by another and the *last* of earth's great convulsions and burnings."

Weary with the fatigues of the day we now slept, but rising

before the sun, made haste to prepare for our visit to the cavern. We had engaged two athletic looking Diggers to accompany us, promising them our blankets on taking final leave of them.

Everything in readiness, we pushed out upon the lake and though not less than fifty of all ages had assembled to witness our departure, not a cheer, not a word was uttered, but a mysterious fear or doubt seemed to have made them dumb; even our Digger canoemen had lost much of the loquacious activity exhibited the night before.

We had been making in a direct line for the cavern for more than an hour and a half, till on looking back it appeared that we were nearly or about halfway across, when a spirited conversation commenced between the Diggers. At length the foremost, laying down his paddle, rose to his feet, and for some moments, as the canoe slowly proceeded, carefully scanned the depth of water directly under the bow of the canoe; at length, with a yell and a bound, he leaped into the water, and stood upright with folded arms, the water hardly breast high. It appeared they were previously aware of the existence and position of this now submerged island. On careful examination, we found it to be the smooth surface of a rock that on all sides sloped downwards with a rapidly increasing curve. At the center the water was not more than two feet deep, while at a distance of twenty feet either way, it was six feet deep, and then dropping off suddenly, so that at a distance of only thirty feet further all around, the bottom could not be reached with all the line we could command, a little more than forty feet in all.

It is probably an immense boulder of some species of rock, that has been worn by the elements into a nearly rounded form, at least upon its upper surface, and probably resting upon another rock at no great depth below the surface. And yet the first thought, even before we had made the careful examinations we did, suggested the possibility of its identity with that of the dome of the temple as described to us by the old and blind oracular father of his tribe the evening previous. Our curiosity was only heightened by the answer we invariably received from the Diggers concerning it; and which consisted in placing their fingers firmly upon their compressed lips without uttering a word. An hour more and we were fast nearing the prison of the Genii.

Cave Rock
Library of Congress, Prints and Photographs Division,
Lawrence & Houseworth Collection

An irregular wall of rock, nearly perpendicular, rose upward from the water at least three hundred feet high, with an immense opening that seemed to extend far back into the mountain, and which undoubtedly had its origin in the falling together, at some greatly remote period, of the upper portions of an immense canon or deep gorge, that supporting each other have formed the mysterious grotto of the Digger. It is nearly two hundred feet wide upon the surface of the water, and more than two hundred feet high, as it reached full two-thirds the entire height of the mountain. On entering it, we could see no bottom, though we could see with singular distinctness, a small tin cup at the end of a forty foot line, so perfectly clear were its waters.

ELLEN OSBORN

Behind us lay the lake, bright and beautiful, though not entirely tranquil, for within the last half hour, a light breeze had started up, and smooth and gentle swells were setting into the entrance of the cavern. Before us, apparently at no great distance, an almost total darkness alone appeared, while over our heads, pendent from the roof, were innumerable stalactite, looking like enormous icicles, and gave to the place a feature almost of enchantment. As we advanced, the cavern sensibly decreased in height and width, but on the contrary, the gentle swell at the entrance, narrowing as it proceeded, became immensely increased in height, though rolling with a perfectly smooth surface onward into the deep darkness.

We were not entirely without apprehension for our safety, in case the swells continued to increase as we advanced; the two Diggers became greatly alarmed, for now we could hear with an almost alarming distinctness, those sounds that have ever been the terror of the Digger, but which we were curious to examine, and if possible to determine the mystery of their origin.

We had now penetrated this hitherto unexplored cavern nearly half a mile; it had decreased in width nearly half; its height we could not determine on account of the darkness; we had reached soundings at a depth of ten or fifteen feet. We observed, soon after entering the cavern, a strange increase of all sounds, whether from the voice or the splash of the paddle, but now it had increased to astonishing loudness, and it seemed as though the reverberations from the report of a pistol would never cease except in intensity. There were two, three and sometimes more, distinct sounds emanating from the cavern; one such as we would suppose would be made by a fall of water or small cataract within an immense grotto or cavern, where the sides gave echo from unequal distances. Another, so unlike any we ever heard before, so varied in intensity, now like a low murmur and then again so fearfully loud, at intervals accompanied by a short shrill cry, it taxed our reason to account for it, and not a little our *courage* to proceed; added to which was now almost total darkness by which we were surrounded, and as if to increase our misgivings, there was a constant repetition, though at irregular intervals, of a heavy splash or plunge, as though an animal the size of a large dog had leaped from a height into the water; nor could we by any effort we could make, either by an increase of speed or the deepest quiet, while moving along, obtain the least glimpse of the cause.

On approaching either side of the cavern, we found at intervals, instead of a perpendicular wall, tables or shelving portions of rock that permitted us to land, taking care to watch the swells as they swept by. These landing places were, in every instance, the repository of large quantities of bones, mostly the head and vertebrae of fishes, many of which were three feet in length and in every stage of decay. This discovery seemed to be one of profound astonishment to our Indian helpers, inspiring them with a strange dread and a horror of any further prosecution of our enterprise. In addition to this, we were amid total darkness, having turned a bend in the cavern, shutting out entirely the little light that had before reached us from the entrance. The increase of unearthly sounds emanating from the darkness beyond, the incessant plungings of which we have spoken, all combined to render it a scene difficult for us to adequately describe. It became necessary to light a large torch we had provided in order to avoid contact with the rocky sides of the passage; there was no difficulty in advancing, as there seemed no increase in the size of the smooth heavy swells yet setting into the mountain.

Suddenly we came to where the roof was distinctly visible, and but a few rods further, so great was its depression, that standing we could touch the ends of some of the larger stalactite. There was no apparent diminution in the width of the cave. Slowly and cautiously advancing, our torch-light gleaming before us, we saw but a few feet in advance, a stony bank or beach upon which the surf broke with much force, the water being shallow; as it appeared to have considerable extent of surface, and our ardor for further discovery much cooled, though as yet we knew nothing of the origin of the sounds, that, as we advanced, only increased in volume, we resolved to make a landing, and if nothing like a solution of the cause, could be obtained without a further advance in our canoe, in case an opening offered, to return, leaving it for others to explore more adventurous than ourselves. By getting into the water, which here was not two feet deep, and watching our opportunity between the swells, rushed our canoe to the shore and secured it above the reach of the surf. On examination we found the beach to extend only about half way across the cavern, and turning, ran almost parallel with its sides, giving about fifty feet in width of surface entirely covered with fallen stalactite and innumerable fish bones. The other half is a continuation of the water portion, and along which sweeps, at intervals of a few seconds, the strange and ceaseless swell of water; and this is the character of the cave for nearly fifty rods further on, when the roof, by gradual depression, is brought down lower and lower, until it reaches the surface of the rolling swells, shutting off all further advance.

Beyond this, it seems to be for a long distance level with the water of the cave, the under surface of which has been wrought by the action of the water or other causes, into irregular and many deep cavities, and it is the constant striking of the heavy swells against this cavernous roof that produces the varied sounds that are heard. At this place the roar is almost deafening, its violent twanging and hissing, as though, at intervals, water and air together were forcibly driven through narrow apertures, and now and then a sound as though the word *boom* had been uttered with great power by nothing less than the mouth of a volcano far on in the gloom. The terrific darkness of the place, the occasional shrill cry from the mysterious occupants of the cavern, their ceaseless plunge, as we move from place to place, together with the immense accumulation of the relics of the finny tribe, all conspire to render it, as it truly is, a cavern of darkness, of doubt, of terror and mystery.

Note—Have not these heavy swells, thrown at intervals into subterranean passages, some connection with those remarkable springs in the vicinity, upon the eastern slope of the Nevada, that at intervals of a few seconds, throw a jet of water from two to four feet above the surface of the ground?

Editorial Notes On The Lake Bigler Story

This amazing and entertaining story presents us with several puzzles. First, the actual author can't be confirmed. It was probably F. Wadsworth, the editor of the *Placerville Herald*. How much is fact, how much is Mr. Wadsworth's fiction, and how much the tale was embellished by J. C. Johnson in his role as interpreter cannot be determined. The rock in the center of the lake, and even the cave itself are impossible to locate today, if indeed they existed in 1853. The closest place is Cave Rock, but it is now thirty feet above the level of the lake. There are several possible explanations, such as an earthquake that could have destroyed the cave, but the contemporary newspapers would surely have noted such an event.

The Digger Indians referred to were probably Washoe. The remarkable clarity of the lake and the abundance of fish are well-established facts. The litter of fish carcasses inside the cave may very well have been Kokanee salmon, which die after reproducing. Anyone who has visited the Stream Profile Chamber at Taylor Creek Lake Tahoe has observed this. The action of the water within the cave sounds like what is known as a blowhole.

This story is most notable for the description of how the lake and the surrounding mountains came to be. The story told by the old chief (or invented by the men), fairly closely follows what modern geologists think actually happened. The eastern sea mentioned could have been Lake Lahontan, a huge prehistoric lake that filled much of the Great Basin in Nevada. All that remains of it today is found in Pyramid Lake. Perhaps some future researcher can solve these puzzles.

The naming of Lake Tahoe is a story unto itself. The first person to take note of it and give it a name was John C. Fremont, who named it Mountain Lake in 1844. He later tried to amend the name to Lake Bonpland to honor a member of Humboldt's geographic team. In 1852 friends of California's third Governor, John Bigler (of whom Johnson was one) decided the lake should be named in honor of Bigler.

An article that appeared in the January 29, 1870, *Mountain Democrat* newspaper suggested the choice of "Bigler" was not politically motivated, but was rather because Governor Bigler had been with Colonel J. C. Johnson, Colonel Rogers, Monroe Reed, and others when they discovered that the lake was not the Lakes of the Mountain as previously believed, but was a single magnificent lake.

The California legislature and mapmakers adopted the name Lake Bigler. Surprisingly, although nearly everyone was calling it Lake Tahoe, it took until 1945 before the California Legislature made that appellation official.

APPENDIX B
The Known Dead and Wounded
of
The El Dorado Indian Wars, 1850-1851

Dead

Dr. Hugh Dixon of St. Louis

Dr. Dixon was killed on November 3, 1850, twelve miles east of Placerville (Sly Park?). The body was retrieved, but badly mangled. He is buried near his brother in Coloma, California. Sources: *Sacramento Transcript* newspaper, also *Buckeye Rovers in the Gold Rush* by Scamehorn.

Delaware Ebert (Calvin Evarts?)

An article in the March 27, 1875 *Sacramento Union* listed Ebert as the first fatality of the war. He took an arrow through the heart at close range. In 1850 the following deaths were reported: one Delaware, one soldier on November 4, 1850. Sources: "Indian War Papers" California State Archives, *Sacramento Daily Union* newspaper.

Major Leslie Hutchison McKinney from Illinois

Shot with an arrow (according to the *Sacramento Union* March 27, 1875) he was wounded on November 3, 1850, and died on November 4, 1850. His date of birth was February 5, 1822. He was a veteran of the Mexican War, deputy sheriff under Rogers in 1850, and county clerk of El Dorado County at the time of his death. He is buried in Coloma. Sources: *Sacramento Transcript* and *Sacramento Daily Union* newspapers, "Indian War Papers" California State Archives, El Dorado County records, Book A and Probate file, El Dorado Historical Museum, Placerville, CA.

ELLEN OSBORN

J. B. Wade from Rochester, Wisconsin

His death was reported by the *Sacramento Daily Union* on May 13, 1851, stating his ashes were found. The *Alta* (May 5, 1851) reported his home as Racine, Missouri. Jane Voyles interviewed John W. Winkley in 1949. He recalled an "ancient story" that a groups of miners—Davidson, Morris, Toombs, Esterbrook, Kerkuf and Wade—went on a prospecting trip to the middle Fork of the Consumes, where they were attacked at night by Indians, and Wade was killed. The others escaped to Johnson's Ranch. The Indians cremated Wade's remains on the spot. Sources: The Jane Voyles Scrapbook #2 page 203 El Dorado County Historical Museum, *Alta* and *Sacramento Daily Union* newspapers.

Mr. (B. F.?) Clark from Clay County Missouri

He was reported missing and presumed dead, by the *Sacramento Daily Union*, on May 13, 1851. Source: *Sacramento Daily Union* newspaper.

Edwin Jenks from Roscoe, Illinois

The *Sacramento Daily Union* reported on May 28, 1851, that Jenks was killed in ambush (near the Johnson Ranch according to Fyffe) by the Indians. He was with Captain Tracy. The May 28, 1851, issue of the *Alta* quoted the *Placer Times* as reporting that on May 25, 1851 in a battle on the South Fork, volunteer Edwin Jenks of Roscoe, Illinois was killed. Fyffe didn't record his death until July 14, 1851. Sources: *Sacramento Daily Union*, *Alta* newspapers and the diary of James Perry Fyffe.

William Jenkins of Ohio

His death was announced in the *Sacramento Daily Union* and *Evening Picayune* newspapers on June 6, 1851. The Sacramento *Daily Union* further stated that he left a wife and child. He was thirty-three years old. Is he possibly the man Mrs. Ivy Miller of Oakland mentioned to Jane Voyles as being her grandfather? Mrs. Miller recalled a story that her grandfather went out to fight the Indians and never came back. Sources: *Sacramento Daily Union* and *Evening Picayune* newspapers, Jane Voyles Scrapbook #2 page 203 El Dorado County Historical Museum Placerville, CA.

William Decolas

He was reported killed near Johnson's Ranch on July 14, 1851. Source: Unpublished diary of James Perry Fyffe.

Sergeant Matthews

James Fyffe reported him as killed on July 19, 1851. He was buried at Diamond Springs on July 21, 1851. In his account Fyffe stated: "Some of the boys wanted to bury him where he lied (sic). I could not consent to it. Got one of the boys to walk and strapped him (Matthews) on the mule. Took him to camp." Source: Unpublished diary of James Perry Fyffe.

Private Morton

Private Morton was reported mortally wounded in the same battle as Sergeant Matthews. It is unknown if he died of his wounds. Source: Unpublished diary of James Perry Fyffe.

James Craig

From Oneida County New York. He was reported drowned May 28, 1851. Source: *Sacramento Daily Union* April 15, 1852.

Unnamed War Dead:

There were four. One each was reported on: November 4, 1850; May 13, 1851; May 23, 1851; and one man reported drowned, without a specific date. He fell into the South Fork while crossing the log bridge. Any or all of the anonymous dead might be duplicates of the above named individuals. Sources: *Sacramento Transcript* and *Sacramento Daily Union* newspapers.

Note: $176 was allotted by the state to bury the war dead in 1851. Source: "Indian War Papers," California State Archives.

Wounded

Captain Francisco de Allison

He was identified as Fremont's guide. November 3, 1850 he was severely wounded and disfigured in the lower jaw. Sources: *Sacramento Transcript* newspaper and "Indian War Papers", California State Archives.

Delaware Indian

An unnamed Delaware Indian was reported wounded in the same battle in which Ebert was killed on November 4, 1850. Source: *Sacramento Daily Union* newspaper March 27, 1895.

Marion Lamb

He was reported as wounded on June 2, 1851, while engaging in battle under the command of Captain Tracy. He was nineteen years old. Sources: *Sacramento Daily Union* newspaper, and probate file of his father William Lamb.

Marion James

He was reported as injured by the *Alta* newspaper on May 28, 1851. This may be the same person as Marion Lamb. Source: *Alta* newspaper.

Richard Thomas

On May 26, 1851, he was severely wounded while engaged in battle under the command of Captain John C. Tracy. Sources: The *Sacramento Daily Union* and *Alta* newspapers.

William Nichols
On May 26, 1851, he received what were thought to be mortal wounds. He was later reported as recovered. Sources: The *Sacramento Daily Union* and *Alta* newspapers.

Humbolt (first name unknown)
On July 22, 1951, he was reported wounded during a battle in Carson Valley. Source: The unpublished diary of James Perry Fyffe.

P. B. Freeman
On July 22, 1951, he was reported wounded during a battle in Carson Valley. Source: The unpublished diary of James Perry Fyffe.

Not included in this list are a number of reports in the newspapers of miners and other citizens killed or wounded in encounters with the Indians during the time of the El Dorado Indian Wars.

APPENDIX C
Johnson Cutoff
Bartlett's Guide to California as printed by the *Placerville Herald*

(Author's note: the numbers indicate distance in miles.)

From the Eagle Ranch in Carson Valley, through the Sierra Nevada Mountains, by Johnson's Cut-off, from actual measurement and survey. By Payne, from Wisconsin, civil engineer.

- Commencing at the intersection of Johnson's Cut-off with the old immigrant road, at the foot of Eagle Valley, in a S. W. direction to Eagle Ranch.   3 3/4
- Plenty of grass and water. Passing up an arm of the valley, to a creek.   2 5/8
- Ascending gradually, pass water in abundance, to the summit of the ridge.   2 1/2
- Descending to good grass and small springs.   1/2
- Continue descending, but passing over sandy hills, on the south of the road, to good grass and water.   2
- A gradual ascent, the latter portion in a ravine, to the top of a ridge.   2 3/4
- Road rough, to a large meadow of grass and water.   1
- Over ridges and ravines, often in sight of Bigler or Truckee Lake, with plenty of water and small patches of grass, to the summit of a ridge.   5/8
- Descent sandy and steep, to the foot.   1 3/8
- Road good to intersection of trail from Mormon Station.   1 3/4
- Good road, with grass and water plenty, by going a short distance to the north, crossing two creeks to the third, which is bridged.   5 1/4
- Rise to and follow on a low ridge, with grass and water on each side, to Mr. Smith's in Lake Valley.   3 7/8

- Grass and water plenty along Lake Valley to a tributary of Truckee Lake, over which is a log bridge.   1 5/8
- Good road, grass and water to the foot of a mountain ridge. 5/8
- Ascent steep, crooked and stony, to the summit.   7/8
- Gradual descent to good meadow, quite large water plenty. 1/2
- Along the meadow west.   1
- Fair road, but occasionally stony, to Messrs. Brockless post.   3
  Here beware of a cut-off that takes to the left, down a deep and bad ravine. Inquire for Bosworth's post.
- To a small valley, some grass, water plenty.   1
- Cross a rocky ridge, road stony, rough and crooked, to bridge at Slippery Ford.   3/4
- Rough road, stony in places, to Strawberry Valley.   3/4
- Along Strawberry Valley, parallel with a creek, near which is a little grass.   1 1/2
- Across the creek, opposite the valley, are a series of granite bluffs rising to an immense height, almost perpendicular. Following along near the creek to the foot of the mountain. 3/4
- Ascend the side of a ridge, on a rough, sidling road, crossing numerous ravines. Water plenty, but little or no grass, to Silver Creek Ranch. [178]   5 1/4
- Pass around and ascend a small hill to good grass and water, a little north of the road.   1/2
- The Half Way House.   1 5/8
- Water plenty, and grass a little north of the road. Pass over a good road, and then several rough ridges, to the descent of Peavine Hill. Descend to Peavine Springs.[179]   5 7/8
- A little grass below the road. Road uneven to Sears' post. 3 7/8

---

178 This might be Wilson Ranch on map now
179 This might be called Granite Springs now

- Some water and a little grass. A little water and grass, early in the season, about forty rods north of the road.   4 7/8
- Road good on a ridge.   1 1/2
- Leave the summit of ridge, descending south to Walker's post.   1 5/8
- Still descending to the bridge which spans the South Fork of the American River, to Bartlett's trading post.   1 3/4
- Ascending on the south side of the river, road steep and crooked, to summit of ridge.   2 1/8
- To intersection with old immigrant road   1/2

On which are posts nearly every mile, water plenty, but grass scarce. Between Placerville and Bartlett's, there are distance boards every two miles; between Bartlett's and Eagle Ranch, every five miles.

William Bartlett.
Placerville, August 13, 1853.
From the original in Bancroft Library, Berkeley, CA

APPENDIX D

The Agricultural and Mining Association of El Dorado County Memorial to the Congress of the United States[180]

To the Honorable [of the] Senate and the House of Representatives of the United States: The undersigned, a committee appointed by a convention of the citizens of El Dorado County, California, held at Placerville, on the 3rd of March, 1866, would most respectfully represent—that they are citizens of the United States and many of them have been residents of said county more than sixteen years, pursuing the business of mining, agriculture, the mechanic arts, and the varied occupations growing out of these industries; and that the result of their labor has been the accumulation of property in the shape of mills, artificial water-courses, tunnels, shafts, and drifts for mining, farm enclosures, buildings, orchards, vineyards and wine vaults, public and private edifices, and manufactories in towns, all of which are of great and permanent value, and are situated on that portion of the public domain withheld from sale. Therefore recognizing in the humane and sagacious policy, long since adopted by your honorable body, in its regulations for the disposition of the public lands, whereby the humblest may obtain the fee simple[181], guaranteed by the enduring title patent of the Nation, that policy which has given

---

180 *Mountain Democrat*, March 10, 1866
181 Definition of a "fee simple" as it appears in *Black's Law Dictionary, 5th Edition*, page 554: "The estate which a man has where lands are given to him and to his heirs absolutely without any end or limit put to his estate. The word 'fee' used alone, is a sufficient designation of this species of estate, and hence 'simple' is not a necessary part of the title.... Fee simple signifies a pure fee, an absolute estate of inheritance clear of any condition or restriction to particular heirs.... It is the largest estate and most extensive interest that can be enjoyed in land."

population, wealth and power to the great West, your memorialists[182] would respectfully, but earnestly, urge upon your honorable body, the removal of all restrictions whereby your memorialists are debarred from acquiring a legitimate title of record to the lands whereon they have become residents with their families, and have expended many years of industry, and that they be placed on an equality, so far as title is concerned, with other more favored communities on the public domain. Your memorialists would respectfully show that under the local regulations, prevailing in mineral districts, conflicts of individual rights are of constant occurrence, which not only involves expensive litigation, but interferes with the harmony and peace of whole communities, unsettling the permanence of population and subjecting the fruits of industry to a precarious tenure. This want of a fee simple in the soil, whether it be to a mining claim, town lot or a farm, has a direct tendency to make our people migratory in their habits, as may be painfully seen within our limits, by witnessing the suddenness with which mining camps spring up, to be as rapidly deserted. For more than sixteen years this policy has had undisturbed sway, and its obvious results are, that in every portion of our county where mining has been the paramount occupation, there may be seen the spoliation of timber, dilapidation and decay.

Your memorialists are aware that industrious efforts have been made to make it appear that the lands in the mineral districts are entirely worthless for agricultural purposes, and therefore that the Nation should expect them to be vacant, for the free use of those searching for the precious metals. To disabuse your honorable body of so grave an error, your memorialists may be permitted to state that, not withstanding the insecurity of agriculture, where a pretence of mining can be made, there are in eight townships of El Dorado County, according to the report of the Assessors, 84,433 acres of enclosed land, and 20,464 acres under cultivation. In the same districts there are 1,126,331 bearing grape vines and 150,803 bearing fruit trees.

---

182 Memorialist is a person or persons who present a document, such as a short note, abstract, memorandum, or rough draft of the orders of the court, to a legislative body containing a petition or a representation of facts.

Your memorialists are of opinion that if the title patent of the United States could be acquired to the lands in the mineral districts, that there would be not only a more satisfactory feeling of security among those who are in possession, but that with an assurance that the labors of a lifetime would find safe transmission to rightful inheritors, there would spring up very greatly increased developments of both the mineral as well as agricultural resources for the county. For all of which, as to duty bound, your memorialists will ever pray.

J. C. Johnson, Chairman

ELLEN OSBORN

APPENDIX E

Brief of John C. Johnson, Contestant, Patent No. 199

In the United States Land Office at Sacramento, California
Before the Register and Receiver
In the Matter of the Claim of Alburn J. Blakeley,
Applicant for Patent No. 199
Against
John C. Johnson, Contestant
Brief of John C. Johnson, Contestant
G. J. Carpenter and
Geo. E. Williams
For Contestant Johnson
Sacramento
H. S. Crocker & Co., Printers and Stationers
1872

Brief of John C. Johnson, Contestant

The attorney for mineral claimant endeavors, in his brief, to avoid the discussion of nine-tenths of the issues raised in this case. It would be a difficult matter to determine from his brief that his client was seeking to purchase the land, or that his client has caused the citations to issue and had compelled Johnson to defend his rights.

I

Before entering upon the discussion of the questions at issue, we would call the attention of the officer to the "Diagram" which is attached to the paper filed and marked, "Adverse claim of John C. Johnson." This diagram was made by William Sabine, a surveyor, and he testified to the correctness of it. See Sabine's testimony, pages 71—83. It was received in evidence by the Register and Receiver. (Page 83.) The diagram was used by all the witnesses on both sides. Blakeley, in giving his testimony, used and referred to the diagram as being correct. (See B's testimony, page 507.) As the testimony was given as to ten acres tracts and not forty acre subdivisions, it becomes necessary constantly to refer to the diagram in order to understand the testimony.

II

Blakeley's Case

A. J. Blakeley seeks to purchase the following lands, to wit: W. 1/2 of N. W. 1/4 of the S. E. 1/4 and S. E. 1/4 of N. W. 1/4 of the S. E. 1/4, and E. 1/2 of S. W. 1/4 of the S. E. 1/4, and S. E .1/4 of Sec. 35, T. 11N., R. 11 E., and lots 1 and 2 of N. E. 1/4 of section No. 1, T. 10 N., R. 11 E.

His application is made as a mineral claimant. The first question, therefore, that properly arises, is, did Blakeley, before causing the citation to issue to Johnson, comply with the Third Section of the Act of July 26, 1866, as to the posting of notice and diagram? The evidence on this point shows that a cabin stands on the S. W. 1/4 of the S. E. 1/4 of section 35; this cabin has been used by Blakeley to store his tools and mining apparatus when not in use. As the water gives out in June of each year, the ground is not worked from that time until the rains come in the fall or winter. (Johnson's evidence, page 69.) The cabin was closed during the months of July, August, September and October. Blakeley posted the notice and diagram on the inside of the cabin and on the back of a door that was fastened with a padlock. The cabin had two doors, both of which were kept fastened. (See Myer's evidence, pages 117—123; also Peachy, 274—277; also Linder, 331—334; also Johnson, 66—69.) About two months after Blakeley had posted the notice and diagram inside of the cabin, Johnson heard that a notice and diagram had been posted; he went over the ground and could not find it. (Page 64.) He was then informed by a man by the name of Lewis (page 65), that he, Lewis, had heard that a notice was posted in the cabin. Johnson then went to the cabin and endeavored to get sight of the notice and diagram (page 66), but the windows being blinded and the doors fastened, he could not see it. He then went and got some of his neighbors and forced open one of the doors, and found the notice and diagram fastened to the back of the other door. (Page 67.)

It certainly requires no argument to show that such a posting is not in compliance with the Act of Congress.

III

The Act of Congress requires that the Applicant shall show a title to the ground which he seeks to purchase. This Blakeley has not done.

The land had been in the possession and used by Johnson from 1849 to the date of the entry by the Vallejo Mining Company, through whom Blakeley claims, in September 1867. Johnson went first upon the land in August 1849. (See Johnson's testimony, page 5.)

Blakeley was a member of the Vallejo Mining Company, and first went upon the land in September 1867. Johnson had then been in possession and using the land for eighteen years.

Blakeley and the other members of the Vallejo Mining Company recognized Johnson's right and title to the land, and knowing that they could not enter upon the land without his consent, made a written contract with Johnson. This contract was drawn up by the present attorney of Blakeley, and in his brief he should have given us the benefit of his construction as to the intention of all parties who made the contract.

This contract, however, was admitted in evidence (Exhibit A), and a copy of it is attached also to the papers marked "Adverse claim of John C. Johnson." (Pages 22, 23.) This contract on the part of Johnson admits Blakeley into the use of this ground for the period of *four years and nine months from the 20th of September 1867.* That land was to revert to Johnson at the end of that time, there can be no doubt was the intention of the parties. It is true that a notice locating the ground for mining purposes was put up, but it was done to assist the parties in carrying out the agreement.

This is clear from the testimony of Thomas G. Meek, who was present and assisted in putting up the notice, and his testimony is not contradicted by any witness. On page 365 he says, "The agreement was made before the notices were put up." He was then asked the following question: "State if the notices were put up to assist or enable the parties to carry out and have the benefit of the agreement," to which he answered, "Yes, sir; it was put up for that purpose." Johnson, when he gave a deed of his interest in the Vallejo Mining Company, limited the grant in accordance with the written contract. (Exhibit B.) Blakeley, in order to avoid the contract and Johnson's deed, seeks to obtain the title from the Government. The facts relating to the character of the possession of Blakeley and the rights of Johnson are fully set forth in the paper files and marked "Adverse claim of John C. Johnson," and we are now of the same opinion that we were at the time of the filing of the adverse claim of Johnson, that is, that all proceedings should have been stayed, and Johnson have been required to commence an action to determine title.

As the agreement (Exhibit A), may, on the 20th of June, 1872, defeat and destroy any right as to the possession of the ground by Blakeley, the Government will not sell him the land until the question in determined in the local Courts. Section two of the Act of July 26, 1866, say, as to the title and possession of a mineral applicant, that, "in regard to whose *possession, there is no controversy or opposing claim.*"

Blakeley claims title under the mining laws, under three different notices of location. The first notice was put up September 20, 1867, and contains the names of ten persons. Of these Blakeley does not show any conveyance or title from A. M. Meek or J. R. Meek, and the deed from J. C. Johnson (Exhibit B), only conveys the interest of Johnson up to the 20th of June, 1872, at which time it reverts to Johnson. The ground described in this notice of location commences at the embankment in the N. W. 1/4 of N. W. 1/4 of S. E. 1/4 of section 35, and extends up the canon to the junction of the east and west forks, and thence up the east fork to the upper end of Johnson's Ranch. The ground described lies in the bed of the canon and is three hundred feet wide and four thousand feet in length.

The second notice is dated September 20, 1867, and contains the names of four persons, one of whom, J. Likins, Jr., has never conveyed to Blakeley. This ground lies in the west fork of Johnson's South canon, commencing at the junction of the east and west forks and extends up the west fork sixteen hundred feet (see notice). The notice was put up by Blakeley and Thomas G. Meek (Ev. 366), and was not signed by C. F. Irwin, R. Young or J. Likins, Jr. (Ev. 368). It clearly appears from the testimony that Thomas G. Meek, who put up the notice, was interested in the Vallejo Mining Company and was their Superintendent from the 20th of September, 1867, to May, 1868, that the notice was a sham, was not put up with the knowledge of three of the parties, that it was put up for the benefit of the Vallejo Mining Company, but without any intention, on the part of the Vallejo Mining Company, of working it, and for the purpose of preventing other parties from attempting to work it. That no work was done on it whilst Meek was there, which was eight months (see Ev. P. 368 –371). No testimony was given by Blakeley to show that any work was done at any time on the ground located in the west fork. All claim to this ground was forfeited under the mining laws of the district. The seventh and eighth sections of the law declare the ground vacated unless work is done as therein required.

The third location, under which Blakeley claims, is the notice dated August 11, 1870. This is another sham notice. No work was ever done on the ground, and it was long since forfeited and vacated under the seventh and eighth sections of the mining laws. The land described in that notice lies in lots one and two, section one, T.10 N., R. 11 E.

IV

We now come to the consideration of two questions, which we believe have never been passed upon by the Commissioner of the Land Office, and as these two questions are closely connected in this case, we will state and argue them together.

1st. Will the government, in order to give the owner of mining ground, a patent, to that which he holds under the local laws, sell to him agricultural land owned and possessed by a bona fide settler and pre-emption claimant and which was so owned and possessed long prior to the location of the mining ground, and which agricultural land is outside of the mining ground as located under the local laws.

2d.   Will the government sell to a mineral claimant the improvements of a *bona fide* settler and pre-emption claimant, which improvements were made long prior to the mining location and a portion of the improvements being outside of the lines of the mining claim as located under the local laws.

It will be easily perceived from the reading of these two propositions that they involve questions of great importance to those who are settled upon the public lands in the mineral regions of this State. For twenty years the government pursued the policy of allowing all parties to settle upon the public lands in the mineral regions. Under this policy thousands of citizens settled upon these lands and built their homes upon them.

Miners, also, went upon these lands, located their claims and worked them. Being without laws regulating the owning or holding of claims, the miners framed a system of laws, which were, at first, enforced by the power of the majority. Afterwards being recognized by the laws of the State, they became the settled rule of right in all cases. For a few years, after the opening of the mines, the houses and other improvements of those who settled for other purposes than mining were not respected, but gradually the Courts interfered and established the law to be, that the improvements of the settler should be protected. This has been the settled law for more than twelve years past.

Such was the condition of the rights of settlers and miners

at the time of the passage of the Act of July 26, 1866, and the Act amendatory thereof passed July 9, 1870. The purpose of these acts was to give the miner a title to that which he held under the local laws and customs and nothing more. It was not the intention of Congress to allow any one that chose to purchase one hundred and sixty acres of mineral land, even where the land was unoccupied. The Commissioner of the General Land Office has clearly expressed this view of the act of Congress, in the following letter, to wit:

Department of the Interior,
General Land Office, March 1, 1871

Hon. A. A. Sargent, House of Representatives:
Sir—I have the honor to acknowledge the receipt from you, by reference, of the enclosed letter from Geo. E. Williams, Esq., dated at Washington, the 13th instant, desiring to be informed whether a party holding the possessory right to certain placer mining ground in accordance with local customs, may, in making application for patent therefore under the amendatory mining law of July 9, 1870, include such an additional area of adjoining unoccupied or abandoned mineral land as will with the original claim aggregate one hundred and sixty acres.
In response I would state that the 12th Section of said Act of July 9, 1870, provides for issuing patents for placer claims, "under like circumstances and conditions and upon similar proceedings as are provided for vein or lode claims," the law applicable to the latter interest being the Act of July 26, 1866, U. S. Statutes, vol. 14, p. 254, the 2d section of which stipulates among other conditions, that a party to be entitled to receive a patent for a vein or lode, must have previously occupied and improved his claim according to the local customs or rules of miners in the district where the same is

located; and it follows, of course, that an applicant for a patent for a placer claim must come within the same condition. The law giving no authority for granting patents for mining ground not occupied and improved by claimants according to local customs and rules, it would of course be useless to make the application in the manner indicated by your correspondent.

In mining districts over which the lines of the public surveys have not yet been extended, a placer claim held and occupied according to the district regulations and upon which not less than one thousand dollars have been expended, may in the absence of an adverse claimant and after the usual proceedings—be surveyed, entered and patented, whatever may be its shape or area, provided that such claim was located at a date prior to the passage of said statute of July 9, 1870, which interdicts after that date the location of a claim by any person or association of persons, in extent exceeding one hundred and sixty acres, whatever the mining regulations of the district may prescribe; but upon lands which have been surveyed no lot or claim smaller that ten acres can be patented to any person or association of persons under said act, the subdivision of forty acre tracts into ten acre legal subdivisions to be effected in the manner prescribed by the law and instructions.

I am, very respectfully, your obedient servant,
Willis Drummond

The only modification of the views expressed in this letter, is to be found in paragraph 26 of the supplemental instructions of the Commissioner, dated May 6, 1871. And the language therein used by the Commissioner was not, as we conceive, intended to express any change in his views as to the construction of the Act of July 9, 1870, but was intended to indicate, not that the miner had any right to purchase unoccupied mineral land surrounding his claim, to the extent of forty acres, but that the government desired to reserve, the uniformity in the surveys and, therefore, where there was *no adverse agricultural or mineral claimant,* the government would sell to the extent of forty acres. We presume that it will be conceded that where two mineral claimants own each a separate claim of say three acres each, that one of the mineral claimants can not make an application and purchase the ten acre tract, in which the two claims are situated. *In this respect, paragraph 26 very distinctly places the mineral and agricultural claimants upon the same footing.*

If the agriculturalist has any claim upon the land that he is settled upon, his claim to the agricultural land is certainly as good as the claim that the miner has to the mineral land, and he is entitled to equal protection. In addition to the views expressed by the Commissioner in paragraph 26, the latter portion of section twelve (12) of the Act of July 9, 1870, clearly covers the question. The language is as follows to wit: *"And nothing in this section contained shall defeat or impair any bona fide pre-emption or homestead claim upon agricultural lands."*

Apply that language to the facts of this case. Johnson has been living upon the land for over twenty-two years, cleared the land, fenced it, built houses and used it and improved it in every manner that an agriculturalist can use or improve land. In 1867, Blakeley, under a written agreement to surrender the land at the end of four years and nine months, *enters upon and takes possession of a narrow strip, called Johnson's South Canon, in the center of Johnson's Ranch and pre-emption claim.* Thomas G. Meek, who put up the notice of location, testified (p. 364) that the ground described in the notice commenced at the embankment in the N. W. 1/4 of the S. E. 1/4 section 35, and extends up the canon to the east line of Johnson's fence. The length of the ground was four thousand feet, and the width the width of the canon.

It becomes necessary, therefore, to examine the testimony and ascertain the width of the canon. Meek, whilst he was Superintendent for the Vallejo Mining Company, worked up the canon to a point four hundred feet above the embankment (p. 372). He says that the *width of the canon to that point was 80 to 100 feet; from that point to the junction of the East and West forks it gradually widens to two hundred (200) feet; from the junction up the East fork, which was the ground located by the Vallejo Mining Company, for a distance of four or five hundred feet, the canon is three or four hundred feet wide; above that point it gradually narrows down to eighty (80) feet.* (See evidence pages 378—380.) This therefore, was the entire width of the ground located by the Vallejo Mining Company, and not even this width of ground contained gold. Meek says (p. 378), *we worked the ground from 30 to 40 feet wide and that took all the ground containing gold.*

But even conceding that the Vallejo Mining Company obtained a right to the ground the entire width of the canon, whether it contained gold or not, it is not contended by any evidence, that the ground outside the width of the canon contained gold, nor is it claimed by the Vallejo Mining Company located the ground outside of the canon. It becomes necessary to determine, therefore, how much of each ten (10) acre tract within Johnson's Ranch and pre-emption claim, that Blakeley seeks to purchase, did the Vallejo Mining Company locate. We have already seen from the testimony of Meek the width and length of the claim.

Now place the diagram before you and with the testimony of William Sabine, the Surveyor, it will be easy to determine the extent of the claim in each ten (10) acre tract that Blakeley seeks to purchase. Sabine's testimony (pp. 74—82) shows the number of acres, as follows: In the N. W. 1/4 of the N. W. 1/4 of S. E. 1/4 section 35, 1 65/100 acres. In the S. W. 1/4 of the N. W. 1/4 of the S. E. 1/4 section 35, 4 22/100 acres. In the S. E. 1/4 of N. W. 1/4 of S. E. 1/4 section 35, 80/100 acres. In the N. E. 1/4 of S. W. 1/4 of S. E. 1/4 section 35, 3 84/100 acres. In the N. W. 1/4 of S. E. 1/4 of S. E. 1/4 section 35, 3 50/100 acres. In the N. E. 1/4 of S. E. 1/4 of S. E. 1/4 section 35, 2 25/100 acres, and in S. E. 1/4 of S. E. 1/4 of S. E. 1/4 section 35, 1 92/100 acres.

It appears, therefore, from these figures, that Blakeley seeks to purchase over fifty-one acres of land, to which he never had any title under the mining laws, that is, conceding for the sake of argument that he has a title to any as against the contract with Johnson, and which is indisputably agricultural land and to which Johnson has a clear pre-emption right. Blakeley himself admits that a large portion of the land he seeks to purchase is only agricultural land.

Johnson had filed his pre-emption claim upon lot 2 of section 1, township 10 N., range 11 E., and W. 1/2 and S. E. 1/4 of S. E. 1/4 of section 35, township 11 N., range 11 E., being 148 19/100 acres. Blakeley seeks to purchase all of Johnson's pre-emption claim, except thirty acres, and that thirty is separated by the land claim by Blakeley, so that, if Blakeley is allowed to purchase, Johnson can only get twenty acres.

If the facts of this case do not show that the sale to Blakeley would *defeat and impair the bona fide pre-emption claim* of Johnson, then we can not conceive of a case that would come within the language of the latter part of section twelve (12). We now come to the consideration of the two closing lines of section twelve (12) of the Act of July 9, 1870, which are as follows: *"or authorize the sale of the improvements of any bona fide settler, to any purchaser."* It is inconceivable to us how the mineral applicant and his attorney, with this provision of the law before them, and knowing the facts to be that Johnson had fences, houses, and orchards on this land, ever came to the conclusion that Blakeley could purchase this land from the government.

There is but one fact in the case that furnishes any reason to think that the mineral applicant entertained any hope that he would be allowed to purchase the land, and that fact is, *that instead of posting the notice and diagram in a conspicuous place, as the law requires, he put them inside a cabin, locked the door, and blinded the windows.* If Johnson did not see the notice, then he might hope to purchase Johnson's land and improvements, turn his wife and living children from their home, and mine up the graves of his dead children.

Johnson has improvements on every ten acre tract which Blakeley seeks to purchase. On the N. W. 1/4 of N. W. 1/4 of S. E. 1/4, section 35, there is a small building and two hundred yards of fencing and the embankment constructed by Johnson; on the S. E.

1/4 of N. W. 1/4 of S. E. 1/4 there is a house, vineyard, and orchard, pipes laid in the ground for conducting water, and also fencing; on the N. W. 1/4 of S. W. 1/4 of S. E. 1/4 there is a valuable building and barn; on the N. W. 1/4 of S. E. 1/4 of S. E. 1/4 is the graveyard and fencing; on all the other ten acre tracts there is good fencing. (See Ward's testimony, from page 303 to 323; also, Lassen's, from164 to 182; also Johnson's). Johnson, when he settled upon the land, and for many years afterwards, expended large sums in clearing the land and fitting it for cultivation.

V

The only question that counsel for mineral claimant has mentioned in his brief is the mineral and non-mineral character of *that portion of the land which Blakeley seeks to purchase that lies in the ravine or canon.* As this comprises only a small portion of the land which he seeks to purchase, it seems to have been the idea of counsel that if he could magnify the value of that narrow strip to countless thousands for mining purposes, that the value of it for agricultural purposes, and the facts that Blakeley is only there under contract, that it is Johnson's home and land, that he has put all that he has made for the last twenty years in improvements upon the land, has a good and valid claim as a pre-emptor, and that Blakeley seeks to include in his purchase a large amount of agricultural, which he can not pretend contains gold—that all these facts would be over looked and disregarded in the decision of this case.

Whilst Johnson relies on all the questions raised in the case, yet we feel confident that if the case could by any possibility be narrowed down to the question of the value for agricultural or mineral purposes of the land lying in the ravine or canon, that the decision would be that it is most valuable for agricultural purposes. As the evidence proving and tending to prove this fact comprises a great portion of the five hundred pages of testimony on behalf of Johnson, it would be of little practical use to undertake to specify pages of testimony. We will, therefore, confine ourselves to a few of the leading points.

ELLEN OSBORN

And we would here remark that a careful reading of the paper marked, "Adverse claim of John C. Johnson, filed October 16, 1871," will aid and assist very much in understanding the evidence that was taken on behalf of Johnson.

Johnson's possession, use, and cultivation of the land for agricultural purposes for the last twenty-two years is not disputed. But, says Blakeley, the narrow strip of land in the ravine or canon contains gold and in such an amount as to make it more valuable for mining than agriculture, and on that account the Government will disregard all of Johnson's equitable and legal claim to it, and because I am in possession under a mining notice, although that notice was put up only for the purpose of enabling me and my associates to prevent any parties interfering with the contract made with Johnson, sell to me this narrow strip and fifty or sixty acres of Johnson's land, which does not contain any gold.

This particular portion of Johnson's land which lies in the ravine is the richest portion of his ranch for agricultural purposes. The soil is a rich black loam and will last for centuries to come. It produces from four to five tons of hay per acre each year. The hay is worth, at present low prices, from twenty-five to thirty dollars per ton. The clear gain, therefore, from each acre every year is not less than one hundred dollars.

Blakeley has been mining in this ground for four years, and has certainly mined that part which contains the most gold, he having mined in the narrowest portion and below the juncture of the east and west forks of the canon. Thomas G. Meek, who superintended the mining from September 1867 to May 19, 1868, testified that the claim did not pay expenses during that time (p. 375). In the fall of the year, 1870, Meek met Blakeley at Smith's Flat, in El Dorado County, and had a conversation with Blakeley about the claim. Meek asked Blakeley what had been taken out since he (Meek) left the claim. Blakeley told him that from the opening of the claim (September 1867) to that time there had been taken out the sum of sixteen thousand dollars, and that the expenses had been twenty thousand dollars.

In December 1870, there was a trial in the Sacramento Land

Office between Isaac Yoakum and Alburn J. Blakeley, who is mineral applicant in this case. In that trial an attorney residing at Sacramento city, Matt F. Johnson, appeared for one of the parties. He was called as a witness in this case and testified that Blakeley was a witness in the case of Yoakum, and that Blakeley testified that the expenditures, up to that time, in the claim which Blakeley is now seeking to purchase, exceeded the receipts by four or five thousand dollars. (See M. F. Johnson's testimony, page 675). This agrees with what Blakeley told Meek in the fall of 1870, at Smith's Flat. It appears, therefore, that Blakeley had not paid expenses during the time that he has worked the ground.

As the mining washes away and destroys the ground, we are unable to fix upon the basis, consistent with the evidence, upon which it can be determined that the ground is more valuable for mining than agricultural purposes. The hay alone that Johnson has sold from his ranch, the greater portion being from the land in the canon, has not amounted to less than forty thousand dollars ($40,000), and will amount annually to not less than eighteen hundred or two thousand dollars.

VI
Impeachment of Blakeley and his Witnesses

It rarely occurs that a witness is so completely impeached, by the record he has made himself, as Blakeley has been in this case. We assert that there is sufficient in the record to show that his testimony is not entitled to be believed. His affidavit of posting the notice and diagram states that the notice and diagram were posted in a *conspicuous place* on said mining claim, to wit, *upon a certain cabin*; and yet his own evidence, given after the evidence of Johnson, Myers, Linder and Peachy had exposed his attempt to conceal the notice and diagram, showed that the notice and diagram were nailed to the back of a door, which was kept locked, and inside of the cabin.

Blakeley also made another affidavit, which relates to the ownership of the ground he seeks to purchase. This affidavit is marked, filed December 21, 1871. In the affidavit he sets forth, *"That he is now and has been the exclusive owner of the same* (that is the ground he seeks to purchase) *for more than four years past,"* and *"has been in the exclusive possession in his own right for more than four years last past of the whole of said ground."* He swears to substantially the same matter in his evidence on the trial. And yet there is scarcely a particle of truth in the statement. In the first place he sets forth a description of all the land he seeks to purchase and then swears that he is and has been for four years last past the *exclusive owner and in the exclusive possession of the whole of said ground.* This includes some fifty or sixty acres of agricultural land, which there is not one syllable of evidence to show that he or his grantors ever pretended to locate. In the second place he is not now the owner of all the ground that was located as mining ground.

And in the third place, that portion of the land which lies in lots 1 and 2, section 1, township 10 N., range 11 E., was not located, as the copy of notice attached to Blakeley's application shows, until August 11, 1870, less that one year prior to the filing of the application for patent; no work was ever done on that ground. It must appear plain from these facts that Blakeley was willing to swear to whatever was necessary, whether true or untrue, to bring himself within the requirements of the law.

Richard S. Young, one of the chief witnesses for Blakeley, joined with Blakeley in the affidavit relating to the posting of the notice and diagram, and also gave *ex parte* evidence, which will be found in the record immediately following the papers marked "Application for Patent," setting forth the same statements as Blakeley in regard to the ownership of the ground. The remaining principal witness on the part of Blakeley, N. I. Munday, was impeached by about thirty persons.

VII
Conclusion

In closing our argument we must again call the attention of the Register and Receiver to the importance of the case. It may be regarded as a test case on all the points we have mentioned, and a decision in favor of Blakeley would place all the improvements and property of settlers in the mineral regions of this State in the hands of those who would locate the land as mineral, and would be notice to all settlers to leave.

Respectfully, G. J. Carpenter, and Geo. E. Williams, for Contestant Johnson

In the United States Land Office at Sacramento, California, before the Register and Receiver.
In the Matter of the Claim of Alburn J. Blakeley,
Applicant for Patent No. 199,

Against

John C. Johnson, Contestant
Service of contestant, Johnson's brief, acknowledged this 15th day of
April 1872
Geo. G. Blanchard,
Attorney for Minerals

APPENDIX F

The Life of Emily Hagerdon Johnson

Author's Note: In the course of researching and collecting materials, I have acquired five copies of Emily's efforts to write a reminiscence of her early life and travel to California. They are all different. What follows is an attempt to reconcile the different versions into a single, congruent tale. This required a little editing. I tried to keep the editing to a minimum so that Emily could tell her story in her own way.

I was born May 7, 1834, to Luther and Fanny Hagerdon on Bank Street in Cleveland, Ohio. When I was six weeks old my parents moved to Green Bay, Wisconsin. At that time Green Bay was a small fur trading post. Father took up a small piece of government land and built a comfortable log cabin and into this he moved his family, which consisted of himself, wife and three children—two sons and one daughter.

One Sabbath evening Father strolled from the house down to the river shore. While standing there admiring the beauties of nature and the quiet ripples of Fox River as they murmured by, he thought how wondrous are the ways of our Heavenly Father, and the thoughts of the poet came into his mind:

> God moves in a mysterious way
> His wonders to perform.
> He plants his footsteps in the sea
> And rides upon the storm. [183]

---

[183] "Light Shining Out of Darkness" by William Cowper 1731-1800

Just then he was startled by the heavy hand of a tall and savage looking Indian laid upon his shoulder, and the words "Me got paleface now." Then ensued a terrible struggle, the Indian being armed with a large butcher knife and Father altogether unarmed, but a strong and powerful man. The Indian made several thrusts at him with the knife, but Father with a short stick warded them off, and watched for an opportunity to grapple with him. At last he succeeded; catching him by the throat he threw the native prostrate upon the ground and there they rolled and fought for some time. At last Father succeeded in getting the knife away from the Indian and threw it into the river. Then he gave the Indian a good whipping and a piece of advice and let him go. After that, they were good friends.

Time rolled by and another little brother came to brighten our home. And spring in all her loveliness came and carpeted the earth in a beautiful green dotted here and there with the tiny blue violet and the white mayflower.

Then an old bachelor proposed to have a schoolhouse built and the villagers joined together and in a short time they had constructed a small log house as near the center of the village as possible in which they could have worship as well as school. Then came the question "Who will act as teacher?" At last they determined to send East for a young lady by the name of Mary White, a niece of the old bachelor. In a few weeks she arrived and a more lovely woman I never saw: large dark and thoughtful eyes, a complexion as fair as the lily, and cheeks the color of a delicate pink rose, and an abundance of dark auburn hair, but the best feature of all was her mild and gentle ways. She had a kind word and smile for all. I can see her now, seated in the old log schoolhouse with her little band of juveniles gathered around her, each trying to get a little closer to their dear teacher.

This same log schoolhouse and meeting place was very early etched into my memory. Sabbath was a day of elegant clothing and cold dinners. The ladies wore their very best dresses extended over hoops, long enough to reach below the ankle, from under the skirt peeps of lace pantaloons and tiny feet appeared. Often these dresses had been packed unimaginable distances through Indian infested wildernesses.

ELLEN OSBORN

Weekdays we wore calicos and cotton stuffs, which were durable and easily managed in frontier households, but Sundays we were civilized.

Father had just been on a trip back to Cleveland on some business and had brought back some wonderful new clothes for us. Mother had an awesome creation of bottle green silk. I can remember it very clearly. He had also brought many lengths of material, which were to make dresses for me, and others for Mother and some for Sunday suits for the boys. Mother was busy here and there, excited by the new dress. I did not feel in any hurry and was not ready by the time the others were. I was told to leave on my everyday dress and stay home. This was severe punishment.

After the family had left, I went down to the river and pondered upon it. In my wandering, I finally reached the little settlement. There was no one stirring. I could hear a hymn being sung. I wondered if the wife of our next-door neighbor had a dress nearly as pretty as Mother's. I walked up to the door and peeked in. I became too interested and peeked too far. One of the elders took me by the arm and escorted me to my parent's pew. It did not occur to me to resist.

[Section missing?]

At this time an incident occurred, which greatly amused the white people of the fort. The Indians had been greatly attracted to the fort at Green Bay, which was a thing many of them had never seen. The soldiers, seeing that the Indians were not warlike, paid no attention to them. They later crept closer and closer until at last they were quite near a large cannon that stood on the brow of a small hill with its muzzle pointing toward the river. Of course their curiosity was aroused and they became very anxious to know all about it. The gunner, being a practical joker, loaded it with a blank cartridge and then told the natives to take hold of the chains and pull it along. Well, about a dozen of them took hold and began to draw it down the hill. After they were well underway the gunner touched a match to the touchhole and it went off. So did the natives, tumbling down head foremost into the river screaming "Manito! Manito!" which means,

The devil! The devil! They swam for their lives to the opposite side of the river. When they reached their wigwams they told their chief, who called a meeting of all his braves.

"My noble braves," said he, "these our brothers have just returned from the paleface settlement and as you see are wet and exhausted. The palefaces have brought a Manito that shoots fire out of his mouth. Now what shall we do: join with the Chippewa and kill them all off or make peace with them? Black Bear, you are wise, what do you say?"

Black Bear rose and said, "My noble brothers, to make peace with the palefaces means to give up our homes and take our squaws and children and travel to the west whither they are pushing us all the time. No, let us join the Chippewa and clean them out. But let us hear what our brother Grey Wolf thinks."

So Grey Wolf spoke, "Warriors and braves, you all know how we have been hunted down by the whites, our homes broken up, and our land and hunting ground taken from us. Shall we give up without a struggle? No, I say no! Let us join another tribe and exterminate the white man who comes here to desecrate our peaceful homes and kill our buffalo and deer. No! We will kill and scalp them and the white squaws will be the wives of the most brave."

"We will now sleep," says the chief, "and with the rising sun we will be on our way to join our friends, the Chippewa."

[Section missing]

This escaping Indian remembered these things and knew he must use strategy. He plunged into thick woods, dismounted, and gave his pony a sharp cut with his rope, which sent the horse flying through the woods. The Indian put on the wolf skin he had used as a saddle and went in another direction until he had reached a small stream of water. He took off the skin and waded across the stream. He entered the underbrush and crawled several miles. At last his pursuers gave up the chase. He heard them returning to camp declaring vengeance upon the whites and their traitor. After they had passed out of hearing, the messenger of warning re-crossed the creek to make great haste, part of the time walking and part running.

About noon of the next day, he reached the settlement of the whites and came direct to our house. He stepped quietly in. The family was at dinner, but his form threw a shadow across the floor and Father and Mother sprang to their feet and welcomed the Indian who was the one who had attacked Father and afterwards became friendly because Father had spared his life. We called him Dido.

They gave him dinner and after he had finished eating he told my parents that the Chippewa and Menominee had joined together to kill all the palefaces and that they would be upon them by the setting of two suns and Father must tell all his people.

Then there was great commotion in the settlement. Men taking their families, provisions, and such possessions that could be quickly moved. The garrison was astir getting their implements in readiness.

The eventful night came, but all had not reached the protection of the fort. These were taken by the savages and cruelly treated. Infants were taken from their mother's arms and their brains dashed out against the side of a house or tree. The parents were tomahawked and scalped. Houses where the inmates had barricaded themselves were set on fire and surrounded by the savages whooping and dancing. After they had finished their work of horror, they moved on to the outskirts of the town, and finding it vacated, they held a council and decided to first set fire to all the buildings and then attack the fort.

Anxiously and bravely the male inmates of the garrison were watching for the advance and attack, determined to sell their lives dearly. Their wives and daughters were making litters and bandages for their wounded ones. The Indians came in a fearful army, outnumbering the whites three to one. It was discovered that among them were a number of Canadian French traders and that they had supplied the savages with firearms and ammunition. On they came, yelling and whooping, their faces painted with red, their heads bedecked with feathers; it was a hideous sight.

At last came the onslaught. Many a brave father and son fell to the ground to rise no more, and many were carried by their comrades to the women of the fort, who dressed their wounds and gave them restoratives.

You are wondering how fared the natives? Well, they fought bravely until the cannon was sighted upon great numbers and then there was a fearful slaughter. Among the slain were the treacherous traders. As soon as these, their leaders, were killed they began to retreat, but the soldiers and men of the garrison followed them and killed a great many more until they cried for mercy, at which time they were permitted to go to their homes. There was great sorrow and weeping by those natives who had lost their dear ones for, although they are savage and barbarous by nature, they are very devoted and affectionate to their own.

After this there was peace, and Father bought more land and built a very nice large house and furnished it up very comfortably. Into this he moved his family, of which there were now six. Then he turned the log cabin into a soap factory and Mother took in boarders. Together they worked and planned and saved.

Thus year after year rolled by and our little village became quite a town. Father had made a great deal of money in speculating in one way and another and concluded to build a boat. He, with a few men, went into the woods and got out timbers, and hauled them down to the river shore. He then employed ship carpenters and the result was that in a few months the brig "Rocky Mountain" slid from the skids onto the peaceful bosom of the Fox River, thence down the bay into Lake Michigan and on she went until she came to the beautiful city of Cleveland, where he sold her. He then returned and built a gristmill. Our family increased until there were eight of us: five boys and three girls.

Then our dear mother's health gave way and after a long and painful illness of eighteen months on the eighth of June 1849 at two o'clock in the afternoon she bade us all farewell and requested us to meet her in that happy home to which she was going.

I never can forget how dreary and desolate the house looked when we came back from the cold and silent grave in which we had left our dear mother. Oh, dear children, you who have parents treat them with honor, tenderness, and love that when they are taken from you, you can feel that you have been kind and obedient while they were with you. It was so sad to feel our dear mother had been taken from us just at the time when we needed her most to counsel and lead us in the right way. Her teachings were always to remember our Creator and love and serve Him to the best of our ability.

Then began the breaking up of the family as our grandmother Perry, who had come to take care of mother during her illness and had been there several months, felt that she must return home to her aged husband. When she left, she took our little sister Mary. You who have lost your dear ones will realize what a desolate home ours was with three dear ones taken out so closely together.

I, being the eldest girl, had the duties of mother and sister fall upon me, as Mother had left an infant a few months old to my charge saying, "My dear Emily, take good care of little Hattie." I did my utmost to fulfill the duties imposed upon me. Of course Father hired a housekeeper and then there was discord in our once peaceful home all of the time. The five boys did not like to come under the government of a housekeeper.

Father became despondent and as he had in youthful days sailed on the lakes, he decided to go on the water again. He bought a vessel, manned her, and went sailing. It would be two weeks or a month at a time before we would see him again, but on his return he always brought us some nice presents. It was a habit of his to walk in and scatter sugarplums and other candies on the floor. The children would make a mad scramble each to get as many as he could. I could make a balloon of my skirt and cover a great number of goodies. Then the boys would quarrel as to whether I should be allowed to keep them or not.

At one time, Father brought home a raccoon to the boys. He proved to be a terrible nuisance, as every time he saw the pantry door open, he would run to the sink and stand upon his hind legs, wet his forepaws and then run to the sugar barrel and get his paws full of sugar. Then he would run into the attic over the wood shed. In the summer when it was very warm, we were obliged to leave the windows open.

That was before we had screens. The raccoon would climb up the lattice and into the bedroom and pull my hair, setting me screaming with pain and fright. Then he would run away and not show himself for a couple of days. This he would do, knowing that he would be punished by the housekeeper.

For two years Father remained a widower, hiring this one and that one to keep house and keep his family together. Those were unhappy days, for in our Father's absence we were scolded and cuffed about and our once nice and happy home was a living hell. At the expiration of the two years, Father married a young lady twenty years of age[184]. She was the daughter of a Methodist minister. When our new mother came, things were much pleasanter, and she did her best to make us happy, so for two years all went well.

Then came the voice of the Golden West, "Come one, come all, here is a fortune for everyone." Father caught the fever and in the spring of 1853 started for Council Bluffs, leaving his property, which consisted of by this time, farms, a foundry, and gristmills in the hands of an agent.

On the eleventh of April, 1853[185] we started, leaving Green Bay, Wisconsin, for Placerville, El Dorado County, California. We went to Council Bluffs and laid in a six-month supply of provisions. Father bought horses, oxen, cows, and wagons before starting on our long, tedious, and dangerous journey. For in those times the Indians were quite hostile and cruel, killing the men, abusing the women and

---

184 Zilpha Ann Reynolds, daughter of Daniel. The marriage took place in Cuyahoga County Ohio.

185 Among the various versions one serious inconsistency is dates. The start date for California was given variously as April 11, April 20 or May 25. More importantly, the year also is inconsistent. The earlier versions say 1853. Later versions say 1850. 1853 is probably correct, because Emily consistently states she married Johnson three months after arriving in California. Their wedding date was announced in the *Empire County Argus* newspaper as January 1, 1854.

children, driving away cattle and committing other depredations upon the emigrants.

All went well until we reached the alkali deserts, then our stock began dropping off until out of seven span of horses we had but three horses left, and of cattle I know not how many we had when we started, but when we came into California we had three horses, two cows, and two yoke of oxen, but I am ahead of our journey. Those were rough and trying times. Everything seemed to go wrong; stock dying, children sick, wagons breaking down, and every one of us discouraged and wondering what would come next.

One day as we were going along we saw an Indian coming towards us and my Father said, "Boys, I think we are in for trouble, so get ready to do the best we can." In a short time we met. The Indian carried a paper which he gave to Father to read and it told him to beware a certain bunch of willows that we would come to the next day on a stream that we would have to ford, as there was a band of Indians secreted there who robbed and killed the whites when in small numbers and that there were eighteen in number and to be sure to treat this Indian kindly and to send him on to warn other emigrants.

So Father gave him something to eat and a red bandanna handkerchief, which the Indian wrapped around his head and went on his way with the warning. Well, the next day we came to the ambush of this band of robbers and out they came, with spears, bows, and arrows and ordered Father to stop. He did so and then one of them that could speak a very little English told him that if he would give them a span of horses, provisions, and a white squaw, they would let him go on.

While this conversation was going on a very large Indian came to the back end of the wagon I was sitting in, caught hold of me and was lifting me out of the wagon when I gave a yell, which called the attention of Father and brothers to me. Then they all drew their guns on the Indians, who gave a grunt saying, "White chief got pop-pop," meaning revolvers. "Yes," said Father and he shoved his under the leader's nose and said, "I'll pop you if you don't leave here." The rest of them had taken to their heels and hid in the willows. When the old fellow found he was left alone, he very hastily left. The youngest of the boys took charge of the teams and drove on while Father and the older men walked in the rear with their guns pointed towards the willows.

A few days later Mother and I were walking in advance of the teams (we were in the Rockies), and up on the mountain we saw a bear and her cubs. There were three, and these little fellows were playing and boxing like boys. After a while they got too rough and began to fight each other. The old mother who had been watching their frolic got up and went to them, gave each a box on the head and then sat down again. They were quieted a while, and then went on playing. I thought such is nature.

The scenery in these mountain and plains is the most beautiful eyes ever looked upon in the spring. Beautiful shrubs and flowers as far as one can see, which look as if man set them out in beautiful gardens and planted the seeds. Day after day we traveled through these lovely gardens. Plenty of wild game, herds of buffalo in the foothills, antelope, and deer along with the sage hen furnished us with an abundance of fresh meat. We had two cows to give us all the milk and butter we needed. We put the milk into a large can that we used for that purpose and at night there would be a large lump of butter churned by the motion of the wagon and the milk quite sweet.

Sometimes we were where there was a large company of emigrants. If the ground was level and free from rocks, we would get up a dance of quadrilles and waltzes, there being a number of musicians along with their violins, horns, accordions, and harmonicas. If it were late we would have a cup of coffee and some hard bread and the time passed very pleasantly.

ELLEN OSBORN

One day, we came to what was called Echo Cave[186] and camped there for the night. In the morning we all visited the cave. It was up on the mountainside, a small footpath leading to it. As you entered the cave you soon learned why it was called Echo Cave. In walking on the earthen floor it would rattle and rumble like distant thunder. Upon the wall of the first chamber, written in charcoal, were the names of the emigrants who had visited the cave. Some of them showed scholarship, and others you could scarcely decipher. One of these names attracted my notice and I called to Mother to come over and look at the writing. The name was J. C. Johnson, and underneath the name was drawn the bird of our country, the grand old eagle. I remarked to her that that man is a scholar and a lovely scribe.

On the 13th of July we camped on the Humboldt River and about two o'clock in the morning were awakened by the loud barking of our dogs. One of them, which was a bloodhound, swam the river and was gone until daylight, then he came back all wet and tired out and looked at us as though he would say, "I have had a hard time to save you this time." Then we had breakfast and packed the wagons and were just hitching up the horses when the dogs began to make a fuss again and started for the river.

Brother Charles, seeing some ducks on the water, thought it was those that the dogs were after and went to shoot some of them. As he raised the gun, up jumped an Indian out of the bushes close by him and began shaking his buckskin, which is a sign of peace with them. Then he came into camp and wanted something to eat. Mother gave him some bread and meat. Then he wanted some ammunition and Father told him he would not give him any, but he begged so hard that Father gave him a very little powder and told him to go. Father went

---

186 Echo Cave is probably what is also known as Cache Cave in Echo Valley, Utah. Emily described it much as other emigrants described it. It is located on private property. On a current list of legible names in the cave, J. C. Johnson is not among them. For a complete description of the site, see *Historic Inscriptions on Western Emigrant Trails* by Randy Brown. Published 2004 by Oregon-California Trails Association Independence, Missouri.

on hitching up his team and when all was ready bid the boys drive ahead and he walked behind, leaving Mr. Indian standing there. We traveled about twenty miles that day over terrible roads, sometimes very rocky and other times nearly up to the hub in sand.

That night we camped in a desolate looking place: sand, rocks, and sagebrush all around us. It was a beautiful night. The moon and stars came out in all their splendor. All was quiet as the grave, not a breath of air stirring. All except myself locked in the arms of Morpheus, and I was busy with my own thoughts. Presently the bulldog and the hound both jumped from their beds snarling and barking fearfully. Instantly we were all on the alert and waiting to see what was to come next. At last we heard a voice calling to us, "For God's sake, call in your dogs and give us aid!"

Father called the dogs away and bid the travelers welcome. It seems that they came to our camping ground of the night before, and as they were anxious to get into company with someone, they stopped there to cook their supper, intending to rest their team a short time, and then try to overtake us. While they were sitting at their evening meal, they were startled by the report of a gun and one of their number, of which there were nine, exclaimed "Oh, my God, I am shot!" and fell backward. On examination, they found that the ball had entered and lodged just over the left hip. They hitched up their team, put the wounded man into the wagon and started.

About one o'clock they reached our camp and Father went to the wagon in which the young man lay. There he saw a youth about eighteen or nineteen years of age rolling and moaning in terrible agony. He examined the wound, which by this time was fearfully swollen and inflamed. He asked the young man if he thought he could stand it to have the ball extracted without being under the influence of a sleeping potion. He said he thought he could. Father began probing the wound and the patient fainted. He then made use of restoratives, under the influence of which he soon recovered consciousness and consented to take the opiate.

Again Father set about the painful task of reaching the ball. In about fifteen minutes he succeeded in extracting it. Then came a slow fever and for several days it was very doubtful how it would go with him. But youth, kind and tender nursing with the blessing of God at last gained the victory. In two weeks he was able to be on his feet.

Scarcely had he recovered when Father was again called upon to attend to two wounded men who had been shot by Indians. It happened in this way: it was a very large train and they were bringing through a large drove of stock: sheep, cattle, and horses. In the night and in a few moments they were surrounded by Indians. Several shots were exchanged, in which these men received their wounds. The Indians gaining the victory, drove off their cattle and sheep, destroyed their provisions and taking such things as they liked or suited their fancy, left these men to die. The rest having mounted their animals rode away for help, and one of these, having seen our wagons in the distance came as fast as he could, neither sparing himself or horse.

For twenty-four hours he had not tasted food, and with this fasting and his long journey he was hardly able to speak, so we took him into the wagon, gave him some refreshments, and hastened on as fast as possible to help the wounded.

On reaching the spot, what a terrible sight met our eyes. There lay the wounded men out in the scorching sun. There were two women with their little ones, almost frightened to death and not anything to eat. They begged Father to stay with them. He told them that he would until they could get their stock back or get assistance from some of the emigrants. He then looked at the wounds of the men and found that one of them had his arm broken and the ball glanced upward and lodged in the shoulder. This he also extracted and then bound up the wound. He next examined the wounds of the other man. His proved to be but flesh wounds, one in the leg and the other in the arm.

The next day there came along a very large train. We told them the trouble these people had gotten into and entreated them to lay over a few days and assist them in getting their stock. They consented to do so. So Father then told them he thought the best thing they could do was to go to the next water hole and wait for the other men in their party to bring their stock in. We proceeded on our journey.

Our horses and cattle died off until we were so reduced in stock that those who were able to do so had to foot it from Carson to California. As the men Father had hired to drive the teams were not needed any longer they joined other trains, leaving Father and my two brothers to do the driving.

One night we camped at what was then called Sportsman's Hall[187] and in the night two of our cows strayed off and they could not be found in the morning. My brother stayed there to look for them and the rest of us traveled on. We had not gone more than two miles when there came up a terrible storm and the dust that was knee deep became that much mud. Father found that he could not manage two teams, which he was trying to do in the absence of my brother. I saw how hard it was for him and offered my services.

He looked at me and smiled and said, "Why daughter, you could not drive these steers."

"Well, Papa, please give me the gad and let me try."

So he gave me a whip and at first I found it quite difficult to keep them in the road. At last I succeeded and got along very well until my skirts became so very heavy with the mud I could scarcely walk, so I tore my dress skirt off about four inches below the waistline and my underskirt being quite short it made it much easier for me to travel.

Well, after we had gone a few miles we came to a cottage called Mountain Cottage that had a long and wide porch in front and on it were about 30 or 40 men. A man by the name of J. C. Johnson made the remark, "There goes the girl I will make my wife."

All unconscious of this remark I drove along and about six o'clock we stopped at a wayside inn that was kept by an old English couple.

We had our supper and were about to retire when my brother came in. He had found the cows and was very tired and hungry, so I

187 Sportsman's Hall was a well-known stop along the trail. It is located at 5629 Pony Express Trail, Camino, CA. It is somewhat unique, as it has been continuously operated as an emigrant way station, inn, or restaurant since 1853. The current building is the third on the site. The name Sportsman refers to the presence of professional gamblers. For more information, see *The Pollock Pines Epic*, by Marilyn Parker, 1988.

set about getting some supper for him. While doing so, a gentleman came in and seated himself quite near the cooking stove, and while passing him, I stumbled and fell on his back. You can imagine how embarrassed I was. I apologized and left the room.

As I passed by the lady of the house said to me "Young lady, that is the man for you. He is a lawyer and the father of the land."

I didn't care who he was and I never wanted to see his face again.

The next day we came to Blakeley's Ranch where we intended to stop a few days to rest and feed up our stock. We had the consent of Mr. Blakeley to use a log cabin that was vacant at the time. Our cooking utensils, bedding, soiled clothes, and provisions were piled out on the ground preparatory for a general cleanup, when who should come along but the very man I didn't care to see. He bade me good morning and passed into the cabin. I went to the spring for a bucket of water.

On my return Mother and the boys were putting the things back into the wagons, and I said, "What does this mean?" Then she told me that Mr. Johnson had arranged with Father to go over to his ranch which joined the one on which we were. As he, Mr. Johnson, wanted a housekeeper and Mother thought the offer a good one and accepted.

We drove over there and turned our cattle and horses into the green fields where they could get plenty of feed and rest. The boys went to work on the ranch. Mother and I took charge of the house, which was a very nice one. At the expiration of three months I became the wife of Colonel J. C. Johnson, whose signature we had admired in the cave.

APPENDIX G

John and Sophronia Phillips

John Calhoun Johnson's partner at the ranch was John Hancock Phillips. Phillips and his wife, Sophronia lived at the ranch from 1850 until late 1851. Their time in El Dorado County was brief. Both of their lives were cut short by the diseases that ravaged the West in its early days. It is important to remember the fine people, such as these who, although their time was short, contributed to the creation of California.

How Johnson and the Phillips met is unknown, but from what record is left, it is easy to see that they were very good friends. Living and working together on the frontier, they had to be able to trust their lives to one another.

Like Johnson, the Phillips were originally from Ohio. They were both born in Wooster, Wayne County, Ohio. Sophronia's maiden name was Smith. They also shared an adventuring spirit.

Aware that the journey would be hazardous, they left their two young daughters, Melissa Ellen, age five, and Isadora Abigail, age three, behind in Ohio while they traveled overland to California in 1850[188]. They arrived just in time to become deeply involved in the El Dorado Indian Wars that erupted around them in their new home.

Several letters written by John Phillips have become part of the official record of the wars. These letters spoke of the constant state of fear those living at Johnson's Rancho experienced on a daily basis. Written under duress, those letters still show remarkable penmanship and evidence of a good education.

---

188 Native Daughters of the Golden West Pioneer Roster of California Pioneers

Sophronia left for Ohio in the fall of 1851 to fetch their young daughters and bring them back to California, where they would all be reunited as a family in their new home. In those days, the round trip journey from California to the East and back again could take close to a year, a long and dangerous journey with many hazards to be met along the way. It is amazing to imagine the courage of a young woman to undertake such an adventure alone.

It is possible, however, that she was not alone. The 1850 U. S. Census listed the miners at Johnson's Ranch, where the Phillips lived, two of which were William E. Smith, age twenty-eight, and Elliner Smith, age twenty-five. It is likely they were Sophronia's brother and sister-in-law. Smith was one of the few miners willing to stay at Johnson's Ranch during that time of trouble with the Indians. Could that have been because he was Sophronia's brother? Did he stay to be near his sister and offer her his protection?

During the tense days of the winter of 1851, in a letter published in the *Sacramento Transcript*, Phillips mentioned that J. C. Smith of Wooster, Ohio was shot in the left hip by an Indian while working at his claim near Johnson's Ranch on the 20th of January, 1850. Phillips recorded the man's name as "J. C." Smith, and he was more likely to be correct than the Census, that gave Mr. Smith's first name as "William."

In late May of 1851, Company B of the militia was presented with a flag made by Mrs. Phillips and Mrs. Smith[189]. If Mr. and Mrs. Smith had made some money mining and were ready to return home, Sophronia might have seized the opportunity to accompany them. It is also possible that Mr. Smith's injury was debilitating enough that he needed to return home.

What is known is that Sophronia made the trip to Ohio successfully, probably by ship. By November of 1852, Sophronia had said her goodbyes to her friends and family in Wooster and begin her trip back to California. She and her children traveled to New York, and on November 20, 1852 the little family boarded the steam ship, the

---

189 *Sacramento Daily Union* June 1,1851

SS Star of the West.[190] The ship took them to Nicaragua where they made their way by pack mule west to the Pacific Ocean where mother and daughters boarded another ship bound for San Francisco.

Sadly, this is where Sophronia's luck ran out. She contracted a tropical fever that stayed with her for the rest of her short life.

Meanwhile, things were not going well with her husband in California. While he was hurrying to complete the house he was building for his family in Placerville, he contracted one of the deadly diseases so common in those days.

Just thirty years old, John Phillips died tragically on October 17, 1852, when he succumbed to typhoid fever. At the time of his death he was treasurer of El Dorado County and a Democratic candidate for

SS Star of the West, the ship that carried Sophronia and her daughters from New York to Nicaragua. Later the *Star of the West* was chartered to the War Department during the Civil War.
Author's collection

---

190 *New York Daily Times* November 22, 1852 passenger lists

the State Assembly[191]. He was also engaged in constructing a house in the growing new town of Placerville for his family.

Since the building was incomplete at the time of his death, many mechanics' liens were filed, giving a good idea of what it was intended to be: a two-story building with a print shop on the lower floor and living quarters for the family above. The house was located on the west side of Coloma Street near the bridge over Hangtown Creek. Phillips himself had just constructed that bridge.

John Phillips was buried in Placerville, California. Today, the exact location of his grave is unknown. His death was a great loss for his family, but also a loss for El Dorado County and California. With his education and youthful energy, in all probability he would have made many contributions to the development of the state. Indeed, shortly before his death he was one of the petitioners working to create the town of Placerville.[192] Because he died unexpectedly while serving as treasurer of El Dorado County, there were concerns that the financial accounts were not in order. This issue wasn't resolved completely until 1854, about the same time his estate also finally settled.

The will of John Phillips offers confirmation of his love for and faith in the future of California; he provided for California war bonds to be purchased for his girls, and money to buy land in the west for his brother and nephew[193]. He made generous bequests to a number of family members.

Although at the time of his death Phillips had a respectable amount of cash and property, he also had a sizable number of unpaid bills and a mortgage on the house he was building. This resulted in a protracted settlement of the estate, which appeared to have been mismanaged by the executor, George S. Phillips of San Francisco. George was probably a relative of John Phillips. George did at least see to it that his widow, Sophronia got her share first.

Disembarking in San Francisco, it is easy to imagine

191 *Sacramento Daily Union* newspaper October 25 1852 page 2 col 6
192 *Minute & Judgment Book B* page 59 September 10, 1852
193 El Dorado County Probate file # 10/17/1852 El Dorado County Historical Museum Placerville, CA

Sophronia's eagerness to see her husband's smiling face again, his arms outstretched to his daughters, exclaiming, "How big you have grown!" That would have been the triumphant conclusion to her daring undertaking.

George Phillips probably met them when the ship arrived, and gave Sophronia and the girls the sad news that their husband and father had died. Would she have left Ohio if she had known her husband had already been dead for over a month?

The little family stayed in San Francisco for two weeks, so Sophronia could recover some of her strength from the fever before resuming the final stage of their journey to an empty house.

Arriving in Placerville, she found nothing to be as she had expected. In attempting to settle her husband's estate, she was challenged as being ineligible to inherit his estate on the grounds she had deserted her husband! It took several of the town's leading citizens to vouch for her, to convince the court that she was a devoted wife and mother.

On October 15, 1853, almost one year to the day after her first husband's death, Sophronia married James H. Predmore[194], a successful businessman and owner of a sawmill in Placerville. She had undoubtedly known him for some time, because John Phillips had been a partner in the sawmill. The new family moved to Marysville, and then to Shasta County where she died in 1862.

Just prior to her death, Sophronia, knowing her end was near, made provision for her daughters, Melissa and Dora, by placing them in the Convent of Notre Dame boarding school in Marysville, California. The girls stayed there for three years. Both of the girls married, raised families, and lived out their lives as Californians.

---

194 *Placerville Herald* October 15, 1853

BIBLIOGRAPHY

Secondary Sources

Adams, Richard C. *The Delaware Indians: A Brief History.* Saugerties, NY: Hope Farm Press, 1995, originally published in 1906.

Anonymous. *Biographical Record, Harrison County, Ohio.* Chicago: J. H. Beers Co. 1891.

Bancroft, Hubert Howe. *The History of California Vol VI 1848-1859 The Works of Hubert Howe Bancroft, Volume XXIII* San Francisco, California The History Company 1890

Barnes, Will C. *Arizona Place Names.* Tucson: University of Arizona Press, 1960.

Beals, Ralph. *Ethnology of the Nisenan.* Berkeley: University of California Press, 1933.

Bennett, William P. *The First Baby in Camp.* Salt Lake City: The Rancher Publishing Co., 1893. Berkeley: A. Edwards, 1978.

Black, Henry Campbell. *Black's Law Dictionary 5th Edition*, St. Paul: West Publishing,1979.

Borthwick, John David. *Three Years in California.* Edinburgh, Scotland, 1857. Oakland:California Biobooks, 1948.

Brown, Randy. *Historic Inscriptions on Western Emigrant Trails.* Independence: Oregon-California Trails Association, 2004.

Buck, Don, Andy Hammond, Thomas Hunt, David Johnson (Chairman) and John Maloney. *Mapping Emigrant Trails MET Manual.* Independence: Missouri Office of Historic Trails Preservation Oregon-California Trails Association, 2002.

Caughey, John Walton. *California.* 2nd ed. Englewood Cliffs, NJ: Prentice-Hall, Inc.,1940.

Cooke, Philip St. George, Lt. Col. *The Conquest of New Mexico and California in Historical and Personal Narrative.* New York: G. P. Putman's Sons, 1878.Oakland: California Biobooks, 1952.

Coy, Owen, PhD., *California County Boundaries.* Berkeley: The California Historical Survey Commission, 1923. Revised edition. Fresno: California Valley Publishers,1973.

Cross, Ralph Herbert. *The Early Inns of California 1844 – 1869.* San Francisco: California Cross and Brandt, 1954.

DeVoto, Bernard. *The Year of Decision 1846.* Boston: Little, Brown and Company,1943.

Drury, Will. *To Old Hangtown or Bust.* 1912. Reprint by the El Dorado Historical Society, 1975.

Ensign, D.W., ed. *History of Berrien & Van Buren Counties Michigan.* Philadelphia: .W. Ensign & Co., 1880.

Fitch, Thomas, ed. *Directory of the City of Placerville 1862.* Placerville, CA: Placerville Republican Printing Office. Reprinted El Dorado County Museum, 1975.

Giovacchini, Shirley. *Snowshoe Thompson.* Minden, NV: The Carson Valley Historical Society, 1991.

Glasscock, Carl Burgess. *A Golden Highway.* New York: Bobbs-Merrill, 1934.

Goodwin, Grenville. *Western Apache Raiding and Warfare.* Tucson: University of Arizona Press, 1971.

Gudde, Erwin G. *California Gold Camps.* Berkeley: University of California Press, 1975.

Gwinn, Professor J. M. *History of the State of California and Biographical Record of Coast Counties of California.* Chicago: Chapman Publishing Company, 1904.

Hafen, Leroy R., Ph.D. *The Overland Mail.* Cleveland: Arthur H. Clark Company, 1926.

Hanna, Charles A. *Historical Collections of Harrison County in the State of Ohio.* New York, privately printed, 1900.

Harwood, David S. *Sierra Nevada.* Menlo Park: CA: United States Geological Survey, 1981.

Haskins, C. W. *The Argonauts of California.* New York: Fords, Howard & Hulbert, 1890.

Hinkle, George Henry and Bliss McGlashan Hinkle. *Sierra Nevada Lakes*. Indianapolis: Bobbs-Merrill, 1949. Reno: University of Nevada Press, 1987.

Holliday, J. S. *Rush For Riches Gold Fever And The Making Of California*. Berkeley: University of California Press and Oakland Museum of California, 1999.

Hoover, Mildred Brooke, Hero E. Rensch and Ethel G. Rensch. *Historic Spots In California*. Stanford: Stanford University Press, 1932.

Howard, Hugh. *How Old Is This House?* New York: The Noonday Press, 1989.

James, George Wharton. *Lake of the Sky Lake Tahoe*. Chicago: Charles T. Powner Company, 1956.

Johnson, Ben S. Jr. *Progeny of Captain Griffith Johnson(1734-1805) of Allegany County Maryland and Some of Their "In-Laws."* Aiken, SC: Self-published,1988.

Johnston-Dodds, Kimberly. *California and the Indian Wars The California Militia and Expeditions Against the Indians 1850-1859*. Sacramento: California State Library, 2002.

Kraus, George. *High Road to Promontory*. Palo Alto, CA: American West Publishing Company, 1969.

Leeper, David Rohrer. *The Argonauts of Forty-Nine*. Columbus: Long's College Book Company, 1950.

Lewis, Oscar. *Sea Routes To The Gold Fields the Migration By Water To California, 1849-1852*. New York: Albert A. Knopf, 1949.

Loomis, Patricia. *A Walk Through The Past San Jose Oak Hill Memorial Park*. San Jose: Argonauts Society of San Jose, 1998.

McAlester, Virginia and Lee. *A Field Guide to American Houses*. New York: Knopf, 1984.

Norton, L. A. *Life and Adventures of Colonel L. A. Norton*. Oakland: Pacifica Press Publishing House, 1887.

Orton, Richard H., Brig, Gen. *Records of California Men in the War of Rebellion 1861 to 1867*. Sacramento: California State Printing Office, 1890.

Paden, Irene. *The Wake of the Prairie Schooner*. New York: The MacMillan Company, 1943.

Parker, Marilyn. *The Pollock Pines Epic*. Placerville, CA: Self-published, 1988.

Peabody, George W. *How About That! Anthology of Historical Short Stories About Pleasant Valley, Oak Hill, Newtown, and Sly Park*. Placerville, CA: El DoradoCounty Historical Museum, 1989.

Platt, P. L. and N. Slater. *Traveler's Guide to California Upon the Overland Route*. Chicago: Daily Journal Office, 1852. Reprinted San Francisco: John Howell Books, 1963.

Porter, Lillie. *The Lillie Porter Collection of Harrison County Ohio Vol I and II*. Hilliard, OH: The Harrison County Genealogical Society, 1990.

Powers, Stephen. *Tribes of California*. Berkeley: University of California Press, 1976.

Robinson, W. W. *Land in California*. Berkeley: University of California Press, 1948.

Sanborn, Margaret. *The American: River of El Dorado*. New York: Holt, Rinehart and Winston, 1974.

Scamehorn, Howard L. *Buckeye Rovers in the Gold Rush*. Athens: Ohio University Press, 1965.

Schaffer, Jeffrey P. *The Tahoe Sierra A Natural History Guide to 106 Hikes in the Northern Sierra*. Berkeley: Wilderness Press, 1984.

Scott, Edward B. *The Saga of Lake Tahoe Vol I & II*. Crystal Bay, NV: Sierra-Tahoe Publishing Company, 1957, 1973.

Sherman, Edwin A. ed. *Fifty Years of Masonry in California Vol I*. San Francisco:George Spaulding and Company, 1898.

Shinn, Charles Howard. *Mining Camps*. New York: Alfred A. Knopf, Inc., 1948.

Sioli, Paolo, ed. *Historical Souvenir of El Dorado County*. Oakland: Oakland, Calif. Sioli, 1883. Reprinted Georgetown, CA: Cedar Ridge Publishing,1998.

Spinazze, Libera Martina, Charles Warren Haskins, et al. *Index to the Argonauts of California*. New Orleans: Polyanthos, 1975.

Stone, Irving. *Men To Match My Mountains*. Garden City, NY: Doubleday & Company, Inc., 1956.

Swanson, Clifford L. *The Sixth United States Infantry Regiment, 1855 to Reconstruction*.Jefferson, NC: McFarland & Company, Inc., 2001.

Trimble, Marshall. *Arizona*. Garden City, NY: Doubleday & Company, 1977.

Upton, Charles Elmer. *Pioneers of El Dorado*. Placerville, CA: The Nugget Press, 1906.

Warriner, John and Ricky. *Lake Tahoe – An Illustrated Guide and History*. San Francisco: Fearon Press, 1958.

Webster, Noah. *Webster's Dictionary Unabridged*. Springfield, MA: G. & C. Merriam, 1861.

Wilson, Elinor. *Jim Beckwourth Black Mountain Man and Chief of the Crows*. Norman,OK: University of Oklahoma Press, 1914.

Wilson, Norman L. & Arlean Towne. *The Nisenan*, 1982, and *Nisenan Geography* by Hugh W. Littlejohn 1928, an expanded version of the Chapter on the Nisenan published in volume 8, California, Handbook of North American Indians. Smithsonian Institution, Washington D.C., 1978, p. 387.

Yohalem, Betty. *I Remember . . ..*Placerville, CA: El Dorado County Chamber of Commerce, 1977.

Primary Sources

Emigrant Diaries or Reminiscences

Anonymous. "Fayette County Boys 1850." Nebraska State Historical Society. Typed transcript.

Bailey, Washington. *A Trip to California in 1853...Recollections of a Gold Seeking Trip by Ox Train Across the Plains and Mountains by an Old Illinois Pioneer.* Leroy, IL: Leroy Journal Printing Company, 1915.

Bradley, A. B. "Diary, 1850." Berkeley: Bancroft Library. Manuscript.

Brown, J. Robert. *Journal of a Trip Across the Plains of the U. S. from Missouri to California in the Year 1856.* Columbus, OH, 1860.

Cook, William. "Gold Hunters Diary." *Unionville Republican.* Missouri Historical Society.

Daily, Robert S. "Diary." Placerville, CA: El Dorado County Museum collection.

Dickenson, D. C. "Journal, 1852." Berkeley: Bancroft Library. Manuscript.

Farrar, John C. "Diary." Independence, MO: Merrill Mattes Memorial Library. Manuscript.

Fyffe, James Perry. "Diary." Unpublished, privately held.

Gobin, William. "Letter." Unpublished, privately held.

Ingalls, Eleazar Stillman. *Journal of a Trip to California by the Overland Route Across the Plains in 1850-51.* Waukegan, IL: Tobey and Company Printers, 1852.

Jones, Evan O. "Diary." Berkeley: Bancroft Library. Manuscript.

Kilgore, William H. *The Kilgore Journal.* Joyce Rockwood Muench, ed. New York: Hastings House, 1949.

Kreps, Simon Peter. "Journal." San Marino, CA: Huntington Library. Manuscript.

Lane, Samuel A. *Samuel A. Lane's 1850 Journal of the Emigration A cross the Plains to California.* Sacramento: California State Library. Manuscript.

Langworthy, Franklin. *Scenery of the Plains, Mountains and Mines.* Paul C. Phillips, ed. Princeton: Princeton University, 1932.

Lewelling, Seth. "Excerpts from the Journal of Seth Lewelling, March 23, 1850–September 10, 1852." Sacramento: California State Library. Manuscript.

McKinstry, Bryon N. *The California Gold Rush Overland Diary of Byron N. McKinstry, 1850-1852, with a Biographical Sketch and Comment on a Modern Tracing of his Overland Travel by his Grandson*. Bruce McKinstry ed. Glendale, CA: The Arthur H. Clark Company, 1975.

Millington, David Azro. "Journal of a California Miner." Sacramento: California State Library. Manuscript.

Newcomb, Silas. "Journal of a Trip from Darien, Wisconsin to California and Oregon, 1850-1851." San Marino, CA: Huntington Library. Manuscript.

Pigman, Walter Griffith. *The Journal of Walter Griffith Pigman*. Ulla Staley Fawkes, ed. Mexico, MO: 1942

Rhodes, Joseph. "Joseph Rhodes and the California Gold Rush." *Annals of Wyoming Vol. 23* Jan. 1951.

Riker, John F. *Journal of a Trip to California by the Overland Route*. New Haven, CT: Yale University.

Rodolf, Jacob Caspar Frederick. "Frederick Rodolf's Gold Rush Diaries1850-1852."Placerville, CA: El Dorado County Museum.

Rothwell, William R. "The Journal, Letters, and Guide of William R. Rothwell, Being the Narrative of His Trip Across the Plains in 1850." New Haven, CT: Beinecke Library, Yale University. Manuscript.

Scheller John Jacob. "Extract from the Autobiography of J. J. Scheller." Copied and translated from published German version by W. Zander. Copy in Sacramento: California State Library.

Shaw, David. *Eldorado; or, California as Seen by a Pioneer*. Los Angeles: B. R. Baumgardt & Co., 1900.

Shepard, George. "O Wickedness, Where Is Thy Boundary? The 1850 California Gold Rush Diary of George Shepard." *Overland Journal,* Vol 10 No. 4, Winter, 1992.

Shepherd, James S., Dr. *Journal of Travel Across the Plains to California, and Guide to the Future Emigrant.* Racine, WI: New Haven, CT: Yale University, 1851.Privately published.

Shoemaker. "Two Argonauts on the Oregon Trail Diary of 1850." Amargosa Valley, NV: Armagosa Valley Library, 1931. Manuscript.

Smith, G. A. "Journal of G. A. Smith Describing his Journey from St. Joseph, Missouri to Weaver, California, April 15 to July 16, 1852." St. Louis, MO; Missouri Historical Society Library. Manuscript.

Thissell, G. W. *Crossing the Plains in '49.* Oakland, CA: Bancroft Library Berkeley, 1903.

Thompson, Jesse Clark. "Diary: St. Joseph, Missouri to Hangtown, California April 22, 1850 to September 1, 1850." Sacramento, California State Library. Manuscript.

Wright, Robert C. "Journal of Robert C. Wright of an Overland Journey to California in 1850." Chicago: Chicago Historical Society. Manuscript.

Newspapers

Arizona Citizen. Tucson, Arizona Territory.
Arizona Weekly Star. Tucson, Arizona Territory.
Bedford Gazette. Bedford, PA.
Berrien County Record. Berrien, MI.
California Farmer & Journal of Useful Sciences. San Francisco, CA.
Daily Alta California. San Francisco, CA.
El Dorado Republican. Placerville, CA.
Empire County Argus. Coloma, CA.
Evening Picayune. San Francisco, CA.
Leavenworth Times. Leavenworth, KS.
Mountain Democrat. Placerville, CA.
New York Daily Times. New York, NY.
New York Times. New York, NY.

Oakland Tribune. Oakland, CA.
Placerville Herald. Placerville, CA.
Placer Times. San Francisco, CA.
Sacramento Bee. Sacramento, CA.
Sacramento Daily Union. Sacramento, CA.
Sacramento Star. Sacramento, CA.
Sacramento Transcript. Sacramento, Ca.

Online Sources

Anonymous. *Sowing the Wind.* Online essay
Anonymous *The Pike's Peak Gold Rush.* Ch 3 The Argonauts.
    Available online.
Nichols, Deborah, and Laurence M. Hauptman. *Warriors for the
Union.* http://historynet.com>
Winn, Albert Sacramentoabout.com

Periodicals

California Highways & Public Works Centennial Edition
    September 9, 1950. Official Journal of the Division of
    Highways, Department of Public Works, State of California.
California Historical Society Quarterly. "Tom Hill-Delaware Scout."
    Vol 25, 1946: 139-147.
Grizzly Bear, The. R. G. Dean Brentwood. "The Naming of Lake
    'Taho'." Vol. VII, October, 1910.
Pony Express Courier. January, 1948.
Sunset Magazine. Nonette V. McGlashan. "The Legend of Tahoe."
    November, 1908.

County Records

Civil Case #236 H. A. Oldfield vs Milo Oldfield. El Dorado County
    records. Placerville,CA.

El Dorado County Book A Leases. El Dorado County Historical
Museum Placerville, CA.

El Dorado County Deeds Book I. El Dorado County Historical
Museum Placerville, CA.

El Dorado County Minute & Judgment Book B. El Dorado County
Historical Museum Placerville, CA.

General files. El Dorado County Historical Museum, Placerville, CA.

Johnson Blakeley Deed Book Q 351 and 352. El Dorado County
Historical Museum Placerville, CA.

Oral History tape # 74 El Dorado County Historical Museum
Placerville, CA.

Probate File #1008A. Placerville, CA: El Dorado County Historical
Museum Placerville, CA.

Probate file # 10/17/1852. El Dorado County Historical Museum,
Placerville, CA.

"Sawmills." Scrapbook. El Dorado County Historical Museum
Placerville, CA.

California State Records

California Blue Book, Or State Roster 1895. Comp. L. H. Brown,
Secretary of State.

California State Archives records, Sacramento, CA.

California Supreme Court case #2537 *California Decisions* Vol 74.

Coloma State Park Archives. Coloma, CA

Daggett's Scrapbook. Sacramento: California State Library.

George H. Goddard, Civil Engineer. *State Wagon Road Survey of the
Johnson Route, 1855*. Report.

*Journals of the Senate and Assembly of the State of California, at the
Second Session of the Legislature, 1851-1852.* San
Francisco, CA: G.K. Fitch & Company and V. E. Geiger and
Company. State Printer, 1852.

Journal of the Sixth State Assembly of the State of California.
"Exhibit C: Claims Acted On And Claims Rejected by the
Board of War Examiners." Sacramento, CA: State Printer, 1855

Pioneer Files. Sacramento, CA: California State Library.
Records of the Adjutant General –Indian War Papers California
    State Archives Sacramento, CA

Records of Other States

County of Berrien, MI: Probate file #2509. Records.
County of Harrison, OH: Probate record for Nathan Johnson Sr.
Ohio Court records. Cadiz, OH.

United States of America Federal Records

Abstract of Declaratory Statements. San Bruno, CA: National Archives.
Act of Congress 10 USSL
Blakeley, Alburn J. Mineral entry file #5273. Washington, DC:
    National Archives.
Blakeley Patent #199. Washington, DC: National Archives.
    California Census, 1852.
Decisions of the Commissioner of the General Land Office &
    Secretary of the Interior. San Francisco: A. L. Bancroft and
    Company,1874.
Indian Depredation Claim #8317. Washington, DC: National
    Archives.
Land Entry Files Homestead Claim #3681. Washington, DC:
    National Archives.
Metals in the United States. Washington Government Printing Office,
    1883.
Records of Bureau of Land Management. Sacramento office.
Records of New Camp Grant, Arizona.
Report of the 44 Congress, Second Session, 1876.
Report of the 51 Congress, First Session, 1890.
Report of The Commissioner of Indian Affairs. Report of the
    Secretary of the Interior.

Report of the Director of the Mint Upon the Statistics of the
        Production of the Precious
U. S. Federal Census, 1850, 1860, 1870, 1880.

Maps

Army Mapping Service Corp of Engineers Fairbank, Arizona, 1952.
        1:25 scale
Belli, Anthony. Map of Western El Dorado County, 2000.
Bowman, Amos. Map for the California Water Company, 1873.
        Placerville, CA: El Dorado County Museum
Cochise County, Arizona Territory, 1900. Tempe, AZ: Arizona
        Collection, ASU. Hayden Library.
Ferdinand, Leicht and Hoffman. Topographical Map of Lake Tahoe
        and Surrounding Country, 1874.
Granite Chief Wilderness Study Area and Adjacent Parts of the
        Sierra Nevada. Geographical Map by David Harwood, 1981.
        USGS
Happy Valley,1945. Washington, D.C: Arizona Army Map Service,
        Corps of Engineers, U. S. Army. Scale 1:50
Historic Forts of the Old West. San Francisco: The Office of the
        Chief, Public Affairs, 6th U.S. Army, Presidio of San
        Francisco, CA, 1976.
Rand-McNally, Arizona, 1881 (partial) *Topographical and Railroad*
        maps of the Central Part of the State of California and Part
        of the State of Nevada. Comp and Pub. C. Bielawski, J. D.
        Hoffman and A. Poet,1865. Sacramento: California State
        Library.
United States Army Commanding Department of Arizona, 1878.
        Record group 77 W275, sheet 10. South East Arizona
        Territory National Archives.
United States Geological Survey Quadrangle maps for Johnson's
        Cut-Off in California: Camino, Echo Lake, Freel Peak,
        Kyburz, Placerville, Pollock Pines, Pyramid,Peak Riverton,
        Slate Mountain, Sly Park, and South Lake Tahoe.

ELLEN OSBORN

United States Geological Survey Quadrangle maps for Johnson's
Cut-Off in Nevada: Carson City, Genoa, Glenbrook, and
Minden.
USGS Fairbank, Arizona Quadrangle, 1952. 7.5 minute scale
USGS Galleta Flat East Quadrangle, Arizona, 1973. 7.5 minute scale
USGS Happy Valley, Arizona, 1958. 1:62 scale, and 1973 1:24 scale
Western Portion of El Dorado County Map, Showing Mining Claims
by C. A. Logan, 1938.

Unpublished Sources

Anonymous. William Johnson's "Resolution of Respect." San Jose, CA.
Barewald, Ina. "The Johnson Family." Cadiz, OH: Cadiz Library.
Manuscript.
Carpenter, G. J. and Geo. E. Williams, Attorneys for Contestant
Johnson. *Brief of John C. Johnson, Contestant in the Matter
of the Claim of Alburn J. Blakeley, Applicant for Patent No.
199.* Sacramento: H. S. Crocker & Co., 1872.
El Dorado Lodge F&AM. Placerville, CA. Records
Grand Lodge of California F&AM. San Francisco, CA. Records.
Hill, Dorothy J. "A Collection of Maidu Indian Folklore of Northern
California." Unpublished manuscript, 1969.
Hudson, Dr. J. W. Chicago: Department of Anthropology, Field
Museum of Natural History. Unpublished field notes,
original on file.
Johnson, George "Papers." Berkeley: Bancroft Library. Manuscript.
Knudsen, Thelma, "Descendants of Griffith Johnson." Unpublished
genealogy.
Morris, Lloyd. Unpublished letter dated January 17, 1998. Original
in the possession of the USDA Forest Service
Morris, Milt. Unpublished diary, in the possession of the USDA
Forest Service.
"Names on the Plains." Data Base of the Oregon-California Trails
Association.

Native Daughters of the Golden West. Roster of California Pioneers.

Oak Hill Cemetery Records. San Jose, CA.

Palmyra Lodge F&AM records. Placerville, CA.

Pitts, David. "The Story of David Pitts." Tucson: Arizona Historical Museum. Filed under "Tres Alamos."

Rieber, Joralemon Dorothy. "To Live Strivingly 1849 – 1942." Berkeley: Bancroft Library. Manuscript.

Seceder Cemetery records. Deersville, OH.

Smith, Herbert L.. "The Placerville Road The Romance of the Trails to the Comstock 1858 to 1878." Berkeley: Bancroft Library, 1934.

Society of California Pioneers records. Sacramento, CA.

Supernowicz, Dana. "Surmounting the Sierras." USDA Forest Service, 1993. Unpublished manuscript.

Trumbly, Claibourne W. "El Dorado Road History 1850-1980." Placerville, CA: El Dorado County Historical Museum.

Vallejo Mining Company Ledger, San Marino, CA: Huntington Library.

Informants

Cola, Beverly. Personal Communication.

Knudsen, Thelma. Personal Communication.

Larsen, Irene. Letter.

McBride, Edna. Personal communication.

University of Cincinnati dated August 28, 1980. Letter.

Plates and Photographs

Ancientfaces.com

Arizona State Library, Archives and Public Records, History and Archives Division. Phoenix, AZ. 97-2652

Author's own collection.

Cole, David. *U.S. Army Uniforms, Weapons & Accouterments.*

ELLEN OSBORN

Delaware Scouts. Woodcut from *The Soldier in Our Civil War*
    Volume I page 410. Ed. Paul F. Mattley. New York: The J. H.
    Brown Publishing Company, 1885.
Dreamstime.com image #101131187
Goddard, George. Woodcut of Lake Bigler. Carved from James
    Hutchings' *Scenes of Wonder and Curiosity in California.*
Johnson, J. C. Sacramento, CA: California State Library. Photograph
    from collection.
Johnson, J. C. and Nathan. Sacramento: Sutter's Fort. Photograph
    from collection.
Lawrence & Houseworth collection. Library of Congress.
Military Department Adjutant General Indian War papers, F3753.
    California State Archives.
Payne, of Wisconsin, Civil Engineer "Bartlett's Guide to California."
    Printed by *Placerville Herald*. Placerville, CA, 1853.
    Berkeley: Bancroft Library. Oakland: Oakland Library.
Photos #10332, #10964, #2072, #15895, #2106, #1233, #10952,
    #15895, #4402, #8687. Placerville, CA: El Dorado County
    Historical Museum. Photographs from collection.

Index

A

B

C

Grand Lodge of California 130, 164, 266. See also California Masonic
      Grand Lodge
Grange 139-141
Grant, Ulysses S. 95
Grayhorse Valley 87
Great Basin of Nevada 205
Greeley, Horace 95, 96, 97
Green Bay, Wisconsin 168, 234, 236, 241
Gum, Elmer, Sheriff 174

H

Hagerdon, Albert Edward 169
Hagerdon, Charles Luther 14, 169-171, 173, 179
Hagerdon, Eber Adam 100, 169
Hagerdon, Ella Mariah 169
Hagerdon, Emily 11, 20-22, 26, 112, 168-170, 193, 234, 240-241, 244. See
      also Johnson, Emily
Hagerdon Family 168
Hagerdon, Fanny 234
Hagerdon, Frances Leroy 168
Hagerdon, Harriet Ann 169
Hagerdon, James Knox 100, 169-170
Hagerdon, John O. 168
Hagerdon, Luther 168-169, 234
Hagerdon, Mary 169, 240
Hagerdon, Zilpha 168-169, 241
Half Way House 213
Hall, Gaven D., Major 57
Hall, Major 25
Hamilton, N. A. 124
Hand, Charles 120
Hangtown 20, 55, 252
Hangtown Creek 252
Harrison County boys 18
Harrison County, Ohio 14, 17, 148, 160-161, 163
Harvey, Obid, Dr. 58
Haskins, Charles Warren (C. W.) 65, 73, 104, 255, 258
Hattie Tom (Nisenan woman) 7, 11-12, 15, 72-81, 183, 240. See also Tom, Hattie
Hazlet, Margaret Jane Johnson 161

CPSIA information can be obtained
at www.ICGtesting.com
Printed in the USA
FSOW04n0019240316
18213FS